Back to the Keys

A Florida Keys Novel

MIKI BENNETT

This book is a work of fiction. Any references to historical events, real people, or real places are used fictitiously. Other names, characters, places, and events are products of the author's imagination, and any resemblance to actual events or places or persons, living or dead, is entirely coincidence.

First Edition

ISBN: 069284919X
ISBN 13: 9780692849194
Library of Congress Control Number: 2017902588
WannaDo Concepts Publishing, Charleston, South Carolina

To all the dreamers out there: just go for it.

■ ■ ■

5, 4, 3, 2, 1 – "Happy New Year!" shouted the crowd at Times Square, seeming like one giant voice. Then, the confetti came raining down on them. It was nothing like Everly had ever experienced in her life. It was exhilarating, even though she was cold.

But when she looked at Blake, he placed one of his hands on each side of her face and gently brought his lips to hers. The kiss was magical. A warmth spread through her entire body, and she no longer felt the cold. She only felt his soft lips and his body pressed against hers.

"Happy New Year, Everly," he said, only inches from her face.

"Happy New Year to you," were the only words that would come to her shocked mind. He had her speechless, and so happy. And then, she kissed him back, as gently as he had kissed her.

■ ■ ■

Drew watched the celebrating crowd below. He sipped on his glass of wine and wondered where she was. Somewhere down there, Blake was with Everly, and he hoped that she was safe. He couldn't stop thinking about how Blake could hurt her emotionally, and he wanted to make sure she didn't get hurt. Everly was important to him.

■ ■ ■

1

The ballroom was crowded as Everly sat at the table and watched the festivities around her. People were milling about. Family members hugging, smiling and catching up with each other. There were a few children playing and pretending to dance on the wooden area that was designated just for that purpose. The bride and groom were making their way through the gathering, talking and hugging people along the way.

With the soft music playing in the background and the warm glow of the lights from above, the room radiated with romance. The tables were set evenly apart throughout the room with the bride and groom's table prominently up front for all to see. In the middle of each table, there were tiny flowers surrounding a crystal bowl. Tiny candles floated inside the delicate vessels that were lined with seashells beneath the water that held the glowing flames. At each place setting, there had been little goody bags for the guests to take home, little reminders of this special evening of celebration.

The church wedding had been as beautiful as something she would have chosen for herself. Since she had lived in Key West her entire life, Everly had seen over the years that most couples tended to get married on the beach or outside in one of the beautiful local parks. Her friends, Abbey and Zach, however, had decided to tie the knot in a small, quaint church, then have their reception at the ballroom of a local hotel on Mallory Square. It was stunning, with windows that looked out over the waters of the Atlantic.

This was very different from other nuptials she had attended because every part of the lovely celebration, from the wedding to the reception, was indoors. Abbey and Zach had always done things differently from the moment they had met, and that was something she loved about the both of them. Their love story was a beautiful one, of finding and helping each other through the good and the bad, especially after Zach almost lost his life after being hit by a car. But now, as Everly watched the pair dance for the first time as husband and wife, she wished for a love story of her own. But there was another goal more pressing in her mind. She was almost ready to move to her dream city of New York.

Everly had only been to New York City once, for a family vacation. Key West and the Keys had been her life and playground since she was born. She even stayed at home while attending college, after her father became ill and was unable to work. During that time, she helped her mom with the house and finances. Now, though, as her father continued to improve, things were looking brighter for her parents. Everly dearly loved them but she was also desperately wanting to move away from the Keys and explore other places, like New York.

She was eight years old when they took that vacation to the big city, but to this day, Everly could still remember the excitement of that trip. The tall buildings that seemed to reach into the clouds. The street food that smelled wonderful on every corner. The lights at night, twinkling so brightly, that truly made her realize that it was the "city that never sleeps." With her degree in computer science and her nearly flawless skills designing websites, Everly was sure that securing a job would be no problem in a city so large. But she was still saving money to make the monumental move, and she was so close to her goal that it was hard to contain her excitement.

"Can I have this dance?" the man asked, breaking her trance. She recognized that it was Mr. Isler, Zach's dad, and Everly was happy to oblige.

"What are you doing, sitting by yourself? You should be dancing to every song," Justin Isler said as he spun Everly around.

"I was just thinking as I watched the happy couple. I'm so glad they finally said 'I Do'," Everly remarked, glancing over at Abbey and Zach.

"We are, too. They have come a long way––so glad they took the next step. What about you, my dear? Anyone special in your life?"

"Not right now. To be honest, I've not really been looking. I'm hoping to move soon, so starting a relationship wouldn't be the best thing."

"You want to move? From here? It's hard for me to believe that anyone would want to leave this paradise."

"But you see, I have lived here all my life. Born and raised. And while I agree it's beautiful, I'm just ready to go somewhere else. See some new sights," Everly answered, as she instantly saw in her mind the bright lights of the city.

"I can understand that," Mr. Isler said. "My children were the same way, even though some of them have moved back to our hometown. You just never know how things will be until you try." Suddenly, he was interrupted.

"Can I cut in?" The voice was just slightly familiar.

Everly looked to see the man she had been introduced to yesterday. It was Drew Wallace, Abbey's younger brother. As soon as she met him, Everly wanted to talk to him. Not only because he was sexy and very handsome, which he was, but he lived in New York City. He was a journalist there, and Everly wanted to know everything she could to help her make her big move soon.

"So, Everly Meyers, are you having fun?" Drew asked, just as the song changed to a more up-tempo beat.

"Yes. The wedding was beautiful and they have picked the best place for a reception." *He remembered my name*, she thought, and it made her smile inside. As they danced, there was something about Drew that gave Everly that fluttery feeling inside. His smile was sexy and his appealing personality tugged at her in a way she hadn't felt for a long time.

Everly wished she could immediately ask him questions about the city in which he lived, but as she looked around the room once more, she knew right now probably wasn't the appropriate time. Everyone always said she had a one-track mind when it came to moving away. It wasn't that she didn't love Key West, but that burning desire for new experiences was one thing she couldn't extinguish.

Everly loved her hometown. It was a beautiful city with the friendliest people. She could ride her bike everywhere, was close to the beaches she loved, and could practically swim all year round. She lived in shorts, t-shirts and flip-flops all the time, and the atmosphere of the island town was almost always relaxing. It was what everyone dreamed of, right? But Everly just had that indescribable desire to do something different, even if everyone thought she was crazy for leaving this slice of paradise.

■ ■ ■

Drew looked at the girl who was dancing with him. So, this was Everly, the girl his sister had told him about. The one that wanted to live in his city. Drew had to admit she was beautiful, just as Abbey described. Everly's long, silky, light brown hair and her beautiful chocolate brown eyes caught his attention immediately. She was alluring in the form-fitting bridesmaid's dress that showed off her soft, caramel-colored skin. He wanted to get to know her a bit, but she seemed quiet and shy, not at all what he had pictured in his mind when his sister had told him about the girl she worked with and her grand plan to move away from Key West. This made him wonder for a split second if this girl would be able to make it in his city.

New York was exciting, but also aggressive. He had found that out the first month of living there. It was very different from the slow pace of living in the Smoky Mountains of Asheville, North Carolina, where he and his siblings had grown up. After college, Drew had been able to secure a job as an assistant to an editor of a small newspaper in New York. He was excited about moving to the city, even if it wasn't the dream job he had desired. He wanted to work as a reporter for one of the largest newspapers in the city, but had found out quickly that it wasn't something that someone could just step into. Drew would have to work his way into the position, but he wanted it so badly that in his mind, he could feel and see his desk in a beautiful corner office overlooking the city below.

Drew had loved to write since he was a little boy in school. His parents were amazed when his teachers told them their son had a "gift" for writing, and to encourage him as much as they could. He took the usual route in school for someone who aspired to be a journalist: writing for the school newspaper. But Drew also went almost daily to the newspaper offices in Asheville. When he was old enough to get a job there, everyone already knew who he was. And Drew didn't care what kind of task they asked him to do, even if it was cleaning the offices. When the paper had any type of writing contest or feature for teens, he seemed to be the first one to enter.

He also had his own blog on the Internet. It began when Drew wrote about teenage life in the Smoky Mountains, and he treated it like his own mini newspaper of sorts. It had a huge following, which was now even bigger since he was writing about living in New York. It even supplemented his income, but Drew still wanted that elusive corner office at a large newspaper in the big city and was determined to get there.

He remembered when he first moved to New York. Compared to living in the relaxed, homey feel of the North Carolina mountains, the city was non-stop. Drew found an apartment with four other people, even though the entire living space was smaller than he could have imagined! He had been warned that it would be tiny, and was glad that he had pared down to only the bare essentials that he needed. To say he was shocked when he opened the door, with its eight locks, was an understatement. Also, making the adjustment to living with so many people he didn't know was strange at first, but soon, they were all friends. Drew had decided he would make it work, and he did.

In the last four years since Drew had moved, he was finally writing his own articles for a small newspaper that focused on the environmental impacts made by the large city. And he had made the move to live in Manhattan instead of across the river in New Jersey. Again, as he had told himself before, it was another stepping-stone to reaching his goal. At least now, he was writing articles instead of being an errand boy. He now had two roommates instead of four, and had been able to move to a slightly bigger apartment that allowed him a bit more leg room- and a few visitors.

Abbey had made the visit north once to see him and couldn't believe that he lived in a "tin can," as she put it. It didn't help that his place was a mess, with a lot of his stuff strewn everywhere in his room. He had been working feverishly on his first major writing piece that would be the headline article for his paper, a major feat for him. Though Drew had used that as an excuse for the cluttered space, his sister gently reminded him that his room had looked the same when they were living at home. And Drew had smiled and agreed with a laugh.

When Drew heard that his sister had moved to Key West, he couldn't believe she would go to such a remote place. Yes, it was popular and tropical, but to him, it was too far away from the exhilaration of living in a big city. Had she decided she was moving to Miami, he would have thought that was more his type of lifestyle. But, try as he might, living in the Florida Keys held no excitement for him whatsoever.

But now, after being here for only a few days, he was beginning to see why Abbey loved it here. It was beautiful, warm, sunny and relaxed. It seemed like no one hurried anywhere, like they did in New York. Drew hadn't been able to explore much yet, but the history, the clear, aqua water, and certainly the bars that lined Duval Street were interesting and fun. The thought had even briefly crossed his mind that maybe he could write for a paper here, but then he laughed. There was no way he would leave his beloved New York. He would just have to visit more often now, since he could see the draw of these beautiful islands.

"So, Abbey told me you want to move to New York one day. Do you mind if I ask why?" Drew asked the beautiful girl he had been dancing with as they were walking off the dance floor.

Everly suddenly became tongue-tied. This is what she had wanted to talk to him about since she heard he would be here, but as she had danced with Drew, all she could think about was how good-looking he was. But she finally found her voice.

"Well, I've lived my whole life on this island. I haven't traveled much, but the one place I remember the most was New York. I loved it there, even if it was so long ago. I just want to go somewhere, do something different. Explore. Don't get me wrong because I love the Keys, but on the other hand, I'm so ready to leave." *Okay, now I sound desperate,* Everly thought. That was not how she wanted to come across to this man.

Before she had even met Drew, Everly had already hoped that he could be someone that would help her when she got to the big city. Her words just weren't coming out like she had hoped, because Drew looked so good tonight in his groomsmen's suit and Everly was having a hard time concentrating.

Abbey had shown Everly pictures of her baby brother, but in person, he was much different. The brother and sister looked similar, but not as alike as Everly would have thought. His hair was short and blond, and it accentuated his angular face. He had dimples that graced his cheeks every time that he smiled. He was only a few inches taller than Everly and had a very muscular build. She had seen that yesterday when they were introduced. At that time, he wore only a t-shirt, shorts, and flip-flops; it was the casual dress of an islander, minus the slight tan most people had that lived in the islands of the Keys. He had been so charming that Everly instantly pictured herself walking around New York City with this man, possibly hand in hand. That sudden image yesterday threw her off the main subject that she wanted to talk to Drew about: information about moving to the city. Everly had determined that she wasn't going to bring the subject up today since it was a wedding, but since Drew asked her, she didn't hold back.

"I could understand that. I told Abbey when I found out she had moved to Key West that she was crazy. But now that I'm here, this little island town is a nice getaway. As for New York––that's my city. I was like you in a way, before I moved.

I wanted to go there because I just knew that my chances of becoming a top journalist would be the best."

"And how is that working out?" Everly asked as they sat back down at the table.

"So far, so good. In the last four years, I've worked at three different papers, each one better than the previous. Now I'm writing lead articles. The paper is small, though it does have a large readership. I'm hoping to make another step up in the next year," Drew said, even though he was thinking more about Everly's beauty and personality.

"Lance, our boss at work, has a few connections and said once I make the move there, he will be able to help me secure a job as a graphic designer or website tech. I love doing both."

"You certainly shouldn't have a problem there. It seems everything is going digital, even my newspaper."

"Hopefully, I'll be able to make my move by the end of the year. My parents aren't thrilled, but at least they are supportive. My Dad has been very sick, but since he is doing so much better, I think I can leave and my parents will be okay. That is the main reason I haven't left before now, but it also gave me time to save more money. I know it is going to be strange at first, but every time I think of Times Square, the tall buildings, even snow, I get so excited. I have already bought myself a warm coat. When it came in the mail, my mom thought I had lost my mind," Everly said with a laugh. " But then, she quickly knew why it was there, because it certainly isn't needed here in the winter. I usually can wear my flip-flops year-round down here."

"There is my baby brother," Abbey said, suddenly standing beside Drew's chair. "Would you please come and dance with your sister?"

Drew stood up and took his sister's hand. "We will talk more later, Everly," Drew said softly, giving her a smile that caused Everly to shiver inside. *He is way too cute*, she thought to herself, and smiled.

"You got the hots for Abbey's brother?" Zach asked as he extended his hand to Everly for a dance. His other hand was still using a cane for support, as he continued to heal from his wounds from the car accident. When they were finally on the dance floor, Everly could talk.

"Definitely not!" Everly said as soon as she could. "Just asking him information about New York. I have enough money to finally move there. But so I don't upset my parents too badly, I'll probably wait till after Christmas. I'm very excited to go and yet, nervous as a cat."

"To me, you looked a little dreamy-eyed back there, and not about New York City," Zach said quickly, teasing her. "As for your Dad, he is doing terrific––even back at work. Think it might be *you* that is holding back? Don't get me wrong - we want you to stay here, but I kinda know how you feel. I remember I was ready to leave Galveston as soon as I had that degree in my hand, but I never wanted to move to a city as large as New York. But I think you are going to do fine. And it will be nice that you have someone you know there. Drew seems to be a good guy. Plus, he seemed a bit interested in you. Just giving you a guy's perspective."

"What do you mean? How can you tell?" Everly asked, feeling a little giddy inside at the thought that Abbey's brother could be interested in her. They hardly knew each other.

"Just the way he looks at you and how he is acting. Trust me––it's a guy thing," Zach said as they continued to dance. Even though Zach was using his cane for walking and balancing, he didn't let it get in the way of doing the things he wanted. And since he was like a big brother to her, she took his words to heart.

"I will admit he is cute, but I really just wanted to know more about New York."

"You certainly have a one-track mind, Everly. Why don't you try maybe talking and making friends to begin with at first? Just might be a blessing in disguise," Zach told her.

"I'm sorry. It's just…." Her voice trailed off.

"What?"

"I don't know. I'm not the best when it comes to friendships. I'm more of a computer nerd than I want to admit. I guess you could label me an introvert. I've always been a bit nervous in social gatherings like this. That is one thing that concerns me about New York. What if I don't fit in?" Everly voiced her concern, glancing around the ballroom instead of looking at Zach.

"No, you have that wrong. You make a wonderful friend. The problem is that you have built this wall around yourself because of one bad relationship from your past. Even though some idiot guy hurt you terribly one time, doesn't mean everyone is like that, Everly."

Zach knew why Everly had practically closed herself off from relationships. She had fallen head over heels in love, right about the time of her twentieth birthday, with a man that had just moved to Key West. It seemed like everything was almost perfect, but as they were about to celebrate their one-year anniversary, Everly found out that he not only had another girlfriend on Marathon Key, but also another woman in Key Largo. It was only by accident that she found out about the other two women. Everly was devastated and was in a deep depression for what seemed like months. Since that time, she had guarded her heart where everyone was concerned. The only exception was the day Everly met Abbey, when she began working with her. It was the first time in so long that she felt comfortable talking to someone new on a personal level.

"I know it's scary, believe me. I didn't want to let Abbey back in my life when I thought that my injuries from the accident would keep me from being the type of man she deserved. But I'm glad I let my guard down. Now, I have the love of my life by my side," Zach said, looking over at his beautiful bride as she danced with her brother.

"I know you are right, and I promise I will do better. Or, at least try," Everly said softly.

"Then get to know Drew. As a friend. When you are living in a big city, it will be nice to know at least one person." The music ended, and suddenly, a call came from across the ballroom for the bride and groom to cut the cake. Everly watched as the two met at the table that held the four-tiered cake that was covered in tiny candied seashells that seemed to sparkle.

"Now we can talk again. Had to dance with my sister because I certainly didn't want to irritate her, especially on her wedding day." Everly looked up to see Drew was standing beside her.

"I can't imagine Abbey getting upset like that. Do you know a side of her that I don't?"

"Let's just say, when we were kids, she was definitely the princess." Drew laughed. "But then, as her brothers, we were protective of her." Drew was watching as the newly married couple smashed cake on each other, but Everly found herself staring at Drew. But before he could turn to her, she caught herself and quickly focused her attention back to the wedding cake and the couple standing behind it.

"So, what are you doing tomorrow?" Drew asked.

"Me?" Everly was a little shocked by the question.

"Yes, you. There is no one else around us."

Drew smiled at her, and that tingly feeling returned all over again. *Is he asking me out*, she asked herself.

"No special plans. Why?"

"I was wondering if you would mind showing this city boy your island town."

"Sounds like that could be fun. Any place in particular you would like to go?" Everly asked nervously, but spoke in the most confident voice she could muster.

"This is your island. I'll let you decide."

"Then let's meet here at your hotel at ten o'clock tomorrow morning, and we will go from there. Are you opposed to bike riding?" Everly asked with a sly smile on her face.

"I think I can remember how to ride a bike," Drew answered returning her smile.

"Then I will bring my bike and we will rent one for you. That's the best way to see my town," Everly said.

"Then it's a date," Drew said, moving a little closer to her.

2

Everly stared at her reflection in the mirror. She was nervous about this "date," if she could call it that. Yes, she was spending the day with Drew and showing him around Key West, but was it a date or just time spent with a friend? Everly had purposely avoided relationships for so long now, staying focused on her goals and helping her family. This was the first time in what felt like forever that the idea of going out with a guy even came to her mind. It was also the first time that she was truly excited about meeting a man to spend the day together.

As she continued to stare at the mirror, her nerves started to take control. Why was she so jittery? It was just Abbey's little brother, and they were riding bikes around town. That's all!

Everly then went to her closet, glancing through her clothes, wanting to look her best. She picked out her favorite jean shorts, a colorful tank top, and slid on some sneakers. She put her bikini, a towel, and some items from her handbag in her back pack so that she could carry it with her or put in the basket on her bike. Since Everly didn't own a car, her bike was her baby. The beautiful blue aqua frame with the white basket always made her smile every time she saw it.

She checked the mirror one last time, then peered at the clock on the wall. Everly noticed that she had just enough time to get to Drew's hotel. As she made her way through the city streets, there was a feeling of anxiety and excitement coursing through her body as she thought about the day ahead. When Everly reached the entrance, there he stood.

Drew was waiting on her, leaning against the post near the door of the hotel. Everly couldn't help but notice that he looked incredibly handsome. Drew didn't see her approach, so she was able to check him out more thoroughly. His blond hair was a bit unruly this morning, compared to how neat it was at the wedding yesterday. He also wore a tank top and shorts that looked like they could double as swim trunks. Although he was from New York, the few days he had been here had given him just a bit of color to his skin, which accentuated his muscular frame. Everly knew that any girl would give him a second, even third glance. She was finding it hard to concentrate as she approached him.

"Hi there," Everly said as she brought the bike to a stop in front of him.

"I thought that was you, but wasn't sure. With your hair in a ponytail and those sunglasses, I couldn't tell," Drew said. "Plus, you're dressed much differently than yesterday." He flashed her a smile that made Everly melt just a little inside.

"Well, this is more like me," she replied, standing next to her bike. "Tank tops, shorts, flip-flops, bathing suit and towel. That's how I live, here in the Keys." She paused. "We need to go rent a bike for you."

"Already have it taken care of," Drew said, pointing at a dark blue bike propped up not far from where they were standing. "I asked at the desk and the hotel got one for me. So, where are we off to today?"

"There's a lot to do. Anything you want to see in particular?"

"The first night I was here, I saw a little of Duval Street and Mallory Square, but not much. Then, the last two days, it's been nothing but wedding stuff, so I'm open to suggestions."

"Let's head down the street and I'll just show you around. Then, maybe, we can end up back at Mallory Square for the Sunset Celebration. Have to see that before you leave," Everly said, suddenly wondering how long he would be staying.

"Oh, I'm here for three whole weeks, so there is plenty of time. I'm writing a story while I'm here. My boss thought it would be a great piece for the travel section, especially anything I can find on animal rescues and conservation in this area."

He is here for three weeks! Everly suddenly felt a surge of happiness, a feeling that left her confused. She had only just met this man and had spent so little time with him. Was she attracted to him, like Zach had implied? She shook her head, hoping that it would shake some sense into her.

"No?" Drew looked puzzled.

"No, what?" Everly asked, returning his gaze.

"You were shaking your head. You don't think the article is a good idea?"

"Oh, no! I just...." Everly laughed slightly as she quickly tried to cover up her faux pas. "I'm sorry. I was trying to think of where to go to first. I think we will start at the Tropic Cinema. I love that place." *Great recovery, Everly,* she told herself.

"Lead the way," Drew said, extending his arm out to her.

They began their way down the street that was colorful and relaxing with its pretty trees and colorful flowers. The houses that they passed looked as though you could sit out front and enjoy your the entire day with a drink and a good magazine. Even though Drew noticed the scenery, he couldn't help but stare and think about the girl on the bike in front of him.

Everly seemed to be a totally different girl today. She was much more relaxed and, if possible, more stunning than the day before. Today, she was just beautiful––the only word that came to Drew's mind. Her long, shiny brown hair flowed in the breeze as they rode down the street, even though it was tucked into a ponytail. He also had a clear view of her from top to toes, which he couldn't quit thinking of as they pedaled toward their destination.

Suddenly, a picture of Peyton came to mind. His girlfriend back home. The one person he wanted to come with him on this trip, and she refused. She used the excuse that she had to work, but Drew had insisted that she could just come for the weekend, then fly back home. But Peyton wouldn't budge, saying that when he got back home, she would make sure he had a homecoming celebration he would not forget.

"This is our first stop," Everly announced as she slowed down her bike in front of the cinema on Eaton Street. The exterior gave the illusion of an old cinema from the 1950's, though in reality, it was built in early 2002. The aqua blue color of the building gave it a tropical look that was perfect for this town. The "cinema" sign with its neon lights along with the shiny silver trim made the building look like an old classic theater. "I love coming here. I know it isn't as grand as the big multiplexes on the mainland, but it is so unique." She was nervous as she talked and glanced over at Drew to see him observing the building.

"Love the colors, and it blends in well with the feel of the island." Drew surveyed his surroundings "It's so different here. I'm used to not being able to see the sun, or a rooftop, for that matter," he said, laughing. "It feels good. But right now I need to take a few pictures." He propped up his bike and grabbed his camera. Everly quickly stepped out of the way.

"Where are you going?" he asked her.

"I was moving so you could get pictures for your article."

"What if I wanted you in the picture? 'Local island girl shows the world the enticing island of Key West.' Sounds like a headline to me. What do you think?"

I think you are too handsome for your own good and you are keeping me feeling a little jumbled inside, Everly thought to herself. "Me, in your newspaper in New York City? How much?"

"How much what?"

"Don't people usually get paid for being a model? You know, since you want me in the picture," Everly teased him, moving slowly to stand in the front of the building.

"Sometimes. But mostly, they just like the fact that they are a celebrity, even for a few brief moments," Drew said, as he smiled at her then took pictures of the cinema and of Everly.

"Okay, I guess I'll settle for temporary celebrity status. You'll just have to send me a copy of the article when it comes out so I can put it on the wall of my bedroom at home. I call it my 'City Wall.'" *Oh, why had she told him that!*

"City Wall?"

She rolled her eyes, then put her head in her hands. "I can't believe I said that. It's so embarrassing."

"Can't be that bad!"

"Well," Everly began shyly, "I have a wall in my bedroom that is nothing but pictures of New York City. I've had it since I visited there when I was younger. My friends think I'm a bit obsessed, but I love it. Kinda silly, huh?"

"Sounds cool to me. I would love to see it before I leave."

"We'll see," Everly answered, smiling at Drew, secretly relieved that he didn't make fun of her. They hopped back on their bikes and she led him through the streets of Key West. They stopped at a few other tourist attractions that were considered "musts" for anyone visiting Key West. They went to the Southern Most Point Buoy, where they stood in line for a picture. This was the southern most point in the United States with a sign to let everyone know that Cuba was only ninety miles away.

Next they visited Fort Zachary State Park, riding the bike trails and stopping at the beach for a little rest. Then it was on to the famous Hemingway House, once the home of the famous author and his six-toed cats. They stopped to peer through the iron fence surrounding what was now a museum, opting not to take the house tour. Then, they headed back toward Mallory Square, but not before stopping for a late lunch along Duval Street.

"It's so relaxed down here," Drew said before he took a bite of his fish taco.

"I have to admit, it really is. Everyone keeps telling me that New York City is going to be too much for me, but I really don't think so. I know it's busy, crowded, and people always seem to be in a rush, but that is exciting to me. To have my own place, out on my own, in a new city. Maybe that will lead to a brand new me," Everly said with a smile.

"Well, I hope New York doesn't change you a bit. You are just fine the way you are," Drew said, giving her a wink.

Everly wanted to say something, but her mind was drawing a complete blank. This very handsome guy was flirting with her and she was sitting across from him, staring at him like a silly schoolgirl. This is when she wished so much that she had the social skills that her friends had when it came to men. After being in one hurtful relationship, it had wounded her so deeply that taking a chance again was a moot point in her mind, at least for now. But sitting across the table from Drew seemed to be melting her resolve on this issue for the first time since that fateful day when she found out her ex-boyfriend, Kevin, had two other girlfriends. She didn't want to experience that hurt again.

"It's almost time for the artisans and performers to start lining up at Mallory Square. If your sister were here, she'd be setting up her display right about now. Hope they're enjoying their mountain honeymoon getaway," Everly said, to quickly change the subject.

"I couldn't believe she decided to go back home for her honeymoon. I guess she didn't exactly go home, but to the Smokey Mountains? Let me go to a tropical island down in the Caribbean. That would've been my first choice."

"Remember, she lives here now. Plus, she wanted to show Zach where you guys grew up. I think it's romantic, especially this time of year. According to Abbey, the leaves are changing into their fall colors and the weather is cooler. A cabin in the mountains with a fireplace? Sounds perfect to me!" Everly said, her eyes closed, envisioning the scene in her mind.

"I guess that is how I grew up, and as far as cold weather goes, snow and blustery wind is not real romantic. Especially when you are digging your way out just so you can go somewhere like to work. Wait till you get to New York and experience it for the first time, except instead of having a nice warm car, you have to walk to work. Then, let me know what you think," Drew replied.

"Well, remember, I already have my coat, so that shouldn't be a problem."

"You may want to invest in some hats, scarves, and gloves, too. Even some extra socks. It gets pretty cold."

Everly smiled. "I already have those, also. I told you, I've been preparing for this getaway."

"You are serious. Are you always this intent on getting what you want?"

"Most certainly!" Everly said, as confidently as she could before they got back on their bikes and headed to Mallory Square.

As Everly had predicted, they reached the Square just as everyone was getting ready for the Sunset Celebration. Drew and Everly walked around the surrounding shops, Everly showing and telling him everything she could about each place they went.

Drew listened and watched the enchanting girl. She was cute and bubbly, and something about her had him entranced. Everly was nothing like the girls in New York, and the thought of her being there suddenly frightened him, for her sake. He hoped that she would be okay, and immediately decided that he would be her protector after she arrived. But then, he had the next three weeks to get to know this girl, and suddenly, the trip he hadn't been too excited about was very appealing.

This also made Drew feel very confused. Why was he not thinking of Peyton? Was this a bad thing? He wasn't cheating on her because he and Everly were only friends, but he just had a weird feeling that he couldn't shake.

Together, they sat on the pier to watch the changing sky in front of them. The magnificent colors that displayed as the sun sank below the horizon were gorgeous. The show before them couldn't have been more perfect for someone's first time of celebrating the sunset on Mallory Square.

"Now, that is what we call a sunset, here in Key West. Each evening is always a bit different but special none the less," Everly said. "It might be silly, but it's a really big deal here."

"I can see why people do this. It is relaxing and makes the city even more enticing," Drew responded, nudging her arm.

"Yeah, I guess it is. Sometimes, it's just no big deal to me since I've been here all my life. At least the colors were great tonight. Sometimes, we have too much cloud cover, but that doesn't change the mood down here." Everly sat there quietly, gazing straight ahead over the water, even though she wanted to look at the man sitting beside her. "Hope I was a good tour guide today. We only got to see such a tiny fraction of the island. And then, there are the rest of the Keys. Each one is special."

"Actually, Everly, the whole day was great. Thanks for showing me around. I can tell that it will take more than a few days to really see what this town has to offer. I had already planned on doing more research and traveling to the other Keys, as well."

"Good, then. If I can help you, just let me know. As for me, it's back to work tomorrow. With Zach and Abbey gone for the week, Roger and I will have our work cut out for us, but hopefully it won't be that bad." This time, Everly dared to look at Drew, and felt slightly weak as she glanced at him. He seemed even more handsome in the evening than he had this morning. She could not help but continually notice little things about him during the day. His personality only made him seem that more attractive, as they had laughed and joked most of the day.

"So why don't we go to dinner tomorrow night?" Drew asked, looking at her with the softest blue eyes she had ever seen.

"I'll be working late tomorrow, but I might be able to on Tuesday," Everly said, before she even had a chance to think.

"Then it's a date. Again. This time, I'll pick out the restaurant, but you will have to tell me if I made a good or bad choice. I'll let you know when I pick you up."

"You have a car here?"

"Rented one at the airport."

"I'm so sorry! I had you riding a bike all day long. We could have taken your car," Everly said apologetically.

"I wanted to see your town your way. I just might rent the bike again tomorrow and do some more exploring on my own. It was a lot of fun today."

"I had fun, too. So, hopefully, I'll see you Tuesday?"

"Unless we can sneak a lunch tomorrow," Drew said with eyebrows raised.

"Nope, too much work. Here is my number," Everly said, as she wrote her cell phone number on the back of a Key West brochure and handed it to him. "Give me a call and I'll text you my address. See ya later," she said, before getting on her bike and riding home, but not before looking back to see Drew watching her ride away.

3

"Well, that was an exciting weekend," Roger said as they finally both sat down at their computers. He and Everly, along with Lance, had pored over the work for the coming week, trying to find a way to balance the increased workload. With Abbey and Zach on their honeymoon, this was going to be a busy week. They had known this would be an issue, but what they didn't expect was a big change over the weekend to a web design project for one of their major clients. Everly knew as soon as Lance told them about the design changes that their week had just gone from busy to hectic.

"Yes, it was. I'm just glad to see those two finally married. Now, we won't see wedding stuff scattered all over their desks every day." Everly laughed as she remembered how only last week Abbey's desk seemed to be covered in lace, flowers and a wedding to do list along with her regular work.

"Now, it will be all about the house," Roger said. "I bet she'll change everything Zach has."

"You're probably right."

"And if I remember correctly, I saw you having a nice Saturday evening, yourself."

"What are you talking about?" Everly asked a bit slowly, knowing full well what Roger was hinting at.

"I'm not blind, young lady. I saw you dancing and chatting with Abbey's brother. Nice looking and he's from New York. Do you already have a place to stay?" Roger laughed.

"Ha, ha. He was nice, but I tried to keep my New York questions to a minimum, thank you very much. Can't say that I didn't want to ask him everything I could about moving there. I think I'm going to leave after Christmas. Maybe even be in New York for New Year's Eve," Everly replied with a dreamy look in her eyes. "But don't say anything. That isn't a concrete plan, and I don't want to mention anything to Lance just yet."

"Well, I hope it's what you've always wanted. I've been there and done that. Give me this island town any day," Roger retorted, glancing through papers on his desk. "It's too noisy, too crowded, too cold, too...."

"Hey, don't knock it. I haven't been able to travel the world like you, so give me some slack. I love my hometown, but is it so wrong to want to go and explore a new city? Especially New York?" Everly asked.

"I think you should go. I just want to start a pool with everyone to see how fast you come back."

"Wow, Roger, you have that little confidence in me," Everly said, dejected.

"Oh, I think you can make it there. Just not sure it'll be everything you've dreamed it to be. But then again, I could be completely wrong."

"Hey guys, I love New York, too, but we have some heavy-duty work to do," Everly observed over her shoulder that Lance was coming up behind the pair with more paperwork in his hands.

"We're getting started now," Everly replied, her eyes opened wide at Roger, as if to tell him to stop getting her into trouble. Roger only shrugged his shoulders back at her.

"So, what about Abbey's brother?" Roger asked.

"What about him?"

"Oh, please. Saw you talking to him off and on all night."

"And I thought my parents were nosy," Everly teased. "We did spend the day together yesterday, but it wasn't a date. Just showed him around the island a little bit," Everly said slowly.

"I knew it!" Roger exclaimed.

"Just as friends," Everly quickly said. "He wanted to see the sights and I played tour guide. He is actually here for three weeks, writing some article for the newspaper he works for back home."

"Wow, a quick romance for Everly. It's about time."

"It is not a romance, and you make me sound weird, Roger. I do date, you know."

"Hardly."

Everly knew he was right but didn't want to give in. "I'm just very selective."

Roger snickered at her comment. "That's putting it mildly."

"He asked me to dinner tonight, but I knew we would probably be busy, so we are supposed to go tomorrow instead. But with this work project, I don't see how we will be doing anything but sitting in front of a computer screen for the next week."

"Oh, no! You aren't getting out of this one, Miss Thing. There is time for some dating."

"It's not a date! We're just friends, and barely that. I just met the guy. Honestly, that's all," Everly said, trying to convince Roger, and really herself, that there was nothing more than friendship on her mind as far as it concerned Abbey's dashing brother.

"I guess we shall see," Roger remarked with a grin, and continued to work on the project before him.

■ ■ ■

Drew stared at his watch. It was only noon on Monday. Though there were plenty of things he could do, he found himself still thinking about his time with Everly yesterday, which perplexed him.

He was at the hotel by himself, now. Yesterday morning, he had been the designated driver to take his parents, brother, and sister-in-law to the airport to head back home. All the family was gone, and he was now supposed to be in work mode. He had promised his editor one great story and maybe a few smaller ones about the Keys, the wildlife conservation efforts in the area, and the tourism industry. He knew that he could gather the information he needed in only a week or so, but had elected to take the three weeks offered to him by his editor, James. And after meeting Everly, he was glad for that.

She was different than the many women he had met since moving to New York City. She was cheerful, funny, and beautiful, but mostly down-to-earth. He wanted to be friends with her, but it was confusing him. He needed to talk to Abbey about Peyton. Drew was thinking about asking Peyton to marry him, but he still had questions that he felt he couldn't ask anyone else. Now that he had met Everly, Drew's feelings were scattered. He still loved Peyton, but there was something about this vivacious Key West girl that just drew him into her world.

His ringing cell phone brought him back to the present. He didn't recognize the phone number but in his business, that was an everyday occurrence.

"Hello," the female voice said into the phone.

"Hi, there," Drew replied, instantly recognizing Everly's voice. "Working hard?"

"You have no idea," Everly said, her voice sounding tired. "A big project landed in our laps over the weekend. Usually, it wouldn't be a problem, except Abbey and Zach are gone. Glad their honeymoon is only a week."

"Then I guess asking you if you might have changed your mind about dinner tonight is out of the question," Drew said.

"I'm really sorry. After a day like today, sitting out by the water and relaxing sounds wonderful, but the way I feel right now, I will probably just head home. I just wanted to check on you and see if you were able to do some sightseeing by yourself today."

Drew instantly thought of Everly in silky pajamas, walking sensuously toward a bed. He squeezed his eyes shut and quickly erased the image from his head. No wonder his sister told him not to mess with Everly or he would have to answer to her.

"I've done a little. Are we still on for dinner tomorrow night?" Drew asked hopefully.

"I'm planning on it, but I will let you know later."

"How about I bring lunch to work for you today for helping me so much?"

Everly couldn't help but smile. She had only known this man for a few days but he was certainly getting under her skin. "Thanks for the offer but I brought my lunch. And I'll be working as I eat."

"I have certainly had more than a few days like that myself. So since I'm by myself today, what should I go do?"

Everly told him about the wildlife refuge and turtle hospital on Marathon Key.

"I was hoping that you might be able to fit in a little road trip to the other Keys. Maybe Saturday? I mean, I know I could go by myself, but you know them so well. I thought it would be fun to hear all the information and stories from a local's point of view." Damn, he wanted to be with the girl, but knew it wasn't right. He should stop, but then Drew told himself that he knew they could be just friends. He really liked Everly. *As a friend,* he quickly told himself.

"As for tomorrow night, if we're on schedule, I don't think Roger would mind leaving work on time. But for the weekend, I'll have to wait and see if this project gets done. If it's finished, it might be nice to celebrate with a little trip up to Key Largo and back."

"Who is Roger?" Drew asked curiously.

"You had to have met him at the wedding. He works here with us at the agency. We have two teams here: me and Roger, and then Abbey and Zach. Roger was there with his new boyfriend, John." Suddenly, Drew remembered him.

"That's right, I remember now. Abbey introduced us. I guess I better let you get back to work."

"I probably should, but I just wanted to check on you. Hope you enjoy the sightseeing today. Bye." Drew heard the click of the phone.

He continued to stare at the phone in his hand, thinking about the girl who had just called. And all Drew could do was smile as he thought about Everly and that she had cared enough to check on him. It made him happy, in a way he hadn't felt in quite awhile.

Drew glanced around the hotel room, then out of the sliding doors. The resort was elegant, but he could only stay two more nights. Then, he would be staying at Abbey and Zach's place 'til they returned from their honeymoon. After that, he was still trying to figure out where he would stay for the next two weeks. Abbey said he could stay with them, but he didn't want to intrude on the newlyweds. But depending on what accommodations he could find, Drew decided that he might just accept his sister's generous offer.

Okay, get it together Drew, he said to himself. He always had things planned, and knew what he wanted to do and what needed to get done. But spending some off time with Everly yesterday had really thrown him a curve ball. He had to admit he really didn't even want to work. But he knew he had to present something to his boss by the end of the week, so he decided that instead of taking Everly's suggestions of sights to see, he would work the rest of the day. He would save the tourist time for when he could spend it with Everly. The thought of that made him smile again.

4

"Wow, this burger is delicious" Drew marveled, just before taking another bite.

"I told you they have good food here," Everly said with a smile. "Yes, it can be touristy, but I still love it. I even met Jimmy Buffett a couple of times." She continued to eat her chicken caesar salad and French fries as they sat at the Margaritaville Restaurant.

"You've met him?" Drew asked excitedly. "I love his music."

"He's here occasionally. He has a recording studio in town." Everly had seen many celebrities over the years, as they would come to vacation in the island town. Though there were a few she wanted to talk to, she mainly kept her distance, knowing they were here to get away from everything. But it was tempting, at times.

"So, how are your articles coming along? Were you able to work on them over the last few days?" Everly asked. Since Everly had been so busy, their Tuesday dinner plans had been postponed until Friday.

"Yes, but only from your suggestions. For now, I have two articles in the works. The first highlights the best of the Keys. For the second, I went to the turtle hospital to start my piece on animal rescue. Next, I need to interview some people on what conservation projects are being done down here. I must say, the drive to Marathon was beautiful There's so much to do down here."

Everly noticed as Drew talked that he didn't seem very excited about the subjects he was writing about. There was no spark, nothing like what she imagined for someone that was supposed to be so excited about being a journalist. At least, that was how Abbey had described her brother's love for journalism. "This might be too personal a question, but are these the type of things you want to write about?"

Drew was taken aback by Everly's keen observation. "What makes you ask that?"

"I don't know. You just don't seem too thrilled about your subjects when you talk about them."

"To be honest, not really. But I will say, I'm enjoying writing about what to do in the Keys. Don't get me wrong, I'm all for saving our wildlife and the conservation efforts, but-"

"But what?" Everly asked.

"I'm going to sound like I don't care, but it's boring to me."

"Then why are you writing them?"

"To put a roof over my head and be able to buy some food. Plus, I just see this work as stepping stones to what I really want to write about."

"And what would that be?" Everly asked, now intrigued.

Drew sat back and looked at the girl across from him. She was asking questions that no one had asked before and though it unsettled him a bit, he liked it at the same time. "When I was a boy, my parents couldn't get over the fact that I loved to read the newspaper every day. I would read it before school, and I always read the articles about our hometown first. It didn't matter if it was a crime or a Boy Scout award. I loved learning what was around me. Then, I would read the national news. In high school, I was on the paper, of course, and became its editor in my senior year. Most of my fellow students wanted to do fluff pieces about the school, but I always made sure we talked about our community. And that won me an award from the city.

"In college, it was a bit different. I never became the editor, but was the assistant. We wrote about everything, but mostly about college activities. It was never fulfilling for me. After school, I thought that I would just try to work locally, but I really wanted to get my feet wet in the business. And I figured there was no better way to get experience than to go to New York or Washington, D.C. Out of the two, New York just sounded more fun, so off I went."

"You still didn't answer my question. What do you want to write about?"

"Communities. Families. How to survive in this world. Maybe not just survive, but thrive and make a difference at the same time," Drew said. "Sounds lame, huh?"

"So, you've known what you wanted to do since you were a little boy. That's cool. So, why aren't you writing pieces about the communities in New York City?"

"That's not what my paper specializes in. And finding a job was a lot harder than I thought. I was lucky that I had substantial savings before making the trip there, because I went through almost all of it before I landed my first good job," Drew replied as he thought back to those days.

"That's why I have been saving money since high school. Everyone thinks I'm crazy for wanting to move. And every time I said I was putting my money away for my trip, some would even laugh. But I have enough to make the move now and live, I hope, decently while I find a job. I'm just making sure my family is okay before I go. Like I told you, my Dad was sick for a while, but he's able to work again. It breaks my heart a little when I know my parents don't want me to leave, but they are still supporting my decision."

"I know what you mean. My parents weren't exactly thrilled that I chose New York but they didn't try to talk me out of it either. So, I told you why I wanted to work in journalism, but what is your story, Miss Meyers?" Drew asked as though they were at an interview, giving her a very serious look. She could only laugh.

"I've always been a tech geek. When I was five years old, my mom came into the kitchen to find me fixing our weather radio. I had my Dad's tools all spread out on the kitchen table, and the radio was in pieces. At first, she was going to punish me, but instead sat there and told me that I needed to ask permission before I did such things. Then, she patiently watched me put the radio back together, and by the time my Dad got home, it was all in one piece. And working!" Everly said proudly.

"I gravitated toward all things technology, but loved computers. I would take them apart, then put them together. Then,

I started learning coding and designing my own programs. In high school, I started building websites, and it was an extra plus that people were paying me to do something I loved. I still do side jobs to this day, and that has helped me build my savings up for my move to New York. When my Dad got real sick, I decided to go to college online so I could stay home for my parents, but it also led me to working for Lance. He's been like a second father to me, and has already called a few web design firms in New York on my behalf. I have interviews waiting when I get there."

"Then you shouldn't have any trouble making it in the big city," Drew said. "But won't you be leaving anyone else behind, besides your family?" He had wondered if she had a significant other since the day he met her, even though it shouldn't have crossed his mind.

Everly laughed again. "If you mean a boyfriend, no. Getting a little personal there, Mr. Wallace."

"Once a reporter, always a reporter. We have to ask these questions." Drew smiled and Everly couldn't help the sudden tingly feeling in her stomach. She felt excitement just by being with him. He made her happy and she enjoyed his company. But this wasn't in her plan. And of all people, Drew was the last person she should develop any feelings for. He was Abbey's brother! Everly wanted them to be friends. *But would I be able to be only friends*, she wondered.

"So, are you working this weekend?" Drew asked.

"No, thank goodness. Roger had plans to go to Miami, so that's why we were working late every night. He had this trip planned for weeks, so I put in the hours with him to make sure he could go. But it also let me have a free weekend. It seems like it's been nothing but wedding stuff for quite a while, not that I'm complaining. I loved helping Abbey and Zach. Speaking of, when do they get back?"

"Sunday afternoon. I have to pick them up at the airport. But until then, I need to explore some of the other Keys. I know we talked about it earlier in the week, but would you like to go on a day trip with me tomorrow, all the way to Key Largo? Just take our time, and you can show me the places I need to go back and visit for my stories. I have a list, but I'm sure you can tell me what's good and what's not."

Everly sat across from him, trying not to show the giddiness she was feeling. "That sounds good. I can pack some snacks for the day and show you around."

"So, what time do you want to leave in the morning?"

"Pick me up at eight o'clock. Might be a long day, but it's supposed to be nice this weekend so we'll have lots to see." Everly tried to make a mental list of the places she wanted to show Drew but the excitement of spending the day with him had her mind drawing a complete blank.

"I can't wait. This should be fun," Drew said, giving her that handsome smile.

I can't wait either, Everly thought to herself as she stared at the gorgeous man across the table.

5

"I'm so glad it turned out to be a beautiful day. I wasn't sure after the rain we had yesterday, but it seems the weather guy got it right this time," Everly said from the passenger seat.

Drew had picked her up right on time. Even though it had been earlier than she normally got up on a Saturday morning, she found herself dressed and ready to go at 7:30 A.M. Her parents asked her what was going on because of her early departure. Though they meant well, it was one thing she was looking forward to when she moved out: no questions about what she was doing or where she was going. Just the thought of that kind of independence made her smile. But, so did the nice-looking guy driving the car.

"So, where should we stop first?" Drew asked, looking over at his passenger. Everly looked so alluring, and very much the island girl, with her floral tank top, white shorts and flip-flops.

"Bahia Honda State Park is really nice. Beautiful beach, great place for picnics and watersports. They also have camping too," Everly continued. For some reason, she was nervous, even though she knew this man now. The more she was around Drew, the more she liked him. Not only was he good looking, but he was sweet and seemed genuinely interested in her.

"Then the state park it is."

"This is where Zach and Abbey had their first date. Well, I wouldn't call it a first date. Zach met Abbey here for a picnic before her first day at work. He claims that's when Abbey decided she wanted him." Everly laughed at the memory, and how Zach always made a big deal about that first meeting.

"I've heard the story, but my sister tells it a bit differently. Abbey did tell me this was one of her favorite places to go." Just as he finished his sentence, the state park sign came into view, and they were parked and headed for the beach within minutes.

Everly couldn't help but watch as Drew got out of the car. He was so toned and muscular. He had also acquired more of a tan during the week he had been down here, which only accentuated his stunning good looks. Now, as she stood beside him in the sand, she realized that she really enjoyed being with this man. It was the first time in ages that the thoughts of moving to another city wasn't the first thing she thought of upon waking in the morning. Drew had somehow weaved his way into that spot.

"You weren't kidding. This place is awesome," Drew said. Within a few seconds, he was taking pictures with his phone.

"Oh, this is just the beginning. We'll have to drive down through the park. The scenery is beautiful."

They took a short walk along the beach, the water lapping at their feet as they walked on the sand. On their right side was the Atlantic Ocean with its aqua blue water and to their left were rows of green mangrove trees. Everly told him what history she could remember about the park as they walked along the shore. Soon, they were back in the car, driving along the beautiful ocean-lined road in the state park that overlooked the stunning water with its many shades of blue. She loved when she glanced over at Drew to see the look on his face. Everly could tell he was becoming enamored by the Keys, like most people did when they came to the islands.

Everly was glad that she had offered to drive so Drew could actually see the things she would talk about along their road trip. Now, he had the window down, snapping one photo after another.

"You were right. This is pretty cool," he said, looking over at her. "And you say you want to move to New York? I can promise you, there is nothing like this up there."

"But there is snow, tall buildings, Broadway shows, and more. It's sophisticated and has so much culture. Plus, I can always come back to the Keys to visit. Only a plane ride away," Everly remarked as she looked out over the water and smiled.

"There is also a shit ton of people, a high cost of living, and just a tiny bit of crime," Drew said with a laugh. "And I promise, the snow isn't what it's cracked up to be."

"Hey, don't rain on my parade. I know about the not-so-good. Already had a sit-down with the parents, who are still subtly making comments about me going anywhere. Plus, when anyone finds out I want to move, it seems I end up being lectured on everything that is wrong with the city, usually ending with the reason why they had moved here or were visiting."

"So, your parents are that adamant they don't want you to go, huh?" he asked.

"I think they don't mind if I go for an extended vacation. They just want me to be close by and stay here. They are all for me getting my own place on the island. As a matter of fact, when they found out that Abbey's place was going to be available once she moved in with Zach, they practically said they would put down the deposit and first year's rent!" Everly said with a grin.

"I would have taken that!"

"No, you wouldn't. Abbey has told me how you really wanted to move to the city. She even said I reminded her of you."

As Everly made a turn around the parking lot to exit the park, Drew knew her words were right. "So where to next, tour guide?"

"We're just going to ride up the highway. There is so much to see that you'll have to make some day trips, or maybe stay overnight in a few places over the next few weeks. It's probably a good thing your editor was so generous with your time away."

As they rode down Highway 1, Everly made sure to point out the Turtle Hospital, even though Drew had been there already, and then Dolphin Research Center. She gave him general information about the Old Railroad Bridge and the famous 7 Mile Bridge. She also told him of Sombrero Beach that was very popular with turtles as a place to lay their eggs. Then, it was all about the sports fishing that was so popular in Islamorada. Before she knew it, they were in Key Largo.

"Now, this park is great, too. You have to make sure to come back here," Everly said as they reached the John Pennekamp State Park. "You can go snorkeling and scuba diving. They also have glass-bottom boats and a great beach. You would probably love it there, but we don't have time today. But it would make a great day trip."

"Well, it seems that I have a lot to do over the next week or so. I really didn't know these islands had so much to offer. But right now, I don't know about you, but I'm starving," Drew said. "Why don't we get some lunch, or we could grab some food and go to the park to eat? Which sounds better?"

Everly thought and remembered a restaurant in the area that she and her parents loved. "No, we are going to Mrs. Mac's Kitchen."

"Is this somebody you know?" Drew asked warily.

Everly couldn't suppress a giggle. "No, it a great diner."

Soon, she parked the car in front of the eatery. "Now that we are here, I'm hungry, too. But I have to apologize. I'm sorry if I talked your ear off as we drove. I guess I could be a Keys tour guide, for sure." As she glanced over at Drew, the smile on his face took her breath away. It seemed like the more time she spent with Drew, the more mesmerizing he was. And right now, she didn't need some silly crush to get in her way. It would only complicate her life, and that was the last thing she needed.

"Nothing to apologize for. You've been beyond helpful. I wouldn't have half this information if it wasn't for you. But right now, my stomach is certainly talking to me."

As they both walked into the restaurant, Everly couldn't help but picture herself with this man in New York. Spending the day with him was making it hard to not see him as more than just a friend. Drew was sweet and genuine, a gentleman, and funny.

Their lunch together made it more difficult for her. Their time was filled with stories Drew shared with her about his life in New York, causing her to laugh too many times. She told him more about living in the little island town where she grew up. She did elicit a laugh or two from Drew as she told stories of the crazy things she had seen over the years while living in Key West.

"Are we ready to head back?" Drew asked. But as he looked at the scenery around him and especially the girl in front of him, he wasn't sure he wanted to leave.

"I am if you are, but now that I'm full, I'm a bit sleepy. But there are a few more places I would like to show you. If it's okay with you, I would like to go by the marina here before heading back. I want to see a friend of mine. Well, sort of a friend. You probably met him at Abbey's wedding. Garrett Holmes?"

Drew was trying to remember who Everly was talking about, but was drawing a complete blank.

"I thought that he and his girlfriend, Skylar, might be able to help you with some information in this area. Skylar owns a few charter boats and Garrett is a marine biologist in the area. I don't think it will be long before those two get married. Seems like the wedding bug is running rampant among my friends lately."

Drew laughed at the sweet girl sitting across from him. His sister was right. Everly was wonderful, and he only hoped that the big city wouldn't change her. In the short time he had lived there, he had seen many people, friends included, come to the city. It either embraced them or ruined their lives. He'd felt lucky not to be included in the latter group.

When they got to the marina, Garrett and Skylar had just brought their charter boat in from a scuba trip. After chatting with the couple for only a few minutes, Drew knew immediately that he would have to come back to interview them. Especially Skylar, when he found out how she had struck out on her own even though she had come from a very wealthy family in Miami. Between the two of them, Garret and Skylar had a vast amount of knowledge about the area. Garrett could give him the much needed information about the ecosystem in the Keys, something he knew his editor would devour.

The drive back to Key West was nice and, as Everly had promised, she did show him more areas to investigate. But Drew knew that he wouldn't be able to do everything. He would have to stay much longer than the three weeks he had been allotted. But he was glad that he had spent the day with Everly.

Now, Drew secretly vowed that when she made her trek to New York, he would be her big brother protector. He was feeling close to her now that they had spent more time together. It was the least he could do after she had been so gracious with him, showing him so many of the places where she had grown up. And at the same time, giving him more than enough information for several stories that were sure to be front-page news for his editor.

"Thanks for the day trip. My list is now a mile long of what I need to do before I leave this tropical paradise," Drew said, walking Everly to her door.

"Glad I was able to help. I really enjoyed the day. It has been a while since I made that trip for fun. Usually, I drive it to go shopping, since we don't exactly have malls and big box stores. I make the trip to the mainland about once a month or so. When I go, it's just a long drive for me. Today, I was able to share everything with you, and that was nice. Plus, I hadn't been to Mrs. Mac's Kitchen in a while, and that was an extra nice treat. Thanks for the lunch, by the way," Everly said as she reached her front door.

"My pleasure. One more thing. Would you like to go with me to the airport tomorrow to pick up Abbey and Zach? I'm sure they would like to see you."

Everly's heart fluttered just a bit. More time to spend with Drew was just the thing she was thinking of. And he was asking her. Could he be feeling a little of what she was? Was there an attraction between the two of them? Even though she had told herself that it would only complicate matters more, that fear was fading by the minute. Each second that ticked by, Drew Wallace was taking tiny baby steps right into her heart.

"I would love to."

6

"I think their plane is getting ready to land," Drew said as he walked up to Everly. "Seems it was a bit late." They had been watching the stream of people come through security, but had yet to see the honeymoon couple.

"I think it already has," Everly said.

At that moment, Drew finally saw his sister and new brother-in-law. They were both pulling carry-on luggage that seemed to be full, almost to the point of exploding.

"So, how was your mountain honeymoon?" Everly asked giving Abbey a hug as they finally reached them.

"It was wonderful. I got to show Zach where I grew up, go zip lining, stay in a very romantic log cabin with a fireplace, and more." Abbey was glowing, and Everly was so happy for her friend. She suddenly wondered if she would possibly be able to share something like this with someone special. Maybe Drew?

"Why are you shaking your head?" Abbey asked her friend.

"What?" With Abbey's words, Everly realized that she was trying to erase the images of her and Drew that had flooded her mind, but had made her gesture visually. "Nothing really. Just happy for you. I hope you'll share a few more details later," she said to cover up her odd behavior.

Within a few minutes, the foursome was walking toward baggage claim. "So, how has everything been here while we were gone?" Zach asked.

"I've been showing Drew around town. Yesterday, we took a trip up the Keys. I'm giving him some information for work."

"And I definitely have my work cut out for me. Everly has given me more info than I think I can cover while I'm here. I guess that means I'll have to come back. At least I have a place to stay, right?" Drew said, looking at his sister. He expected a smile, but instead, Abbey looked a little dismayed.

"What?" he mouthed to Abbey silently, and she only shook her head back at him. Puzzled by his sister's reaction, Drew didn't know what to say.

"Abbey, let me take that for you," Drew said to his sister, taking the handle to the rolling case. "Man, what do you have in here?"

"You think that's bad, you should feel our suitcases. I think Abbey brought half of her stuff from the mountains back with us. I didn't think there was going to be any room for our clothes."

"I hadn't been back home in a while, and I couldn't pass up the opportunity since we had extra luggage. Did have to pay some fees, but it's worth it. Now, our Key West home will have a touch of the Smoky Mountains once I get Zach's, well, *our* place fixed up," Abbey said with a smile on her face.

But as soon as Zach and Everly were in a conversation and looking for the couple's luggage, Drew pulled his sister to his side. "Why did you give me that look?"

"You know why. You used to do that with all my friends, even though they were older than you. I don't want you to do that to Everly."

"What in the hell are you talking about?" Drew asked.

"Can't you see she likes you?"

"I like her, too. She's a nice girl, and I hope I can help her when she gets to New York."

"Not like that, you idiot. I mean, I can tell she really likes you. Not just as a friend. I don't want to see her get her heart broken. She's already been through one crappy relationship. She doesn't need another," Abbey admonished her brother.

"We're just friends. She's just been helping me with some details about the islands. We're not dating or anything. Just had some lunches and dinners, and a trip through the Keys yesterday." Drew continued to stare at his sister, trying to figure out what he had done that was so wrong.

But before Abbey could utter another word, Zach and Everly were at their sides, two large suitcases in tow.

"I can't wait to see what you brought back," Everly remarked as she sat the luggage on all four wheels. "By the weight of this, it feels like you brought back a piece of furniture!"

"Good one," Drew said with a smile, which made Everly grin even bigger.

"Ha-ha." Abbey rolled her eyes but then watched the face of her young friend and co-worker. Yes, it was just what she expected. Abbey could tell that Everly had a crush on her brother, and she knew Drew had a girlfriend in New York. She hoped that he had shared that tidbit of news with Everly during their weeklong string of activities. "All I brought back was just a few things I wanted for our new home."

They loaded up the luggage in the car and headed back to what was now Zach and Abbey's place. Abbey seemed to talk non-stop about their adventures in the mountains, and Everly clung to every word. She had never seen the Smoky Mountains, and it was a place she had wanted to visit. Abbey had told her that one day, they would take a girl's trip there, but then Zach and Abbey fell in love. But maybe now they would be able to make that trip. Maybe even meet in the mountains for a girl's weekend getaway once Everly was living in New York.

"Drew, if you don't mind, I sure could use some help moving Abbey's things from her place tomorrow. We moved a lot of the smaller stuff already, so we probably only need to make a couple of trips tomorrow. That should have everything moved out. We're cleaning it Tuesday, then it's officially up for rent again," Zach said, smiling at his new bride

"No problem. We can start first thing in the morning. But I have a big question. Can I still stay here for another night? I can always find a hotel tomorrow," Drew asked.

"You can stay here for the rest of your visit, if it's okay with your sister," Zach answered nonchalantly.

"But you guys are still on your honeymoon. I don't want to spoil anything."

"Why don't you stay at Abbey's place? She has the best landlords ever, and I'm sure they wouldn't mind. Sorry if I butted in," Everly said. She had jumped into the conversation and she suddenly saw a picture of her and Drew having a nice dinner at Abbey's old apartment. Just the thought of spending a romantic dinner with this man was so enticing.

"That's really a good idea. I don't mind if you stay here, but it would be nice to spend these first few weeks with my new husband, just the two of us." Abbey slid closer to her husband and gave him the gentlest kiss on the cheek. But in the back of her mind, Abbey was planning the talk she intended on having with Drew. He had to stop flirting with Everly before things got out of hand.

"Well, I'm glad you guys are home safe and sound. And thanks, Drew," Everly said, looking at him very sweetly," for letting me tag along to pick them up at the airport. I have a few things I need to do before work tomorrow. I guess I'll see you two back at work on Wednesday. Let me just warn you that it's been slightly busy, so be ready. Your desks are stacked with projects. Just something for you to look forward to." She then turned to Drew. "Are we still on for dinner tomorrow night? Remember, this is to be your class on Key West history." Everly smiled.

"I don't mean to cause any trouble, but we might need him here, to help with all the moving," Abbey countered quickly.

"I'll call you tomorrow, Everly. Let me walk you out." Drew gave his sister an evil stare as the couple walked out the door.

"Okay, I'll bite. What was all that about?" Zach asked.

"My brother, the flirt. I can see he's worked his charms on Everly. Couldn't you tell how she clung to every word he said? Followed him around, staying close to him?"

"Maybe he likes her, too. That would work, since she is moving to New York soon."

"Listen, I love my baby brother, but his relationship skills are lacking, just slightly."

"What do you mean? They seemed to be getting along fine."

"He's a flirt and truly doesn't know it. Plus, he has a girlfriend in New York." Abbey sat silently for a moment. "I just don't want him to hurt Everly. I can tell from the body language I've seen since they picked us up, Everly has a crush on him and he's just being his overly charming self, seeing Everly only as a friend."

"Maybe he really likes her, and you're reading all the signals wrong," Zach said, trying to understand the situation.

"Just when have I been wrong? I helped Josie and Michael, then Garrett and Skylar." Abbey raised her eyebrows at her new husband. Now, she could tell that Zach was beginning to understand what she was talking about, just by reading his facial expressions.

"Well, I'm leaving this all up to you. I'm not saying a word."

"When he gets back, we might just have to have a little talk."

As if on cue, Drew walked back into the little apartment, a smile spread across his face. But when he looked at the couple before him, he immediately recognized Abbey's look of disapproval.

"Okay, let's go for a walk," Abbey said. "We need to talk."

"I just walked back in! What in the world do we need to talk about?"

"Everly!"

"Abbey, if you haven't noticed, I'm a big boy now and can handle my own relationships. And friendships, which is what I have with Everly. We've just had a great time while you were gone this week," Drew said, defending himself before Abbey could say the words he knew she desperately wanted to throw his way.

"I'll be in the bedroom, unpacking, if either of you need anything. Just remember to be nice to each other. This last week has been peaceful, and I would hate to end it on a sour note." Zach smiled at both of them, gave his wife a kiss on the top of her head, then walked down the hallway.

"Well, if you won't go for a walk, then we'll discuss it right here," Abbey said, sitting on the couch and motioning for her baby brother to take a seat. Now it was Drew's turn to roll his eyes as he sat roughly in the small padded chair across from her.

"Drew, please don't break Everly's heart. She's so sweet, and she's already been through one tough relationship that has her wary of men, anyway."

"Abbey, I can't say this enough: we're just friends. We've had some dinners together, and yesterday we drove up the Keys and back. She gave me some valuable insight for stories I can take back home. But I will admit that I think she's a beautiful girl and a lot of fun to be with. I've thoroughly enjoyed my time with her. What's so wrong with that?" Drew looked at her, puzzled.

Abbey shook her head. Sometimes she wondered what Drew was thinking. "I can tell just by Everly's body language that she likes you. I mean, really likes you! And you – you practically kept to her side the entire time since you picked us up. You act almost like you like her as well. Do you like her like that? You know, more than a friend?"

"You're getting awfully personal here, but no. If you remember correctly, I have a girlfriend in New York. I promise, Everly and I are just friends, and I know that's how she feels, too. There's been no kissing, hand holding – anything. I swear! You're reading too much into this. You'll see. As a matter of fact, tomorrow night, we are going to a book signing because one of her favorite authors is going to be there. She told me all about the collection of books they have at this book store, including rare first editions, and I told her I wanted to see it. It's another good story for an article about vacationing in this area. Then, we're going to get something to eat. You and Zach should come along, and I can prove to you it's not what you think. Not that I should have to, but I will." Drew looked at her very genuinely, and Abbey could tell that he was indeed telling the truth. His radar was out of tune if he couldn't tell what was happening, but hopefully, she would be able to prove it to him tomorrow night.

"We'll go, because now that I have brought it to your attention, I think you'll see things just a bit differently. I want you two to be friends, and if you were genuinely interested in her for a real relationship, I would be thrilled. Everly is a beautiful soul. But I know about your girlfriend back home. Have you told her about Peyton?" Abbey waited to hear the answer, and when it didn't come quickly, what she had suspected was true.

"No, because it's not a big deal. I've only talked to Peyton a couple of times because she didn't want me to stay so long in the Keys and got upset. She accused me of seeing someone here, which was ridiculous because I've never been here before now." Drew had been a bit perturbed when Peyton had accused him of cheating.

"Do you think it might be because you don't stay with a woman very long? It seems there is always someone else for you. I'll give you credit that you break up with someone first, but you've dated more women than I can count!" Abbey said a bit loudly.

"How would you know?"

"Because half the time, you would either bug me or Mark about your latest girl problem." Abbey suddenly remembered one day when her older brother, Mark, came into her room looking like he had just run a marathon. Come to find out, Drew had been talking his ear off about whether to break it off with his girlfriend, because he had just met the girl of his dreams.

"Well, Peyton and I have been dating almost a year now." But Drew had to admit that Abbey was right about that. It seemed he never could make a good decision when it came to women. Or at least, that's how he felt. He envied his sister and brother because they had found that special person that was meant just for them. He wanted so badly to ask them how they knew that the person they were with was the 'one.'

Drew had hoped to have that conversation with Abbey before he left, but after this, he wasn't sure. He didn't dare let Abbey know that just being with Everly these last few days had confused the feelings he thought- no, he *knew*- he felt for Peyton. Not that he didn't love Peyton, because he did. *Don't I?* Drew thought.

"Why so quiet? Are my words true?" Abbey asked.

"No," Drew said quickly. "You'll see, tomorrow night. Everly and I are just friends. And she feels the same way that I do."

"I sure hope so."

7

Everly was so excited about this evening. After she got home from Abbey and Zach's yesterday, she picked out an outfit just for tonight. She was going to meet one of her favorite authors and, once again, spend time with Drew. Even though when they first met, all she was interested in was any details he could share with her about New York, things were different now. She wanted to know all about him. He had such a warm, tender heart and was such a gentleman. Add to that his sweeping good looks, and Drew was the total package in a man, as far as she was concerned.

They had planned to go to the author signing at her favorite local book store, Key West Island Books, then on to Hog's Breath Saloon for dinner. Drew said he had more questions about Key West, and Everly was more than happy to oblige. She only hoped that spending this time together here would help their friendship once she reached New York. Or that maybe, their friendship would become more of a romance.

Everly couldn't help but admit to herself that she was beginning to think more about Drew and what the possibilities could be once she was living in New York. She even daydreamed of romantic nights with him, walking the busy city streets. Going to see a Broadway show. Maybe a carriage ride in Central Park. All these thoughts were making her smile and feel a little weak inside.

"I don't think I've ever seen you smile as much as you have today. It's like it's permanently tattooed on your face," Roger said, bringing her back to reality and to the computer screen glowing in front of her. "Your weekend must have been really nice. I know mine was."

"Actually, it was wonderful," Everly said. "Oh, I'm sorry. I didn't even ask how your trip was."

"Fantastic! We had a blast in Miami, even though the airboat ride was not my idea. But I couldn't tell John no."

"John?" Everly asked softly.

"John, the man I'm seeing," Roger answered, looking at the girl sitting by his side. She was staring at the computer like she was frozen in place.

"Earth to Everly? Where are you?" Roger said, snapping his fingers, which made Everly jump. "By the way you're acting, your weekend must have been over-the-top good," Roger continued. "You can't even concentrate on work. So where is he taking you tonight?"

"How do you know I have a date?"

"So, it *is* a date? With Abbey's brother? Wow, you are moving right along! Wait 'til Abbey finds out."

"I didn't mean date. We are just going to a book signing and then dinner. I'm still helping him with research while he's here in the Keys. Anyway, he goes home soon. Plus, Abbey already knows I've been helping him while they were gone. I went with Drew yesterday to the airport to pick her and Zach up from their trip."

"Wonder what she thinks." Roger leaned toward Everly, giving her a nudge with his elbow. "But it really doesn't matter, because you'll be in New York soon. And if Drew is anything like Abbey, girl, you better latch onto him."

"It's nothing like that, Roger, really," Everly replied, finally starting to concentrate on the work before her. "I'm sure he has a girlfriend waiting for him." It was the first time Everly thought of Drew being with another woman. Suddenly, she couldn't fathom how someone like Drew didn't have a girlfriend waiting anxiously for his return. He hadn't said a word about dating anyone but she hadn't asked either.

"Well, don't you think he would have told you by now if he was attached to someone? If he hasn't said anything, I'm sure he's single. Maybe, he isn't getting the right vibe from you."

"Seriously, Roger, please drop it. We're just friends. I have too much going on to even think about dating or being in a relationship." Everly said the words, keeping her composure as best she could. But in her mind, she was thinking just the opposite. If it were Drew that was going to complicate her life, it would be perfectly fine with her.

"Okay, I'll leave you alone. Seems like you're back to your old self. That one-track 'I'm moving to the city' mind," Roger said, turning to the stack of papers on his desk. "But Everly, let me give you a bit of advice. Reaching your goals is great, and I know you have been looking forward to moving for so long now. But it's always better sharing things with someone.

Don't choose to be alone, because take it from me, it truly is lonely."

With that, Roger turned back to his desk and quietly set about his work, leaving Everly to ponder his words. But with one quick look at the clock, she realized she was off in two hours and would see Drew in three. Those tiny little shivers mixed with happy feelings consumed her once more.

"Everly, you have a call on line one," Lance announced from the open door behind them.

"Thanks." She picked up the phone and pressed the button. "Hello?"

"Hi, there! I didn't know whether I could call you on your cell phone or the work line, so I hope this is okay." It was Drew. The smile she had earlier was gracing her face more broadly now. Everly made sure to turn away from Roger. She could only imagine what he would say next.

"It's no problem. What's up?" Everly asked.

"There has been a slight change in plans for the evening," Drew said. Everly's heart sank just a bit. "Abbey and Zach are going to join us for the book signing and dinner. I hope that's okay. I thought, maybe between the three of you, I could get more research and story ideas."

"That sounds great," Everly said in a voice as cheerful as she could muster. Until this moment, she hadn't realized how much she had been looking forward to more alone time with this man. But they would still be together, and that was what she concentrated on.

"Are we all riding in one car? We can park close to the book store and walk everywhere. That's one great thing about this town," she said, still determined to make tonight nice.

"You and Abbey think just alike, because that's just about verbatim what she said. Not sure if that's a girl thing or a friend thing," Drew said with a little laugh. She pictured him in her mind, with his sexy dimples. "We'll be by at six o'clock to pick you up. Will that still work?"

"That should give me enough time to get home and changed. We're getting caught up at work, so I should be out of here on time. I can't wait to get to the book store. I think you're going to love this place. There will probably be more books there that will help you with your research, I'm sure of it."

"I have to admit that I'm a sucker for a great book store. Maybe, one day, my novel will be sold there."

"I didn't know you were writing a novel," Everly said.

"It hasn't really come up in conversation, and it's slow going. But being here…let's talk about it tonight," Drew said quickly.

"I'm gonna hold you to it."

"See you at six!" The phone clicked off.

So, her time with Drew had now become a foursome. But that was okay. Everly wanted to hear more about Abbey and Zach's honeymoon, and she was sure that she would have more time with Drew before he left the island. Even though there was a bit of disappointment running through her, she wasn't going to let it affect her time tonight. Ever since Drew came to town, it seemed her life had gotten just a bit more exciting.

■ ■ ■

As Everly and Abbey stood in the line, waiting for a signature in her book "Chasing the Water" from one of Everly's favorite authors, T.D. Solener, Zach and Drew perused the bookstore.

Everly watched as Drew found one book after another, proving that he was indeed a writer, through and through. Drew purchased several books, and from the boyish look of excitement on his face, she was sure that he loved the store as much as she did. Watching him made Everly realize they had one more thing in common: a love for books. The more time they spent together, the more things Everly added to the mental list in her head about how much she was drawn to Drew. She hoped that he was feeling the same way, too.

Stop! she said silently to herself. *This can't happen and you are not going to let yourself get hurt again.* But Everly realized that this wasn't some crush anymore. She really liked Drew. He made her happy and she loved being around him.

"I heard that you and my brother had a great time while we were gone," Abbey said.

"We did. Of course, I had to work a lot to make up for you being on your honeymoon," Everly giggled, leaning into her friend. "But we had some dinners, and then the trip up the Keys that he told you about. Seems we have a lot in common. He also gave me some good information about New York. Now, I wish that I could move tomorrow."

"I hope that it's everything you dreamed of. But you can always come home if things aren't like you imagined." Abbey meant it, but she also worried that the big city would take away a piece of Everly that made her special. She was a unique and confident woman. New York was going to be so different from what she was used to. But Abbey knew there was no way to talk Everly out of her big move. Sometimes, letting people follow their hearts was hard, but something that must be done, whether the outcome was good or bad.

"Drew told me that once I got there, he would help me if I needed anything. I'm glad I'll know at least one person when I get there. I'm excited about going, but nervous just the same. It's going to be a completely different world than living here in Key West. But Drew has been a big help this week, giving me lots of advice I know I'll need."

"Everly, I know this really isn't my place," Abbey started, "but I have to say something because you're my friend. I love my brother dearly, but please don't fall for Drew. He's sweet and he means well, but when it comes to women, he's a bit clueless. I keep telling myself that he needs to grow up some more, but I think it's just his outgoing personality. He wants to help everyone, which is admirable, but he doesn't quite know how to read people, especially women." Abbey said the words carefully, not sure how Everly would react.

"What do you mean? We're just friends. Sure, it's been great hanging out with him. I've been to some places around the Keys that I haven't been to in years, so that's been fun. But you know my focus right now is just moving to New York," Everly said. She was trying as hard as she could to convey there were no romantic feelings in her heart for Drew, when she knew the truth was just the opposite.

"You know, this is your friend you're talking to. I've been around you long enough that I can read you like a book. I can see that you like my brother. Don't get me wrong – he's a sweetheart. But that's just it. He has a charm about him that he doesn't see, and it gets him in trouble."

Everly looked at Abbey once more. *Was I that transparent?* Everly thought. There was a small part of her that knew that every one of Abbey's words were true.

Drew hadn't tried to kiss Everly or hold her hand. In fact, as Everly thought about it, there wasn't even any mention of a single word that could be construed that he liked her in a romantic way. The time Drew and Everly had spent together had been like two close friends.

"Abbey, really, I only see him as a friend. I will admit, a very cute and sweet friend, but a friend."

Everly brought her thoughts back to the present, focusing on Mr. Solener sitting at the table. Though she was finally getting to meet one of her favorite authors, the only thing Everly could think about was the fairytale romance with Drew that she had concocted in her imagination. It was still there, but she tried to tuck it back into a small corner of her mind. Abbey had just told her that Drew didn't even know he had such an adorable personality, and she could see Abbey's point. Like she had told herself before, Drew was the perfect guy for her.

"So, where to next?" Drew asked once they were standing outside on the sidewalk.

"It's on to get some dinner. Might be a bit loud, but the food is good. If it's the Key West atmosphere you're looking for, it's one of our most popular landmarks," Everly said in the most animated voice she could muster. Now that she knew where she stood with Drew, suddenly, she felt she could be her complete self.

"Sounds good to me," Zach said as they all started walking down the street.

The restaurant was noisy and crowded, as Everly predicted, but the vibe throughout was one of pure fun. They all had drinks and ate, with Abbey and Zach sharing honeymoon stories that had everyone laughing. For Everly, it was still exciting to sit beside Drew and be with him, but after the conversation with Abbey, she knew a romance was too good to be true. But Everly was going to enjoy every minute of it while she could.

"Hey, Drew, I never got to ask you at the wedding. Why didn't Peyton come with you?" Zach asked before taking a drink of his beer.

"Who's Peyton?" Everly asked.

"Drew's girlfriend. I thought Abbey told me she was coming with you," Zach continued, not knowing the hornet's nest he had just released.

"Ah, she had some modeling shoots and wasn't going to be able to stay the whole time. So, she decided to stay home," Drew said.

Everly felt like she had just been punched in the chest. He had a girlfriend? He hadn't said anything about that the entire time they were together. Abbey was right. Everly suddenly felt like a fool for thinking that there could have been more to their relationship. But she now knew, especially from the way Drew was talking, that she was only a friend to him.

"I really hate to break up this party, but I need to get home. I have to be at work early for a conference call, and you know how Lance is if I'm late." Everly looked only at Zach and Abbey. "I hope you two are ready to work on Wednesday. There's plenty to do."

"We didn't get to talk much tonight. Want to meet tomorrow night? Maybe just go out to the beach and sit?" Drew asked Everly directly.

For a second, Everly was speechless. She wanted to say yes immediately, but the conversation with Abbey and then a quick glance at her friend gave her the courage to say just the opposite. "Actually, I have plans for tomorrow night. But since Abbey and Zach still have another day before coming back to work, they might be able to answer your questions."

"True. Then let's get together another evening this week. Plus, we're still going to the Turtle Hospital on Saturday, right?" Drew's voice was like honey to her. She had forgotten about the plans they had made. She suddenly felt very confused and just wanted some air.

"Sure," was the only word that came from her. Everly told herself that once she was home, she could figure out what was going on in her mind.

"Let me give you a ride home," Drew said, standing up to follow her.

"Oh, no, I'm fine. You guys stay here and enjoy the evening. I'm going to catch a taxi back to my house. See ya later."

Before anyone could say anything, Everly grabbed her handbag and walked out of the restaurant. Once she was walking along the sidewalk, she felt like she could finally breathe somewhat normally. Learning about Drew's girlfriend brought back those dreaded feelings of betrayal from her failed relationship, only a few years ago. And it shouldn't have, because she and Drew were never a couple. But at that moment, Everly realized how much she had fallen for Drew.

What hurt the most though was knowing that he didn't feel the same way about her.

8

"What was that all about?" Drew asked as he watched Everly practically run out of the restaurant.

"You seriously have no clue, do you?" Abbey said sternly to her little brother. Then, she looked at her husband. "And why did you have to bring up Peyton?"

"Why not?" Zach asked.

"Because my genius brother hadn't said a word to Everly this whole time they've been spending time together, have you?"

"No, but what's the big deal?" Drew asked, eyebrows raised as he stared at the couple across the table.

"She likes you, Drew. Tell me you aren't that blind."

Drew sat there, letting it all sink in. He liked Everly too, but now, he could see his sister's point. "I had no idea. I mean, I really like Everly. It felt good to have a friend that was a girl that I could just have fun with, no pressure. I was waiting to discuss Peyton with the two of you. I even considered getting Everly's opinion about a few things I'm going through with

Peyton. I mean, Everly and I get along so well, it's been like we've known each other for years."

Abbey rolled her eyes. Just liked she had revealed to Everly only an hour ago, her brother was clueless when it came to relationships.

"It's probably a good thing you didn't. Don't think that would have gone over too well." Zach was trying to diffuse the tension between the siblings but wasn't sure he was doing a very good job.

"Well, I can see by the look on your face that the light bulb must have come on in that brain of yours," Abbey said. She was trying to not be upset with Drew, but couldn't. He was charming and he'd been this way his whole life. Between that charm and his good looks, even Abbey's friends had been enamored by her younger brother.

"I know you meant well, but that Drew Wallace appeal has struck again, and this time, Everly was the target. She'll be okay, but at least you know where she stands. And now, she knows where your feelings lie, too. She's a wonderful girl and will make a great friend. She's going to need that when she gets to New York. So, I hope that you can repair this situation before you leave."

"I will," Drew said, wondering what he was going to say to Everly. He loved her company and already had ideas of how to help her once she moved. In his mind, he could see all the wonderful times they could have together in New York once he introduced her to his friends and his girlfriend.

"But why would you want to talk to us about Peyton?" Abbey asked as nicely as she could. She was trying to disguise her displeasure about discussing Drew's girlfriend.

"Oh yeah, Peyton," Drew said, the words bringing him back to Abbey and Zach.

"Well, I thought if I ever needed this kind of advice, I might as well ask a newly married couple." Drew took a deep breath. "I'm thinking of asking Peyton to marry me," he said.

Abbey felt like the air had rushed out of the area surrounding them. Drew, married? Hadn't she just told Everly that he was still learning all about even being in a relationship? Not that she didn't trust her brother and love him dearly, but he just didn't seem to be mature enough to get married. Even though it seemed the other areas of his life were organized and spot on, Drew seemed scattered when it came to knowing anything about love.

"Do you think you're ready for marriage?" Zach asked before Abbey could say a word.

"I think so. Peyton and I just seem to click. We like the same things. We both have ambitious goals. And, I love her." The last three words that Drew uttered were a bit hesitant, compared to the others.

"Are you sure? You sounded more like you were reassuring yourself, instead of declaring your feelings for her," Abbey countered, trying to say the words nicely. It was obvious that Drew wasn't sure how he really felt.

"I really do. We have been together for a while now, and it just seems like the next logical step."

"Wow, that sounded very romantic!"

"Abbey, just because you don't like Peyton doesn't mean that you have to be so condescending." Now, Drew was on the defensive. He had felt like he could turn to them for advice. But what he didn't want was a lecture.

"I'm going for a walk." Drew stood up and turned to walk away from the table.

"Whoa, there," Zach said, gesturing for Drew to sit down. "Wait a minute, and let's talk. Don't you think you kinda hit your sister and me with some awfully big news? Plus, you asked for my opinion too. I haven't been able to say anything."

Drew reluctantly sat back down. It felt like the atmosphere around them was suddenly very thick with tension, even though they were sitting outside in the beautiful Florida weather. All Drew could think about was the mixed emotions that were clouding his head. Hopefully, Zach would be of some help.

"First, I've never met Peyton, but she sounds nice," Zach said. He kept his eyes focused directly on Drew but out of the corner of his eye, he saw his new wife staring at him with wide eyes. Zach slipped his hand under the table and gave Abbey a reassuring pat on her leg to help her calm down. "But marriage is such a big step. Even Abbey and I talked about it for quite a while and went through some major hurdles to get here. But it was worth it." This time, Zach looked at his wife and smiled.

"When you think of being married to Peyton, does it make you happy?" Zach asked. It was such a simple question, but when Drew didn't immediately answer, it spoke volumes.

"Drew, I'm sorry if I got a bit defensive. You're my brother and I always want to take care of you. Make sure you are happy and love your life. I'm so lucky that I have two brothers that I feel so close to, because I've talked to many people who barely know or have anything to do with their siblings once they're grown. But if you can't quickly answer Zach's question, then maybe you're thinking of getting married for the wrong reasons. Is there more to this than you're telling us?"

Drew sat back in the chair and let out a sigh. "Peyton's just been talking about it quite a bit. I thought it would make her happy, and then she wouldn't be on me so much when I wanted to do something with the guys or when I go on assignments. You should have seen the fit she threw about me coming here. Not to your wedding, but staying here for the stories. I even asked her to come with me, like a vacation, and she said that if she was going to some beach, it would be Hawaii or the south of France. Florida didn't interest her at all."

"Okay, I'm going to say something- and don't hit me- but why would you even entertain the idea of marrying someone like that?" Zach asked.

"Just seems like everyone has someone. My friends are getting married. Peyton is fun to be with and we have a good time. Her parents even want us to get married. Her father offered me a better job at one of his media outlets as an editor. Corner office and all. Everything feels like what I'm supposed to do."

"Drew," Abbey said softly, reaching across the table and taking her little brother's hand, "this is your life. Not anyone else's. You have to do what makes you happy. Your body language when you talk of getting married is like someone going to their execution. I know you like Peyton, maybe even love her. But you asked for my opinion, so here it is. Give it more time. Don't let anyone rush you. If you and Peyton are meant to be together, it will work. But on yours and Peyton's time, not someone else trying to rush you. And just because everyone seems to have what you deem 'the perfect life,' believe me, theirs isn't. Listen to your gut, because it usually knows best."

"I second that," Zach said, leaning toward him from across the table. "But I do want to add something. When you and Everly picked us up at the airport yesterday, and then again this evening, you seemed so happy. Totally different than how you are right now, as we discuss marriage and Peyton. Maybe that will give you a bit of insight on how you genuinely feel."

"You mean I like Everly?" Drew asked, confused.

"No, not necessarily. But you've been down here, away from your life in the city. You seem much more relaxed, but you're still working. You're enjoying your research and making new friends, like Everly. Take back some of the Keys vibe with you. You have to admit, we're much more laid back here than in New York. It might serve you well when you go back home.

"As for Everly, she's special to both of us," Zach continued, looking over at Abbey once more. "I hope that you two can overcome this little incident tonight, because it'll help all of us here feel better when she moves to the city. We keep trying to talk her out of it, but she's one determined girl. All I ask is, don't break her heart. I think before you go back home, you need to be honest with her. Talk to her about Peyton. That way, when she gets there, she's already prepared. Hopefully, it'll be like she has a big brother watching out for her."

Zach's right, Drew thought. Why was he letting everyone pressure him into marriage? He would have to have a talk with Peyton as soon as he got back, and hope that she wouldn't break up with him. But then, he thought about Everly. She had become a close friend to him in such a short time, and he didn't want to ruin that friendship. She had really made being here in the Keys much more enjoyable than he ever imagined possible. And he couldn't imagine them not talking, since they had at least spoken on the phone or spent time together every day since Zach and Abbey's wedding. Tomorrow, he would fix the situation he had created. He just had to find the right words to say, which should be easy since he was a writer. But right now, for Drew, the words that he needed were nowhere to be found.

9

Everly was looking at the computer screen in front of her, desperately trying to figure out the problem in the coding, but her mind just wasn't letting her think properly today. Last night had gone completely different than she had pictured in her mind, and now these hurt emotions wouldn't stop invading her thoughts. She was mad at herself, because Drew had never said he liked her. He had never done anything to give her any indication that he might be interested in her more than a friend.

Drew had been so charming, doing all the things that Everly had dreamed of. She couldn't remember ever being this comfortable with a man that wasn't a relative or someone she worked with. No, Drew was different. But Everly had dreamed up this romantic scenario in her head of she and Drew dating, walking on the beach or, better yet, the streets of New York. But one word had changed everything: Peyton.

Why hadn't Drew mentioned his girlfriend before? Never once in all the time they had spent together had he ever mentioned someone he was dating, but Everly hadn't asked. She felt so stupid, almost depressed.

"You've been staring at the screen for an hour. What's the problem?" Roger asked.

"Nothing," Everly answered back, the tone in her voice giving her away.

"This must have something to do with Abbey's brother. Did you two have a lovers' quarrel?" Roger asked innocently, but soon wished he hadn't spoken the words. He watched as Everly slowly laid her head back on the chair and stared at the ceiling.

"So, tell me what's going on." Roger wheeled his chair over to Everly's side. She finally looked at him.

"No, it wasn't a lovers' quarrel," Everly said softly. "We aren't dating, remember?"

"Then he must have done something to really piss you off, by the way you're acting."

"I'm not pissed off. You sure are getting a bit nosey, don't you think?" Everly shook her head.

"So, what gives?"

"I don't know. Just, this last week or so has been nice. I...." Everly didn't want to continue her sentence. She just wasn't ready to voice the thoughts that were swirling in her head. Apparently, Roger could tell what she was feeling.

"Listen. When you're ready to talk, just know that I'm here. But I hate to say this – we've got to figure out this problem before we leave. Those were Lance's instructions before he left, and we both know how Mr. Huffton is about this website. So, let's go over everything once again."

Roger took control of the project, and before she knew it, Everly was back in work mode. Then, the website problem became crystal clear. As they were locking the door to leave for the day, her cell phone rang. She picked it up to see Drew's number across the screen.

"Are you going to answer it?" Roger stared at Everly as she was staring at the ringing phone in her hand.

"I don't know."

"Well, I'm not sure what Mr. Wonderful did last night to have you all turned around, but don't jump to conclusions. In other words, don't react too quickly. I hope I'm making sense. I'll see you tomorrow." Roger gave her a fatherly hug and was soon riding on a bike toward his home, leaving Everly standing along the street. The cell phone rang again.

"Hello."

"Hi, there!" came the cheerful voice on the other end. "Thought maybe you might be working late. Was wondering if you want to go get something to eat and watch the sunset again at the square. Or maybe somewhere we can just sit and talk for a bit." Drew's voice sounded so good to her - too good. Her whole being wanted nothing more than to say "yes," but the thought of seeing him hurt inside.

"Thanks, but it's been a really long day. Some problems at work, and I'm just wiped out. Maybe tomorrow?" Everly said.

"Everly, I really think we should talk. Please?"

Everly looked around, desperately trying to decide what to do. "I think tomorrow night would be better. We could meet after work."

"Tomorrow would be fine. What if I get sandwiches and we go to the beach and just relax? How does that sound?" Drew asked.

"I'll see you then." Everly clicked the phone off and tucked it back into her tote. *It does sound wonderful. Especially with a dreamy guy like Drew*, she thought. Everything felt so complicated in her life now, where only a few weeks ago, her plan was crystal clear. She had to get back on that path, the one where she felt stable and knew where she was heading. Falling for Drew had been a mistake. Could she be just friends? Everly wasn't sure.

■ ■ ■

She looked at the clock. There were only thirty more minutes before she was off work. Her nerves going into overdrive, just knowing that Drew would be here shortly.

"You weren't kidding when you said there was a stack of work waiting for us." Abbey had rolled her chair over to Everly, leaned her head back and sighed. "I think all I want to do is go home, take a shower, and crawl into bed. I'm not even hungry. Zach will have to fend for himself. You have big plans?"

"Your brother is actually meeting me here. We're going to the beach to relax a little while and have a dinner of sandwiches. I guess he has more Key West questions to ask me," Everly said with a slight smile on her face.

"He said he had plans, but I was so busy, I didn't even ask what he was doing. I know when we left this morning, he was already working on some articles for work. He's taken over my kitchen table, with his laptop and papers scattered everywhere."

"I would think he'd have enough information by now, as much as we did last week. I can't think of anything else I can show or tell him. But it'll be nice to just sit on the beach and chill for a while. Even if I was by myself. I do know that's one thing I'll miss once I get to New York. Speaking of which, last night, I went over everything and I think I will be able to move in about seven or eight weeks. I've contacted the landlords at three apartment buildings, checked on flights, and I have my personal stuff ready to go. At least, what I can stuff into two suitcases. Everything else, I'll have to buy or order online. Money is in the bank, so I have enough saved to get by for about nine months while I find the perfect job, as long as I stay pretty frugal. I haven't told anyone this, so please don't say anything. I'm hoping to have a concrete plan by next week. Then, I'll let Lance know as soon as possible."

Everly saw the look in Abbey's eyes, the same one she got every time she mentioned the words "New York" to anyone. It wasn't one of sadness, but it was evident that Abbey didn't want her to go. For that matter, it seemed no one wanted her to leave. Did they want her to stay in Key West because they would miss her? Or did they think she wouldn't be able to make it in the big city, having lived here her entire life? Everly didn't know which, and she wasn't sure she wanted to know the truth. She had dreamed about this her entire life, and she wasn't going to back down now.

"Listen, Everly, I'm really sorry about last night," Abbey said. "Maybe I should have told you about Peyton, but I felt like it was something that Drew should have done. And Zach knew nothing about it. He just happened to step right in the middle of this, without even knowing what was going on."

"You're right. Drew should have said something, but I'm fine."

"Remember what I told you last night? I can read you. Just remember that this isn't like what happened to you before. Yes, Drew should have told you he was involved with someone, but from his perspective, you two are only friends."

"Abbey, I'm fine, really. As for tonight, I think I might be the one asking more questions than him," Everly said before Abbey could utter another word. "There are so many things I still need to know about New York, and it seems that every time we've been somewhere, Drew wants to talk about nothing but the Keys. Now, it's my turn."

"You two are alike in that respect. Apparently, he still loves it there, so he should be able to help you. I know I feel better about you moving with Drew there. I know he'll help you with anything you need."

"Even with Peyton around?" The words came out before Everly could censor herself.

"Yes, even with Peyton there. One thing about Drew, like I told you before, is that he just likes to help people."

"I didn't mean to sound so sarcastic," Everly said. "It's just that...."

"You don't have to say another word. I know what you mean. But right now, I hope you enjoy your evening, because someone has come to pick you up."

Everly turned around and there he was, looking better than she thought possible. Or were his good looks magnified because Everly now knew he was unavailable? Her little dream that had come to life so quickly was now gone, disappearing in what seemed like a puff of smoke. It didn't matter. He looked beyond sexy to her right now, so she took a deep breath to calm the weakness she was feeling at just him being in the room with her.

"I hope I'm not too early," Drew said, walking cautiously into the workroom.

"Nope, we're all tired and very ready to go. Everly says you guys are heading to the beach tonight?" Abbey eyed her brother warily.

"Yep. I want to see another famous Key West sunset. I will admit that the sky here, whether it is sunrise or sunset, is amazing. But then again, it could be because we don't see the sky that much in New York," Drew said with a chuckle.

Damn, Everly thought. Why did he have to be so sweet?

"What about in Central Park?" Everly was putting her things in her tote while trying to be part of the conversation. She was nervous about the upcoming evening, but doing her best to exude confidence.

"Well, now that you say that, I've seen the sky there, but I have to admit that it's much nicer here."

"I can't wait to view the skyline of New York." Everly was trying her very best to steer the conversation back to New York and not her hometown.

"You two have a good time. As for us," Abbey said, as she put her hands on her husband's shoulders, "we're heading home shortly. That is, when Zach can pull himself away from the computer screen. We'll see you later Drew. See you tomorrow, Everly."

Drew noticed the look on his sister's face and knew immediately what she was thinking. He rolled his eyes, then he and Everly walked down the steps and out the door, to the sidewalk of Duval Street.

"I rode my bike today. I wasn't thinking when I left for work or I would have walked. I'll need to come back here to ride it home," Everly said, still trying to keep her composure.

"I guess it's too late to rent a bike, or we could have done that tonight."

"I usually don't ride at night anymore. Especially after Zach's accident."

Everly still shuddered at the memory of Zach being hit by a car, leaving him in critical condition. She couldn't remember anything like that happening to someone she knew. Ever since that time, riding her bike at night made her nervous, even though it was so common around town.

"Then I will follow you to your house, then we'll go to the beach from there. How does that sound?"

That would be just enough time to get my thoughts wrapped around the evening to come, Everly thought to herself. She wanted to be in control of this evening and not let her emotions get the best of her. Everly had to make sure the conversation tonight didn't go anywhere too personal, at least not on a romantic side.

"Everly, you okay?" She glanced at Drew to see a look of concern in his eyes.

"Yeah, just got a bit lost in thought. Let me get my bike." She hurried to the little space where she locked her bike up on the days she rode it to work, which was almost every day. She used her parent's car when it would rain, and thought about getting her own. But Everly knew once she left, the car would just be sitting, while she continued to pay insurance. And that was money she needed to take with her to the city.

As she pedaled through the streets of Key West, Everly was self-conscious of Drew following her in his car. There were times he had to pull over to let someone pass him, but he stayed right with her, almost like he was making sure that her ride home was safe. That thought made her smile.

"Thanks for following me home. Now, I don't have to worry about leaving the bike overnight at work."

"The more I drive around this city, the more I like it. No wonder Abbey fell in love with it. It has that small town, homey feel, even though there seems to be people everywhere. It definitely has a personality all its own."

"Yes, it does. I guess, living here my whole life, I'm just so used to it that I don't see it like you do. Or like most of the tourists do when they visit."

"That's the way I feel back home in the Smoky Mountains. Every time I tell someone where I'm from, they ask how I could leave the beauty of the mountains. I'm pretty sure it's the same way you feel." Drew finished his sentence just as they pulled up to Smather's Beach.

There was a gentle breeze blowing, keeping the temperature comfortable. The sun still had about forty-five minutes before making its way below the horizon, but it was beautiful.

Drew took the bag of food and a big blanket out of the back seat, and they made their way to a spot under one of the tropical trees.

Soon, they were eating sandwiches and chips. Drew had even brought her favorite drink: sweet tea. He'd also brought chocolate chip cookies for dessert, one of Everly's favorite sweet treats.

"How did you know that chocolate chip cookies are one of my favorite desserts?"

"Because it seemed every time we ate somewhere since I came here, you always would order the cookies for dessert if they were available. Plus when we went on our ride up the Keys, you had the cookies with you."

He might not feel the same way I do, Everly thought, *but he sure was observant enough to know some of my favorite foods.*

"Did you make these?" Everly asked as she bit into one, savoring the delicious treat.

"Yep. And from scratch, too." Drew's words were muffled as he talked with his mouth full of the chocolate delight.

"You cook?"

"Does that surprise you?"

"I just figured, living in New York, that you would eat out all the time."

"I admit that take-out is a staple at my apartment, but I do try to cook when I can. You'll find out when you get there. It's fun at first, having food delivered, trying the street vendors and the little diners. But then, there is something about homemade food." Drew took another bite. Everly continued to study him.

"So, who taught you to cook?" she asked.

"My mom, of course. I would always ask for chocolate chip cookies. So, one day, she told me that if I liked them so much, I would have to learn how to make them. From there, I went on to learn how to make spaghetti sauce and even chicken pot pie, which is one of my favorites. I even considered going to culinary school, but that didn't last long."

"Seriously?" Everly asked, thinking that Drew never ceased to amaze her. This just added more charm to this sweet man.

"I guess I still could have gone to New York and been a chef instead of a journalist."

Suddenly there was a silence that fell between them. Everly didn't know what to say next, and the air seemed to get thick with tension. Everything she wanted to ask or say seemed to be a jumbled mess in her brain. But she didn't have to worry. Drew began to speak.

"I really want to apologize for the other evening. I've enjoyed all our time together. I don't think I've had this much fun in such a long time. You're so easy to talk to and fun to be with. But I should have told you about Peyton. She's my girlfriend back home. If you couldn't tell, Abbey isn't too fond of her, but Peyton just comes from a different way of life than how we grew up. I can't wait for you to meet her when you come to New York. I have a feeling you two would make great friends." Drew took a breath before saying anything else, wanting to make sure the words were right.

"I also hope that we can still be friends too. I don't want this to keep us from talking, because I've truly grown fond of our time together. I've had so much fun this last week and a half, being with you and going places all through the Keys. And we still have a few places to visit, right?"

Everly wanted to tell this man that they should be together. That they were made for each other. Even though they had only known each other for such a short time, she was the woman for him. Even in her past relationships, she had never fallen so fast for a man. To look at Drew now, knowing that all he wanted was for them to be close friends, made her heart ache.

But Everly knew, deep down inside, that she didn't want to lose him, either. If friends were all they could be, she would accept it. Besides, when she got to New York, her goal was to work and take time for herself and discover her independence. That was what she was going to concentrate on.

"Yes, we do. There are a couple of more places to check out. If you want to take the time, you should go visit the Florida Everglades. Maybe even take an airboat ride. You'd love that!" Everly said, as animated as she could be.

He's just the big brother I never had, she repeated to herself, trying to make it feel a little less hurtful.

"I never thought about that. James, my editor, would love it! But I did receive a call today, saying that I have to head back next week. I thought that three weeks on assignment was too good to be true, but it probably is time for me to get back. I think if I stay here much longer, I'll be like Abbey. Never want to go back home. But can't erase the city out of this boy," Drew remarked with a laugh.

Everly looked at him and smiled. "Hopefully, this girl is going to be the consummate New York girl very soon."

"Do you have an apartment yet?" Drew asked. Everly could tell that his body language seemed to be relaxed, now. He must have been anxious about their little "talk," more so than he appeared to be when they first arrived at the beach. *But then again, why choose such a romantic setting to tell someone you only want to be friends,* Everly thought to herself. This man was certainly complicated.

"I've talked to lots of people over the last few months. It's kinda hard not being able to see the places in person, but I think I've narrowed it down to three apartments. Wherever I stay, I'll be sharing it with three or four other people, which I gather is the norm there."

"I live with two other guys. We all work different jobs, keep different hours, and run in different circles of people, so we don't see each other much. But I lived in several apartments 'til I found this one. If you let me know the addresses of the apartments you're looking at, I'll check them out for you when I get home. Send you some pictures. That might help you decide. You aren't moving 'til after the holidays, right?"

And now, he's being so helpful. This was making it more difficult for her. Everly felt like she was on an emotional rollercoaster right now, and wondered if Peyton knew how lucky she was to have Drew in her life.

"I was going to wait 'til after New Year's, but now, I think I want to get there before the big celebration on New Year's Eve. Maybe even go to Times Square to watch the ball drop. I can't imagine seeing it in person after watching it on TV all these years."

"I've been a few times and it's fun, but the people – wow! Hope you aren't claustrophobic and have plenty of time to walk. Plus, you have to be careful. But then, maybe we can go together," Drew said, eating another of his cookies.

"I'm sure you will be with Peyton at some holiday celebration."

"Well, let's just wait and see. It would be a great way to start out your new year. In the city you've always dreamed of and celebrating with thousands of people. Just make sure you have warm clothes. You're going to need them up there, and you won't be needing *those*." He pointed to her flip-flops. "At least not until summer when you are walking around Central Park."

"I've worn these shoes my whole life so I can't wait to wear my boots. I wear them occasionally here, in the winter, and people stare at me like I'm nuts. But then again, this is Key West. Just about anything – and I mean anything – goes," Everly responded with a laugh.

"I've noticed that, however I've seen a few things in the city that made me stop and stare Just down here, people are way more relaxed."

Their conversation was now more calming, the previous tension having dissipated for the most part. They talked more about Everly's move to the city. Drew started listing all the places, restaurants, and activities that she had to do. As she listened to him talk, many of the things he mentioned were already on her list, but there were several items she'd never heard of. Everly could feel the excitement building and couldn't wait to go. She felt like these next weeks couldn't pass fast enough.

But there would be plenty to keep her busy. Plus, she needed to finish up some side website jobs before she left that would help put some more extra money in her bank account.

As they sat in the sand and watched the sunset, Everly remembered that the night she met Drew, all she just wanted to do was sit down with him and talk about everything they were discussing now. At that time, she wasn't remotely interested in the man sitting beside her. But in a very short time, that had all changed. Drew was special, and even though they could only be friends, Everly felt especially lucky that he had come into her life.

10

The rest of the week seemed to pass in a blur. Drew and Everly either ventured off together each night, or Abbey and Zach would join them as they wandered around Key West to explore the city or took quick trips to the closer Keys near the city. Then, on Saturday, they spent the day at the Turtle Hospital and the Dolphin Research Center, two places Drew had been especially interested in. On Sunday, they made their way to the Florida Everglades and took the airboat tour that Everly mentioned.

"That was awesome!" Drew jumped off the boat, sporting the biggest grin. "I could do that all day long."

"I know you well enough to know that by the third ride, you'd be beyond bored. Remember, I grew up with you," Abbey teased her little brother.

"But the wildlife we saw, and the speed of the boat! I just hope my pictures came out."

"How is your little online photo gallery doing?" Abbey asked as they walked toward the car.

"Photo gallery?" Everly asked.

"Yeah, I make a little money on the side doing photography. I sell prints and stock photos online. I also post them on my blog. Nothing much, but it does help with the expenses. Plus, I really like taking photos. There always seems to be something special every place I go." The way Drew looked at Everly caused her stomach to do a small flip, something that she just couldn't help.

"I knew you were taking a lot of pictures, but I figured it was because you were just on vacation, or for your stories. You never said you sold your work. I think that's awesome," Everly said.

"Yes, my baby brother has many hidden talents. He can't seem to settle on just one."

"Why should I? If I can try different things I think are interesting, then I'll find what I truly enjoy. Too many people just settle. You need to go out. Explore. Try something interesting. Meet people."

"You sound like an advertisement for a motivational seminar," Zach said with a little laugh. "But, I agree with you. Though, there are times that some people think they need to keep searching, when what they want has been in front of them all the time." Now Zach reached over to take his wife's hand, giving it a kiss.

"True, but that's one of the great things about New York City. There are so many things to do, to try. You just wait, Everly. You'll see what I mean once you get there. I wouldn't doubt that you might even meet your Prince Charming there," Drew remarked as he was checking the messages on his phone.

I thought I already had, Everly said to herself as they all drove back toward Key West. It was a three-hour drive, and Everly loved that she was sharing the back seat with Drew. She still couldn't help wondering what it would have been like if Drew had been single when he came to the Keys. Everly imagined what it would be like if they were a real couple as she glanced over at him. But Drew was off in his own little world, still checking text messages and emails.

Friends, Everly, just friends, she reminded herself. But sitting this close to Drew was making it hard to believe those words.

"Well, shit," Drew said suddenly.

"What's wrong?" Abbey asked, turning around to him quickly at the sound of his words.

"James wants me back Tuesday morning. That means I have to fly out tomorrow. Whatever is going on, he's willing to pay the fee to have the flight changed. I had more places to go, but he said that this project is more important and he needs me to manage it. That's a good sign if he wants me to take charge."

Drew sounded excited, but Everly was deflated. She was hoping that Drew being here another week might change his mind about how he felt about her, but now, that wasn't going to happen. But she would be in New York in a few months and maybe, just maybe, things would be different.

Ugh, stop this back and forth, she wanted to scream out loud. Everly knew that perfect dream of her and Drew being together wouldn't come true, but for some reason, it just wouldn't leave her alone, no matter how much she wished it away. Everly was infatuated with Abbey's brother, and it was going to take time or another man to help her get over this love sickness that had overtaken her.

"Well, you have tonight and tomorrow morning to squeeze something in. Anything special you want to do?" Everly asked, trying to be as nonchalant as possible.

"I think I've been to all the most popular places. I was hoping to see some things that were lesser known. I guess that will have to wait 'til my next trip."

"Ha, that'll be a while. It took me getting married to get you down here this time. If I remember correctly, you said I was crazy to move to 'some little out-of-the-way island town.' It was too boring." Drew just shook his head as he stared at his sister.

"I do need to do a little bit of shopping tonight, and I wouldn't mind going to Mallory Square once more. As of right now, if I can book it, I'll fly out tomorrow around noon. Any chance one of you can take me to the airport?" Drew looked at all three occupants of the car, waiting for an answer.

"I don't see why Lance wouldn't let me off for a few hours," Everly said quickly. Hopefully not too quickly. It would be nice to take Drew to the airport and get to say goodbye, just the two of them.

"That would be great. Plus, that shopping I need to do is for souvenirs and something special for Peyton. Would you mind helping me tonight?" Drew asked her.

"Sure." Everly responded with a cheerful voice though she was feeling nothing but disappointment at hearing Drew's girlfriend's name. "All we have to do is hit Duval Street."

"Or Mallory Square," Abbey said. "That reminds me, I need to get my sculptures finished to sell next weekend. I haven't been there in four weeks, with the wedding and all."

"That's right. I didn't get to see my sister in action as a vendor on the square."

"Then that's the first thing on your list for the next time you're in the Keys," Everly said. "We had a blast celebrating her first night there. It was exciting."

"I will say, that's one of my favorite places in Key West. The people I meet and being able to share my artwork is fun and rewarding. Something I never thought I would be able to do back home in North Carolina," Abbey said.

"I know you could've sold your art in New York. People eat that stuff up," Drew said. "I told you that when you came to visit."

"And I told *you* that New York just wasn't the place for me," Abbey said. "Too busy, and way too many people. Key West is my kind of town."

Just then, they turned onto N. Roosevelt Blvd., toward their home. It had been a long day, but enjoyable, and Everly had loved every minute of it. Once they dropped Abbey and Zach off at their house, Everly and Drew went to the shops along the popular Key West street and even walked through a few places at the square. She helped Drew pick out the souvenirs he needed before leaving the next day. And even though it was difficult, Everly helped him select a stunning seashell necklace for Peyton.

As he dropped her off at her home, Everly stood there and watched the car drive away. Drew was going home and she was taking him to the airport.

Everly felt a wave of depression come over her. Why did she agree to do that? The shopping and being his ride to the airport tomorrow? But as soon as she thought of the questions, she knew the reason why. She just wanted to be with him, secretly hoping that maybe, just maybe, one day, he might see her more than just Abbey's friend from Key West.

■ ■ ■

"Do you have everything?" Everly asked as Drew got out of the car. He had his carry-on slung across his back and his wheeled suitcase by his side.

"I think so. I packed that suitcase so tight. Hope it doesn't go over the weight limit. Thanks again for the ride to the airport, and for helping me yesterday. I would have never been able to pick out something so nice for Peyton."

"Yes, you would have. Just, sometimes, it's nice to have a girl's touch when picking out gifts." Once again, Everly kept things as cheerful as she could.

"The guys are going to love the t-shirts. I have a feeling that after they see the pictures and hear what I got to do, we might be back down here for a guy's weekend," Drew said with a laugh.

"Well, hopefully by then, I'll be in New York." This time Everly was able to put a little excitement in her voice. She was looking forward to moving, but at the moment, leaving Drew at the airport to go home had her feeling down. This man had put a stamp on her heart and she was quite sure it could never be erased. At least it wasn't a huge hurtful mark that would leave a terrible emotional scar. It had just been a crush.

She felt good knowing that when she got to New York, she had someone there she already knew to help her if she needed it. Though, Everly had already determined that she was going to do this on her own.

"Oh, you will be," Drew said. "Thanks again, Everly. I mean it. For everything. I couldn't have done a fraction of what I did without your help. And I feel like I've made a great friend. Just like I told you before, you are as sweet as my sister said you were. But she didn't quite describe your determination. One thing is for sure: when you put your mind to something, you go for it. That's admirable. You're going to be fine in the city.

"So, you have my number and email. We'll stay in touch, and when you have a moving date, let me know. I'll pick you up at the airport. When I get home, I'll look at those apartments for you. As for the job, don't think I'll be able to help you there, but if I should hear something, I'll let you know."

"I appreciate the help, but I've already applied to four places and have interviews for when I arrive, so I have that taken care of. It's the apartment thing that has thrown me off. I want to be safe, and it feels weird to meet potential roommates online."

"That's when you call or email me. I'll let you know if it's decent, okay? We'll get you moved up there, safe and sound. That way, your parents can rest a little easier. I remember my mom was in tears the day I left. She was so scared that I was going to get mugged or something. There might be some crime, but it's safer than most people think. My Dad was more supportive, but then, he's always been a bit more adventurous." Drew suddenly stopped talking, just looking at her. She was so adorable, and had helped him more than he could say.

"Have a safe trip," Everly said, then leaned over and gave Drew a quick kiss on the cheek. For Everly, if felt as though electric sparks flew from her lips the moment she touched his skin. Then, the feeling traveled through her body.

Drew gave Everly a hug, said goodbye, and headed toward the boarding area. He turned around once to wave to her, and then he was gone. As Everly stood there, she could still feel the tingle in her lips and the arms that were wrapped around her only moments ago.

But now, she had work to do. It felt like it was finally coming true. Moving away to the big city she had dreamed about her entire life. She let that excitement fill her system as she walked back to the borrowed car she had used to bring Drew to the airport. Now, for some reason she couldn't name, she was ready to go, to solidify all the plans she had made. Everly would be a New York girl by the end of the year.

11

As the plane made its ascent over the beautiful islands, Drew looked out at the sight below. The wonderful clear aqua waters surrounding the tiny green islands looked like a postcard or something out of a magazine. He now knew why people came here. Truth be told, he would come back here anytime he could, especially with his sister here. Abbey told him before he left that he always had a place to stay when he was here, and that was perfect for him. Next time, though, he would rent a car from Miami and drive down to the relaxing island town.

When he finally leaned back in his seat, Drew's thoughts were all over the place, but there was one thought that was very persistent. It was about Everly. He felt so confused. She was like a little sister, but she was also a beautiful, intelligent woman. He'd never met anyone like her before. She was so innocent and sweet, but strong at the same time. He couldn't get her honey brown hair and beautiful brown eyes out of his mind. Her tanned skin on her slender, well-toned body made her appealing, too. Drew knew that most of his friends would be waiting in line to meet this girl once she'd made her move. At that thought, he was suddenly jealous. He immediately felt as though he had to protect her.

Then, a picture of Peyton floated into view. He loved Peyton, he was sure of it. She made him laugh, too. She was also beautiful, but totally opposite of Everly. Peyton had dark, chocolate brown, almost black, hair and blue-violet eyes. Her skin was creamy white, almost as though she never went outside. Both women he was thinking about were polar opposites. But why was he comparing the two women?

Drew took a deep breath and willed himself to think about the articles he was going to write. This back and forth between two women was making him dizzy, when he knew the one that was meant for him. So, he would concentrate on work, or better yet, take a nap on the almost three-hour flight from Miami to New York. He would see Peyton tonight, and that would help him clarify these feelings.

Drew arrived in New York just as the sun had set. He donned his coat as the other passengers gathered their belongings to exit the plane. It would probably be a shock to his system to go out in the thirty-degree weather after standing in the sunshine and heat of tropical islands only hours before. But, this was where he truly belonged. He sat down to let the rest of the passengers exit the plane and looked out at the New York City skyline. He smiled. He was home.

Though he didn't want to, he had no choice but to take the shuttle bus into Manhattan. He usually jumped aboard the AirTrain that led to the subway, but with his suitcase in tow, there was no way he was dragging it and his carry-on up and down the staircases. Peyton wouldn't be at his apartment for almost two hours, and that would give him plenty of time to get home and unpacked.

Peyton had texted him and said she was bringing dinner, which was great because he was sure there wouldn't be food at home. His roommates weren't great about stocking food, and he knew that everything he had left a few weeks ago was sure to be gone. Thank goodness, he stashed a few things away in his room, which he had locked when he left. His roommates were great, but sometimes, the people they brought over were questionable. One day, he would have his own apartment, like Peyton. But unlike her, Drew wanted to do it on his own.

Peyton's parents were paying for her place while she got on her feet. Her photo shoots were erratic, so her income wasn't steady. She'd had a string of jobs since they had met, but had never once wanted for anything. Peyton's parents always seemed to be there, should their only child need anything. But Drew knew she seemed to be trying. Peyton wanted to work in the world of fashion design, and by working as a model, she was making some great contacts. She'd been a successful child model during her younger years, but now, her assignments were not as plentiful. She was doing well as a hand model, but that didn't satisfy her.

Peyton's fashion design drawings had caught the interest of a photographer one day, who had referred her to a friend of his. Now, she was doing an internship at a fashion house, but there was no money attached to it. But that didn't bother Peyton, because her parents were always there to save the day.

Drew sometimes wondered if Peyton would be able to make it on her own. She'd never experienced any of the things he did when he first moved to New York, but in a way, he was glad. It was tough for him when he first arrived, not knowing anyone and learning the ropes of the city by trial and error. Peyton had been spared that.

The two of them had met at an event he was covering for his newspaper and she was modeling. At first, he couldn't believe a New York model had any interest in him, but they hit it off the very first time they talked. Drew had dated a few women already since his move to New York, but none that had ever amounted to any type of relationship. Peyton had been different.

At first, they were together every minute of the day, if possible. And before he knew it, he was meeting her parents. They seemed to welcome him, but there was always something that just made him feel that they were accepting him just for their daughter's sake. He could never tell if they really liked him or not. But he didn't see them that often, which was fine in his book.

Drew had mentioned several times about him and Peyton flying to Asheville so she could meet his family, but there was always an excuse, each one being very plausible. But Drew wondered if Peyton really wanted to make the trip. He wanted her to meet his parents, especially if he was going to propose to her.

But after his time in the Keys, Drew seemed to be rethinking everything. Not that he wasn't looking forward to being with Peyton tonight, but he couldn't quit thinking about his time in the Keys. It was peaceful and relaxing – just the opposite of the big city. And then, there was Everly. They had become such good friends, and he couldn't seem to get her out of his mind.

The apartment was empty when he unlocked the door and walked in. At least, everything seemed to be in place, not the mess he'd found the place in last time he had gone out of town. Once he was in his room, he plopped on the bed and sighed. It felt good to be home. His own bed. His own things around him. But as he unpacked, the little souvenirs he brought back from the tropical islands had him thinking of the bright sun, the trop rock music, and the relaxing vibe. If only he could import that feeling to the city. Then, he would be completely satisfied.

"Anyone home?" Drew heard the female voice and knew she was here. And early!

"Hey, sweetheart!" Drew walked quickly to meet her just as she shut the door.

"Well, it's about time you got home," Peyton said, her hands full with boxes of Chinese take-out.

"Let me help you." Drew took some of the containers from her then leaned in for a very long-awaited kiss. But suddenly Peyton backed away.

"Have you taken a shower yet?" Peyton asked. "If not, I'll take a raincheck on that kiss. Go get cleaned up, and I'll get the food ready. I think I remember where everything is." She turned her back to him and walked quickly to the kitchen.

"I'll be right back," Drew said, a little perturbed at his welcome home, but then again, this was his Peyton. Things like this hadn't bothered him before because he just accepted her as she was. But something inside him was different now. He couldn't quite put his finger on what the difference was, but he felt the little nagging in the back of his head.

He took a quick shower, threw on some clean clothes, and headed back to the kitchen. Peyton had already set up all the little containers holding their favorite dishes, and had plates ready for serving on the little kitchen table. It was times like this that she appeared to be a very domesticated woman, but he knew this was out of the norm for her. No, Peyton was used to being waited on most of the time. And Drew didn't mind, he told himself. He kind of loved that she relied on him, making him feel important.

"Did you get all the information you needed for work?" Peyton asked as they both sat down to the wonderful smells of the Chinese food.

"I think so. Could have used this week for more research, but James wanted me back as soon as possible. Just hope everything is okay at work." Drew took a bite of the delicious food, groaning just a bit. "Boy, have I missed this."

"I can imagine! I'm sure that their food down there in those little islands can't compare to the cuisine here in New York," Peyton said.

"No, I have to admit, the food there was fantastic. Fresh, lots of seafood, and the drinks were amazing. But then again, I think it had something to do with the laid back atmosphere. It was everywhere, not just in one certain place. Peyton, you'd love it."

"I'm not so sure about that. Going to Disney World was enough for me, and that was a long time ago. Just not my type of crowd. When I was there, Florida seemed like nothing but a bunch of old people," she said, taking a dainty bite of the food before her.

Drew couldn't help but laugh at her statement. "I assure you, there are people of every age, especially in the Keys. Next time I go down there, I'd love for you to come with me."

"Are you going back so soon?" Peyton said in alarm. "The holidays are almost here and we have plans, remember?"

"I don't mean right away, but my sister and her new husband have offered me- or us- a place to stay anytime." Drew suddenly had an idea. "Let me show you some of the pictures I downloaded while I was on the plane."

Drew grabbed his computer out of his room and found a spot amongst the take-out boxes to place the laptop, so they could view the photos. It wasn't long before Drew was showing Peyton the beautiful shots he had taken, explaining each one. Even though he could see out of the corner of his eye that she yawned every now and then, he continued to go over each picture, hoping she'd see what he had. The Florida Keys could be a great place for them to have a romantic vacation.

"Who is she?" Peyton's quick question and her glare at the computer caught Drew's attention.

Drew looked at the picture. "That's Everly, my sister's coworker and friend. She showed me around Key West, and then through the Keys. She's the main reason I have so much information to write my articles."

"It seems she's showing up in a bunch of your pictures. Looks like you two spent a lot of time together." Peyton's voice was a bit monotonous and she wasn't looking at Drew, but continuing to stare at the computer screen.

"Peyton, we're just friends. She's the girl I was telling you about that's moving here. As a matter of fact, she'll be here the end of December, just in time to celebrate New Year's Eve. I told her that maybe all of us could go to Times Square to watch the ball drop."

"Oh, no! I did that once, thank you very much. Dad is putting together a wonderful dinner and New Year's celebration at the hotel. We'll have a perfect view of Times Square and the festivities below to ring in the new year. I'm sure some of your friends would be more than happy to escort…what's her name?" Peyton asked.

"Everly. But I think it'd be fun to party with the crowds. Give it a thought, okay? I'd really like her to get off on the right foot here. I didn't have anyone to help me when I moved, so I kinda feel like I need to be a big brother to her. And I know that you two will probably be best friends. She's really nice."

"Hmmm. You sure you two are just friends?"

"Do I detect a note of jealousy in your voice?" Drew teased her.

"Over her?" Peyton said, pointing to the picture on the screen and laughed. "Never. I'm just making sure you know who you're dating." She stretched out her hand toward him and took his. She looked at Drew with a slight pout on her face, then slowly put her arms around him and turned him towards her.

"Are you full yet?" Peyton said the words in a sexy voice then slowly and sensuously, she kissed Drew across the cheek, and then slightly brushed her lips across his mouth. "I'm hungry, but not for food anymore. I'd like to remind you of what you have here." Now, her hands were exploring his chest down to the waistband of his jeans, where she took the hem of his t-shirt and started to gently pull it over his head.

"Maybe, we should continue this in my room, just in case my roommates come home. Let me put the food up first," Drew said, taking his hand and cupping Peyton's cheek.

"No, just leave it on the counter. I don't think this can wait." She led Drew to his bedroom, but not before glancing at his computer screen once more. At a girl that now seemed to have some of Drew's attention. That wasn't sitting well with her at all.

12

Everly looked at the two packed suitcases lying open on the bedroom floor. She'd put as much as she could into each, double- and triple-checking that she had everything she needed to get by. She could buy or order the bigger things she would need once she was moved into the apartment. Though she had been waiting for so long now, the fact that she would be getting on a plane to head north in a few short days had her excited, yet very anxious.

Her last day at work had been yesterday, and it had been bittersweet. She adored every person she worked with and, as promised, Lance told her that if things didn't work out like she'd planned, there would always be a place for her with him. He was like a second father to her, and her co-workers were like siblings. But this is what Everly had planned for over the last few years, and it was finally coming true.

It was Christmas Eve tomorrow, and she wanted to spend as much time as possible with her parents before she left. But Everly was also tugged by a longing to spend time with her friends, too. She would be leaving the 27th, giving her just enough time to get moved into her new place and explore a little bit of New York before celebrating New Year's Eve at Times Square. She had watched it so many times on TV but had never imagined she would be there in person.

Drew had been a tremendous help over these last few weeks. They had stayed in contact, though not as much as Everly would have liked. She had found several apartments online and called the landlords, then Drew had checked them out for her. These places were close to his apartment building, which made it easy for him to do some follow up for her. Each place had been nice, though she would be sharing the rent with at least three other people. Her room would be small, but that came with the territory when living in Manhattan and trying to stay on a budget.

She had talked to her potential roommates; she interviewed them and they asked her questions ranging from work to personal subjects that she would've never asked. But then again, they'd be living together, so she assumed they had a right to ask. This would be her first time sharing a living space with someone she didn't know. The thought made her nervous, but the excitement flowing through her now overrode each new apprehensive thought that popped up in her mind. She was finally moving to New York City!

"Now, I'd say you're taking everything except the kitchen sink." Everly's dad, Gary, had walked through the open door to her bedroom, now watching his little girl pack for her big adventure.

"Actually, I've pared down to the essentials, even though it may not look like it. I'll have to buy a bed, desk, and a few other things when I get there. I've been looking online and there are several flea markets around the city. I should be able to find something. If not, an air mattress on the floor and a lap desk will suffice," Everly answered, smiling up at her father as she stood up and walked over to him.

He was looking so much better these days. After much testing and so much waiting, the doctors were finally able to put his symptoms together and gave him a diagnosis: Multiple Sclerosis. It was a relief for all of them to finally know what had been plaguing her father for so long. And Everly had to applaud him. He had listened to the doctors, took the medicine he needed and changed his lifestyle. He still had days where he still wasn't feeling his best but overall, he was so much better now. She only prayed that things continued to improve.

When her father had become sick, Everly thought her plans of moving were dissolved. She didn't resent her parents for needing her help, but her desire to travel was so strong that sometimes, she would cry herself to sleep. She didn't know what made her want to leave so badly.

Her parents were close to perfect in her eyes. They had been strict, but kind, even when she tested the boundaries of their rules when she was a teenager. When compared to the parents of some of her friends, she seemed to be the envy of her small group when it came to moms and dads. Everyone loved hers, so her friends were always at her house. Everly's parents loved this, and for her, it was fine, but she always had that feeling inside to just get away.

"Are you sure you still want to do this?" her dad asked. This was only the third time he had asked her today.

Everly put her arms around him, giving him a hug. He responded by holding her tightly.

"I'm sure, Dad," she said softly, her words slightly muffled by his chest. "You know, you and mom can always come and see me, but wait 'til I know my way around the city. Then, we'll have a blast as I show you my town."

"That's sounds like a good idea. We'll wait and see, but you know this will always be your home. No matter what. If you want to come back, you're always welcome. I just want you to know that." Everly could hear a slight crack in his voice and she didn't dare look at him. If she did, she knew she wouldn't be able to keep her emotions in check.

"Can this be a group hug?" Everly's mom, Sheila, put her arms around her. "Why are we all standing here like this, not that I mind?"

"Just soaking in a family moment," Everly said softly.

■ ■ ■

"So, luggage is checked in and you have everything else you need in your carry-on, right?" Everly's parents said, almost in unison.

"Yes," she answered as she looked at the small assembly of people that had come to the airport to see her off. She was giddy with excitement, but a little anxious too. It was a surreal moment for her, to finally see something that she had pictured in her mind for years coming true. There was a plane sitting just outside that would take her on the first leg of her journey.

One by one, each person gave her a hug, a bit of advice, and wished her well. By the time Abbey and Zach approached her, she was having a hard time keeping it together.

"So, Drew is meeting you at the airport, right?" Right now Abbey sounded more like her mother than her friend.

"Yes. He said Peyton might be coming, too," Everly answered. She had made peace with the fact that her perfect man was already taken. After Drew had returned to New York and she was by herself again, she realized that what she felt for Drew was just infatuation. She was genuinely okay that she and Drew were only good friends, and felt that there would be someone else in her future. Plus, Everly was going to be too busy for a relationship right now. This was her first true adventure, and there wasn't time for a man right now.

"Just don't let Peyton get to you. I'm not going to be negative, but just remember what I told you. She is, shall I say, different."

"Abbey, you're beginning to sound like my parents," Everly whispered in her ear with a slight giggle. "I can tell you, one day, you'll make a great mom." She gave Abbey a hug and before she could pull away, Everly heard those words again. "You can always come home."

"Everyone keeps telling me that."

"That just tells you how much we love you," Abbey said, pulling away and wiping a small tear from the corner of her eye.

"Come here, you." Before either woman could say another word, Zach pulled her into his arms. "It already feels weird at work without you. I remember the first day you came to the office. I thought there was no way this kid was going to be able to keep up with us, and then you outperformed everyone. Be careful up there. I'm glad you already have someone to look after you."

"I'll be careful, big brother," Everly said, giving Zach a hug. "Now, I just have to work circles around some big city guys."

Everly turned to see her parents standing side by side, her mom with tears sliding down both cheeks. *Please hold it together. Cry on the plane if you have to,* she thought to herself as she came to stand with them.

"Thank you." Everly took each of their hands in hers as she gazed into their eyes. "I wouldn't be able to do this without you. I promise, I'll be visiting every chance I get. I'm only a plane ride away." She hugged her mom first, almost not wanting to let go, but then reached and embraced her dad. "I love you both so much."

"We love you, too. Call us when you get there, and please," her dad said with emotion he couldn't hide, "be careful, Everly. Your mom and I know you can do it. We've seen you accomplish anything you put your mind to, so there's no doubt you're going to take that town by storm. We'd just like to hear from you as much as possible. It would make your parents feel a little bit better about their little girl."

"I promise, Dad," she said. "I love you both." With that, she moved into the security line to wait her turn. Then, with one last look at the people who were sending her off with love, she walked toward the waiting plane.

Once her carry-on was safely stored in the overhead bin, Everly took her window seat. She grabbed her phone and iPad that would keep her busy during the two flights of her trip, but all she could do was stare out the window. She had only flown one other time in her life, when she was a little girl. She barely remembered the flight, so Everly felt like this was truly the first time she had traveled by plane.

She wasn't nervous, but it seemed like the moment she sat down in the plane, doubts crept into her mind. Was she doing the right thing? Would she even like New York? Should she have visited once more before making such a drastic change to her life? Everly began shaking her head back and forth, as if to give her body and mind the signal to shake off these feelings.

"Going back home from vacation?" The words jarred her from her emotional rollercoaster. Everly looked to her side to see that an older couple had taken the seats beside her.

"Oh, no," she answered. "Actually, I'm moving to a new city."

"You mean, you're from here? And you want to move?" This time, it was the woman who asked. They both reminded her of her grandparents.

"I was born and raised in Key West. Now, I'm moving to New York City," Everly said, with more confidence in her voice than she was actually feeling.

"I don't know if I could leave this place. Packing our suitcases last night was hard enough, the whole time trying to find a way to extend our vacation."

"How long were you here?"

"Two weeks, but every time we come, it never feels long enough."

"Where are you from?" Everly asked.

"We're heading back to Michigan," the man said. "From what I hear, we have snow and ice to greet us. That's why my coat has taken up the most space in my carry-on." He laughed as he continued to get situated in his seat. "You're probably going to have a bit of snow in New York, with that last storm that went through on Christmas Day. Hope you're prepared."

"Me, too," Everly said, but she wasn't thinking about only the weather. She looked out the window once more as she felt the plane begin to make its way to the runway. Her heart was beating fast, and she began to feel all sorts of emotions, from excitement to fear. Then, as the plane rose into the air, she let the small tears finally fall from her eyes.

She watched as her hometown came into view below, surrounded by the aqua water around what now looked like a very tiny island. She also noticed the other small islands, or Keys, as she had always known them, dotting the area. It was beautiful. She knew she would miss it, but as Everly wiped at the tears on her cheeks, she felt a surge of excitement. She had been waiting for this for so long, and she was on her way.

13

"I hope she brought her coat on the plane with her," Drew said as Peyton sat down in the chair beside him. "This weather is nothing like what she's used to."

"Goodness, Drew, the girl will be okay. You sound like she can't think for herself. Besides, there will probably be enough people and luggage on that bus ride back to the apartment to keep all of us warm. We should've taken a taxi."

"Way too expensive, and you know it. Besides, I want to help her learn about the city. This is totally different for her."

Out the corner of his eye, he saw Peyton roll her eyes. Why she had come, he had no idea. Drew had originally thought it would be nice for Everly to meet Peyton, another girl living in the city. He was beginning to have second thoughts now. Peyton and Everly were completely different women, so he hoped that this wasn't the beginning of a problem.

Then, Drew saw her. Even though she wasn't dressed in the tank top, shorts and flip-flops he had seen her in almost every day while in Key West, he would recognize her happy smile anywhere. She looked like a tourist coming back from vacation instead of the girl making her way to live in the big city. Drew smiled. He couldn't wait to show her around the city, introduce her to his friends, and take her to see her new apartment.

"You're acting like a little kid about to get a Christmas present. I swear, there's something between you and her," Peyton said, sliding up close to him, snaking her arms around his waist.

"We aren't going through this again. She's a *friend*, that helped me tremendously while I was in Key West. I'm only returning the favor. You're going to like her, and it would be really nice for her to know another woman in town."

"We'll see," Peyton said. Drew could hear a hint of sarcasm in her voice.

"Everly!" Drew called out.

With the sea of people in front of her, Everly just seemed to be moving with the masses, but then, she thought she heard the faint sound of her name. She looked from side to side, only seeing tons of people. But then, she saw the blonde hair and recognized the face. It was Drew. Her whole body went weak, just seeing him for the first time in weeks. Then, she noticed the girl attached to his waist. This must be Peyton.

Everly held up her hand and waved, then slowly weaved her way through the people to finally come to stand in front of the couple. Drew reached out and gave her a big hug, something she wasn't expecting with the girl standing by his side.

"It's about time you got here," Drew said enthusiastically. "You're officially a New Yorker now. Well, almost. Guess you need to get moved in."

"Thanks! I just can't believe all the people. I mean, I've seen huge crowds at our festivals in Key West, but this," she said, looking around, "this is more than I imagined."

"This is nothing," the woman beside Drew suddenly said. "Hi, I'm Peyton, Drew's girlfriend." The woman thrust her hand out toward Everly to shake, and Everly couldn't help but notice that the word "girlfriend" had been stated very emphatically.

"Nice to meet you." Everly was trying to be as polite as possible. She wanted to start this new adventure with as much positive energy as possible, and making friends with this girl who was important to Drew was a priority. Especially if Everly wanted to keep him as a friend. Seeing him again after all this time brought back the desire to be with Drew, but she knew it wasn't to be. It was something she thought she had dealt with weeks ago so the feeling startled her just a bit but quickly faded.

"Let's go get your suitcases. You said you brought two, right?" Drew asked quickly as they began walking toward baggage claim.

"Yes, and I was just under the weight limit on both, thank goodness. I brought as much as I could, but I'm going to have to buy quite a few things. Now I'm so glad that I saved as much money as I did." Moving into her own place was more daunting than she had first imagined, but she had a list and knew that she would be able to get it done. Plus, her savings were substantial. Now, she was glad that she had passed on a few opportunities for trips and nights out on the town, putting her money away for just this moment.

"Well you can definitely find anything you need here. This city lacks for nothing," Peyton said, her tone haughty. "We'll make sure you're able to get what you need, right, sweetheart?" Peyton seemed to be practically glued to Drew's side, so close that Everly wondered how he was even able to walk! Then, it seemed she kissed him just about every chance she could, as though she was making it abundantly clear that Drew was hers.

"We'll be taking the shuttle bus back to my place. One of my roommates is out of town 'til after New Year's Day, so you can stay with me till your place is ready, on the 2nd. Hope that's okay with you."

"Um, when were you going to tell me about this?" Peyton asked rather loudly.

By the way Peyton asked the question, it was abundantly clear to Everly that she wasn't happy with the arrangements Drew had made. She certainly didn't want to antagonize the woman.

"I don't want to be in the way. I have enough money to stay at a hotel 'til my apartment is ready. But I do want to go by there and see if I can meet my new roommates. We've talked through Skype. Everyone seemed nice, but I would feel better to meet in person. Still wondering why I just can't move in, since the room is empty, but the landlord was pretty insistent on waiting," Everly said.

"Peyton, remember, we did talk about this. Donald said it was fine for her to use his room and Blake said it was okay with him, too. You said it didn't matter," Drew replied, trying to whisper in Peyton's ear. When he looked at her face, Peyton only gave him that roll of the eyes, yet again.

"Everly, it really isn't a problem. Except, I must warn you that Blake is a bit of a flirt. But I made him swear to be on his best behavior."

"Maybe, Blake and Everly will get along quite well," Peyton said, now sounding almost too sweet.

"Thanks for letting me stay. I'll be on the lookout for – what's his name?" Everly asked.

"Blake. He's quite cute, and is studying to be a stockbroker. I've been trying to get Drew to change his profession, but he's determined to be a writer," Peyton said.

"I love what I do. I always have, and though it might not be the best-paying job in the world, I'm not giving it up," Drew said.

"Money isn't everything." Everly made the statement as the three stood in the baggage area, waiting for her two large suitcases to come into view. Soon she wished she had not said a thing.

"I think you'll find in New York, money *is* everything," Peyton said. "Just wait and see."

Everly didn't know what to say next. This woman's energy was negative and arrogant. She could see the tension on Drew's face, and she felt sorry for him. He'd never looked like this when they were in the Keys, and she wished she could have bottled up some of that island vibe and brought it to him. Everly certainly hoped that she didn't lose that carefree feeling. She wanted to be a New Yorker, but with the heart of a Florida Keys girl still alive inside of her.

"There they are," Everly said as she made her way to her luggage, with Drew following close behind. "I marked the handles with pink duct tape so I could find them easier once I got here."

"Hey, I just want to apologize for Peyton's remarks. She wasn't very excited about coming here on the shuttle, but I know she wanted to meet you. Especially after I told her all about the Keys and showed her the pictures I took while I was there. She also doesn't like riding shuttle buses, but that's the most economical way to get back to my place." When Everly glanced at him, Drew had a look of apology on his face.

"Why don't we take a taxi?" Everly said.

"It's too expensive!"

"Drew, listen. I've planned for this trip for seven years. I've saved and mapped out everything I could think of to get me started here. And if I've done my math right, I have enough money for us to take a taxi *and* for me to stay in a hotel for a few nights."

Drew looked at the girl standing by him now. This was the Everly he had met in Key West. Relaxed, friendly, and beautiful as ever. Her generous spirit made him smile and he was glad she was here.

"Well, I'll take you up on the taxi ride because it will be quicker, but you have to stay at my place. You'll have a room all to yourself and you can stock any foods you want in the kitchen. We have a small grocery store down the street. Besides, with New Year's Eve coming up, you wouldn't find a hotel anyway."

Everly had completely forgotten about that. Not that she was going to see the ball drop in Times Square, but the chances of finding a hotel were probably slim to none. "With everything else I was taking care of to get ready, I didn't think about the hotels being full for the holidays. And I thought I had everything figured out," she laughed. Everly extended the handle to the first case and started towing it behind her while Drew came up beside her. "I'll take you up on your room offer, but only 'til my place is ready. Might have to get some help to move my stuff on the 2nd."

"I don't go back to work till the 4th, so that's no problem. Plus, you really don't have much. I expected more suitcases," Drew said with a smile.

"Believe me, this luggage is stuffed!" Everly exclaimed as they walked back over to Peyton.

"Everly is treating us to a taxi ride instead of the shuttle," Drew said as they approached Peyton, who was still rooted in place and now texting someone.

"Then, you just became a friend," Peyton responded not looking away from her cell phone. "Maybe I should have asked Dad for the use of the company car, but I didn't think about that 'til just now. Oh, well, next time." With that, she put the phone in her coat pocket and was quickly at Drew's side, practically ushering him to the opened doors. Everly stood there for a moment and stared. If Drew thought she and Peyton would be friends, he really had no clue about women. At that thought, she remembered Abbey's words about her brother only a few months before and smiled. But, she had to admit that Drew had a sweet heart.

The cold air that met her as she walked out the door was stinging her face, but it didn't matter. She was here. When she looked around, there was snow on the ground, like the gentleman on the plane had warned about. She couldn't wait to the see the city lit up and the streets lined with the white flakes. Everly also knew that she had to see the Rockefeller Center Christmas Tree, especially with the snow. And then, there was the ice skating. The smile spread across her face as she continued to look around, excitement building up inside her as she thought of everything she wanted to do and see.

"Are you coming, or do you want to spend the night at the airport?" Drew asked with a grin on his face. She looked to see they already had a taxi, and he was getting ready to put her first suitcase in the trunk. Peyton was inside the car, texting once again to some unknown person.

Everly quickly walked to the car, letting Drew put the luggage in the trunk- except for her tote- and got in the back seat with the couple. Drew was sandwiched between the two women, and for Everly, it was a treat. Even when Drew was in the Keys, they had never sat this close together. She could smell the manly scent emanating from his body and feel the toned muscles of his thigh that was pressed up against hers. This sent a shock of electricity through her that took her by surprise.

But soon, they were on their way through the traffic and Everly saw the city skyline. For the second time that day, tears rolled down her cheeks. These, though, were tears of happiness. She was finally here.

14

"And this is us," Drew said, as the taxi came to a stop in front of his apartment building.

Everly was still mesmerized by all the lights, the people walking the streets, and the snow that had gently started to fall. She hadn't said five words during the drive from the airport, trying to take in all of her surroundings. It was beautiful! Just as she had imagined these last few years.

"Everly, are you getting out?" Drew asked, with a laugh to his voice.

"She's like a country girl lost in a strange world," Peyton said in a half whisper while she stood next to Drew.

"Please, be nice. It's her first time here." Drew sighed and slightly shook his head. "Give her a break, okay?" Peyton just shrugged her shoulders and walked into the apartment building.

Drew took Everly's bags out of the trunk and placed them on the sidewalk. He looked over to see Everly paying the driver and thanking him profusely. The poor man didn't know what to make of her extremely friendly manner and quietly left to find another fare.

"Wow," Everly said. "I'm really here!"

Even though it was cold, Everly stood on the sidewalk and looked in every direction. She even reached down to touch the snow and laughed with excitement.

"It's a bit cold, so we should probably get inside," Drew said, even though he was enjoying watching Everly's childlike reaction to everything around her.

"I'm sorry. I'm just still trying to wrap my head around the fact that I'm here!"

"Don't worry about it. But you do have a collection of snowflakes on your head."

Everly reached up and felt the water on her hair. Then, she reached out and let the snow softly fall into her outstretched hand. Snow! She had never seen snow before, so each ice crystal that fell in her hand and on her clothing was a special treat.

"This is snow! I've never seen it before. It's beautiful."

To watch Everly's reactions was so refreshing, compared to the other people who were in his social circle. Drew wondered if anyone saw him like this when he first moved to New York.

"Come on! Let's get you settled upstairs. And we'll order some food. Then, you can make plans to play in the snow if you want, but maybe, you should save that for tomorrow."

"I'm definitely making a snowman and throwing snowballs. I can't wait to show my parents!" Everly was so excited, she felt like she was walking on air as she quickly moved toward Drew and the opened door to the building. Then, she noticed that Peyton was gone.

"Where's Peyton?"

"I'm sure she already went upstairs. She isn't very patient at times, which is a common trait for some New Yorkers." Drew didn't want her to get a bad impression on her first few minutes in the city, but it did bring back memories of his first day here.

His parents had insisted that they take him to his new apartment, right across the river in New Jersey. They were going to treat the trip as a vacation after they helped Drew move in. At least, that was what they said.

When they arrived at Drew's new apartment, his parents quickly made themselves at home amongst the other two roommates. Drew was embarrassed but didn't say anything, not wanting to upset his parents. He thought for sure that his roommates would think he was a momma's boy after everything his mom did for the three young men living in the apartment.

Instead, the guys loved all the cooking, cleaning, and groceries his parents bought before Drew finally convinced them that he was fine and they could go on their New York City vacation. Instead, they decided to go back to the Smoky Mountains. That's when Drew knew they only wanted to see him safely to the city. He was so grateful that his roommates treated his parents with respect, not at all what he was expecting after the stories he'd heard and read about living in the city. So now, he was doing the same thing for Everly, the little sister he never had. But then, she felt like more than a sibling.

"Which floor?" The words Everly spoke brought Drew back to the present moment. "Where were you?"

"Just trying to get your big ass suitcases in the door," Drew said with a laugh.

"Hey, I did pretty good, bringing only those two. At one point, I thought I might have to rent a car and just drive, but the thought of that long drive wasn't very appealing. Plus, I wanted to make sure I was here for New Year's Eve." Just then, the doors of the elevator opened and they stepped inside, luggage and all.

"Are you and Peyton going to Times Square to watch the ball drop?" Everly asked excitedly.

"No, we have a party we have to attend that Peyton's father has invited us to. It'll probably be pretty stuffy, but I have to impress the parental figures," Drew said.

"So, things are serious between you and Peyton, huh?" Everly wasn't sure she wanted to hear the answer.

"When I was down in Key West, I talked to Abbey about this for a while. I'm thinking about asking Peyton to marry me. I was going to do it on Christmas Day, but things just didn't feel right. I'm just waiting for the right time."

Everly could feel a slight bit of sadness course through her body. Though she had only met Peyton a few hours ago, she honestly couldn't see Drew with this woman. *He deserves better,* Everly thought.

"Well, there's always New Year's Eve, or Valentine's Day," Everly said cheerfully. "Maybe you'll know by then."

"Maybe." Just then the elevator doors opened. "This way." Drew turned to the right and led her down a lighted hallway that had wooden floors and polished walls. The building was older, but had been well kept. It reminded her of some of the older homes in Key West, in a way.

"Welcome to my abode," he said, and they entered a small apartment. As Drew had said, Peyton was already there, drink in hand and chatting with a man in the kitchen.

"I was beginning to think the two of you got lost," Peyton said, striding over to Drew and planting a kiss on his cheek.

"And this must be Everly," the man said. Everly quickly surmised that this was Blake, the flirty roommate from Drew's earlier description. The man walked to her and held out his hand.

"I'm Blake, Drew's favorite roommate."

"Everly," she said. She went to shake his hand, but instead, Blake brought her hand to his lips and gently gave it a kiss. So, he was a flirt. But then, he could probably command any woman's attention. He was at least six feet tall, or maybe more, with hazel eyes that sparkled. His chestnut brown hair was short but a bit unruly, giving him a "bad boy" look. And by the t-shirt and sweatpants he had on, Everly could see this man was all muscle from head to toe.

"Well, Everly, you're here just in time for fun in New York. Do you already have plans for New Year's Eve?" Blake asked.

"She just walked in the door, Blake," Drew said, sounding protective of his friend.

"I know that, but I also know that this girl has been looking forward to moving here for quite some time. Drew told us all about you after he got back from Key West. I'm still wondering why you would leave the sand and warm weather for snow, skyscrapers and sidewalks?"

"We have sidewalks in Key West, too." *Did I just say that*, Everly thought. She instantly felt completely out of her element. She had been emotional all day but while finally standing in the place where she would be staying for a few days, the enormity of what she had done was like bricks were falling on her.

"Where is the bathroom?" Everly asked quickly. She needed a minute to rein in the feelings that were bombarding her.

"First door on the right. You'll be staying in Donald's room, right next door. I'll put your things in there for you," Drew said.

"Thanks." Everly walked to the bathroom, keeping her breathing steady, feeling like she could hyperventilate at any moment. As soon as the door closed behind her, she leaned against it and closed her eyes. She took a few deep breaths to calm her racing heart. She had a panicky feeling all over, and knew that it had to be from all the excitement from the day. But, this was what she needed. Just a few moments to herself in this new place.

"She won't last two months in this town," Peyton said as she sat on the couch.

"What makes you say that?" Drew heard the comment as he re-entered the living room after taking Everly's luggage to the room.

"That's a bit harsh, Peyton. She just got here," Blake said. "She's very pretty, just like you said, Drew. Seems nice too, not like some of these women around here." He glanced at Peyton to see her giving him an evil stare.

"So, you tell your roommates that you were in the Keys with some beautiful girl, and to me, you say it was just a 'work thing' after your sister's wedding?" Peyton was miffed.

"Do we have to go through this again?" Drew gave Blake a disgusted look. "Everly showed me around Key West and the other islands *for work*. I'm not having this discussion with you now."

Everly had only barely cracked the door to hear the words coming from the other room. Peyton clearly thought she was out of her league, Blake thought she was pretty, and Drew had just used her for information. She had only been gone from home a little over twelve hours, and things in her world were totally different.

Everly took a deep breath and looked in the mirror. "I can do this. I'm strong and I have worked hard to get here. No one is going to stop me," she said quietly to herself. Then, she opened the door to join the group in the open room.

"There she is. I already put your suitcases in the bedroom. We're getting ready to order either Chinese or pizza. Since you're our guest, you get to choose. What sounds good to you?" Drew asked.

"Either sounds fine," Everly answered back in a cool voice.

Drew could tell that something was bothering her because she seemed different than the girl who was just outside enjoying the falling snow. He hoped it was only the long day she'd had, but he couldn't tell.

"Well, I'm going home. Neither of those options sound good to me and I have some leftovers in the fridge." Peyton stood up quickly and went to Drew's side. "Why don't you spend the night with me tonight? I'm sure Blake will make sure Everly is okay."

"No, I think I'll stay here. And you usually like Chinese."

"Just not feeling it tonight." Peyton moved toward the door with her coat and purse in hand. "Walk me downstairs?"

"Be right back," Drew said over his shoulder to Everly and Blake, then walked out the door.

"Drew, just a reminder," Peyton said as she slid close to him just outside the downstairs elevator doors. "Where you are right now is because you just happened to run into the right people. Dad really likes you, and I would hate to see you lose all you've worked for because you decide to hang out with the wrong people. That makes sense, right?"

"Is that a threat? And if it is, what the hell for?"

"I saw how you treated Everly. She means more to you than some friend. Just remember that I was here first, and I can offer you a lot more than some little girl from Florida. And, by the way, don't forget about the party on New Year's Eve. I already RSVP'd for both of us." She stood on her tiptoes so she could give Drew a goodnight kiss. "I love you." Then, before Drew could wrap his head around what she had just said, she walked outside, into the snow.

"Love you too!" Drew screamed out in the hall, watching her get in the taxi.

He walked back in to the sound of a lively conversation between Blake and Everly. He was asking her every sort of question about the Keys, and she looked like she was finally relaxing. *Good.* Drew hated to see her so tense, and then realized it was probably Peyton – the girl he wanted to marry. He shook his head as the miscellaneous thoughts flooded his mind.

"We decided on pizza, though I think her first Italian dinner should be out on the town, in Little Italy," Blake said, then looked back at Everly. "We do have some incredible pizza places around here, and the delivery guy is just around the corner. What do you like on your pizza?"

"Anything, really," Everly said. Blake was nice, and certainly handsome to look at, too. Drew hadn't talked much about his roommates so she didn't know what to expect.

"Well then, why don't you get settled in and we will order the food? Should be here in about thirty minutes," Blake said, smiling at her.

"Sounds good. I really need to check in with my parents. I'm sure they're wondering where I am. I promised them a call as soon as I got here. How much do I owe for the pizza?" Everly asked.

"Dinner is on us tonight," Blake said before Drew could utter a word. "Our treat."

"Thanks. I better go make that call." Everly walked to her room, smiling again. *Maybe staying here isn't going to be such a bad idea, after all,* she thought. Blake was nicer than she had expected and in the few moments they had talked, he had made her feel at home in this strange place.

Once Everly's door shut, Blake turned to Drew. "You didn't tell me that your 'Keys' girl was a hottie," he said quickly. "I'd be more than happy to show her around town." Drew recognized that expression on Blake's face and it wasn't one with pure motives.

"No way, Blake. Everly is different from the other girls you've dated, so don't even think about it. She really is a special friend to me. Plus, I promised my sister I would look after her, okay?" Drew was firm and insistent. He wanted to make sure that Blake wasn't going to jump on Everly the first chance he got.

"You sound like her daddy, or maybe, something else. So, you want her for yourself? What about Peyton?" Blake asked.

"Blake, you're an asshole, sometimes! Everly is a close friend. She's like a little sister to me. As far as Peyton, I've been thinking about asking her to marry me, but keep your mouth shut!" Drew said adamantly.

"Are you serious? Marriage? You're too young," Blake insisted.

"Let's just leave it alone. Don't hurt Everly, and don't breathe a word of what I just said about Peyton. Timing just isn't right yet, but I'm already looking at rings."

"Man, you *are* serious. I guess, congrats are in order," Blake said, holding up his wine glass.

"Not yet, but I'll let you know."

"Well, all I know is this. If you're going to marry that girl, you better be on your toes. She's feisty and high maintenance. More power to you."

"Aren't you just a sea of encouragement," Drew retorted.

"Just calling it like I see it. You know I've been with my share of girls."

"Yeah, that's why I'm telling you that Everly is off limits. Don't mess with her."

"I'll be on my best behavior, but I think we should let Everly decide," Blake replied before taking another sip of his wine.

15

"I'm here!" Everly said as she watched the faces of her mom and dad on the screen of her iPad. "Already at Drew's apartment, and we're having pizza for dinner."

"Apartment? I thought you were staying at a hotel for a few days." Everly could tell by the look on her dad's face that he was concerned.

"One of Drew's roommates is gone 'til after the holidays, so he said I could stay here. It'd save me some money. Plus, I forgot to make a reservation, which probably would've done me no good since it's New Year's Eve weekend. But, guess what? I saw snow for the first time! It was all so beautiful," Everly said in excitement.

"Been so long since I've seen snow," her mom chimed in. "Please send us some pictures, okay?"

"You know I will. Probably every day, so your messages on your phone are going to be extremely full. But it's so cold. Glad I wore boots today and had my coat ready, even though a few people gave me an odd stare at the Key West airport."

"How was your flight?" her dad asked.

"It was beautiful. The Keys are stunning from the air. I know the water is clear, but seeing it from above was totally different. I took a bunch of pictures, and I'll send them, too. My flight from Miami was fine. I slept, then read more on what to do when I got here. My first interview isn't 'til next week and I can't move into my apartment 'til Monday, so I've got a few days to explore."

"Sweetheart, I know I'm going to sound like a broken record, but please, please, *please* be careful."

"I promise, I will, Mom. Hopefully, I'll be able to go with Drew or Blake. Maybe, they'll show this newbie New Yorker around town," Everly said with a laugh.

"Blake?"

"Dad, that's Drew's other roommate. Nice guy. As a matter of fact, we're getting ready to have some pizza for dinner. A part of me wants to go out and celebrate, but the other part wants to simply go to bed. I'm tired after the trip and cold, but I still can't believe I'm here." Everly smiled at them, but at the same time, felt a little melancholy. She could see a bit of sadness in their eyes, too, but she couldn't focus on that.

"So, we'll FaceTime again tomorrow, okay? I'll call when I'm out and about. I can't wait to show you the snow. I already told Drew I was making a snowman, and I think I can instigate a snowball fight," Everly said with a laugh.

"We're so proud of you," her mom said. "I can't deny that I wish you were still here, but we both know you've been dreaming about this since you were a little girl. We always knew this, but now, you've proven that you're one determined woman.

Lord help whoever hires you, and whoever steals your heart." Everly watched as her mom wiped a tear from the corner of her eye. That made Everly's own tear up, just slightly, but she was doing her best to keep from crying a third time today.

"I love you guys. I'll talk to you tomorrow, and I promise, you're going to get sick of the pictures and the phone calls."

"Never. Love you, sweetheart," her dad said, and the screen went blank. Everly now sat in the room that was to be hers for the next few days. She was happy. Satisfied. Tired. And a bit cold. Those sweaters, socks and scarves were coming out of her suitcases rather quickly tonight, and she was sure she'd need them tomorrow. But it didn't matter to her. Everything was exciting. And she couldn't wait to explore the city, but right now, some dinner and then bed sounded good after such a long day.

"Dinner is here," Everly heard from the other room. She looked around one more time, stretched, and headed out to have her first New York dinner.

■ ■ ■

When she opened her eyes, she was disoriented at first, but then realized where she was. The room was dark since there was no window, but the light of the clock beside the bed was almost like a night light. It was seven o'clock, and she couldn't believe she had slept in late. She was so used to being up by six o'clock every morning, but then, yesterday had been a full one from the moment she woke up 'til she finally said goodnight to Drew and Blake.

Everly smiled as she lay still in the soft bed, wrapped in the blanket she brought from home. Heavy blankets weren't necessary in the Keys, but this was one she'd ordered online before she left home. She had made sure to sleep with the fuzzy thing in her bed back home before she began her new life here in New York. Now, it was almost like she had brought a piece of her room with her. And she had, in more ways than just this blanket.

Everly brought her favorite bathing suit, a pair of flip-flops, her dolphin ring she'd had for years now, and a little ceramic sea turtle that had held tiny pieces of papers that were her dreams. The little turtle had been given to her by her grandmother, with the instructions to write her wishes on pieces of paper and place them into the turtle's shell. And Everly had. There were lots of little curled up papers in the tiny turtle. Now that she was in New York, she wanted to see how many times she had written about her city of dreams.

Hopefully, today, she would be able to explore the city. Everly had a list a mile long and a map to help her find her way. She would be walking, for sure, and didn't want to attempt the subway before someone could show her the ins and outs of the transportation system. Blake and Drew were both off work until after the New Year, but she wasn't sure of their plans today. She didn't care. Even if it had snowed a foot overnight and she was by herself, she was going out. She was going to see New York, do some shopping, and maybe even try to ice skate at Rockefeller Center, if she could stand up in the ice skates. Everly wanted to give it a try, at least.

Even though she had a list of things to do, she also had a list of things *not* to do, from anyone that found out that she was moving to the big city. And though she would listen and quietly agree, only a few made sense to her, and she had tucked away the information safely in her mind. She might have grown up in a relaxed island town, but she was smart.

When Everly got out of bed, the cold was a shock to her system. She stood, shivering, 'til she put her socks on, along with a long sleeve shirt she quickly pulled out of her suitcase. Last night, she had slept in her usual tank top and panties, but she could tell that she'd probably have to dress a bit warmer each night.

Everly opened the door to smell the scent of freshly brewed coffee. She preferred tea, but would occasionally have a cup, as long as she could douse it with French vanilla creamer and a bit of sugar. She did have a sweet tooth, but with riding a bike almost every day or walking everywhere in Key West, a weight problem never plagued her. She was sure it would be the same way here in New York. Everly might not have her bike, but she'd be walking. Hopefully, her job wouldn't be too far away from her new apartment.

Everly quickly ducked into the bathroom before going out to the kitchen. There, she found Blake, sitting at the kitchen counter and reading the newspaper.

"Good morning, Key West girl," Blake said with a smile. "Hope you were able to get some sleep. Sometimes, people new to New York have a bit of adjustment to the noise from the streets. It's not too bad here, but can be at times. Like this upcoming weekend."

"I kinda figured, so I slept with ear plugs last night. And I can't believe I slept this late."

"When do you normally get up?"

"Around six o'clock. At home, I would get some tea, maybe ride to the beach or get breakfast before work, but I had a bad habit of being late. I was blessed to have a great boss. He's helping me find a job here. I have four interviews next week with people he knows." Everly slowly walked to the kitchen, looking from side to side. "Where's Drew?"

"Went out to get some breakfast food. I'm not very good at stocking the cabinets, or fridge, for that matter. I usually eat out, most of the time. The exception will probably be the next few months." Blake motioned for her to sit next to him. "Want a cup of coffee?"

"No thanks, but I will have some water," Everly said as she held up the water bottle in her hand. "Do you have something big planned?"

"I'm finally, after all this time, finishing my Master's Degree. So, instead of working, going to school, and finishing my internship, I'm taking a leave of absence from my job for the next six months. Then, hopefully, I'll be able to work where I'm interning or my current boss said I can come back and possibly receive a raise."

Everly was impressed that he could live here and not be working without saving like she had.

"So, what are you getting your degree in?"

"International Business. Boring stuff, but I'll be a stockbroker. I've always loved finance and have built my own investment portfolio over the last seven years. Now, it's time to help some others and make money while I do it. So, what about you? Drew said you're in web design."

"Yes, I do a little of all of it. Web design, coding, and more. I've always been a computer geek, I guess you could say. I got my degree online so I could stay home and help my parents when my Dad got sick. I worked for Lance, my boss in Key West, since I was seventeen. I was still in high school, but he gave me a chance after I showed him what I could do. Now, he is helping me, hopefully, land a job here. I'm keeping my fingers crossed because I've never had to interview for a job. I've only worked for Lance," Everly said before she took a sip of her water. Then, she heard a commotion at the door.

"That's Drew, trying to open the door with his hands full. Does it every time." Blake walked to the door and opened it before Drew could finish putting the key in the lock.

"I was hoping you'd hear me and help. Here, grab a bag." Everly heard Drew's voice and instantly smiled.

"What did you do – buy the whole grocery store?" Blake asked, taking hold of two rather heavy bags.

"Well, I wasn't sure what she'd like and we didn't have a thing in this place to eat," Drew replied, walking in and seeing Everly sitting at the counter.

"Ask her yourself," Blake said with a laugh.

"You honestly didn't need to go to all this trouble for me, Drew. We could just go out somewhere and eat."

"It's still snowing outside. Not sure anyone is going anywhere. They say it might stop sometime this afternoon, but I would venture to say there is at least three to four inches already."

"Really?" Everly said excitedly. "Now, I know I'm going out today. I just have to play in the snow. I've never done that before. This will be awesome!"

"I've never seen anyone react to snow like you do," Blake said with a smile. "Very refreshing to see excitement over something us New Yorkers don't like very much."

"Maybe, one day, I might feel like you do, but not right now. I will admit that I'm hungry though. What did you bring from the store?" Everly began pulling things out of the bags the men had placed on the counter. "I can help put these up if you let me know where things go."

"Can we keep her?" Blake asked, turning to Drew then giving Everly a wink. "No one ever offers to help around here. That's the reason I usually eat out. If you stay here, I'll start eating at home, for sure."

Everly was certain that her cheeks had to be a deep shade of red from the way Blake was talking and looking at her. Even the small wink he sent her way had her a tiny bit breathless. He certainly was handsome and a bit sexy this morning, with his day-old stubble that graced his chin and jawline. Everly never expected to meet someone her very first day in New York that had her thinking about something other than moving here. And about Drew. But, this man did.

"Blake, you sound pathetic." Drew felt a strange sensation as he watched the unspoken interaction between his roommate and Everly. He was so protective of her, and he knew of Blake's ways with women. He just didn't want to see Everly be a checkmark on Blake's list. There was more to this sensation, but Drew could not figure it out. All he knew was that he didn't want to see Blake and Everly together.

"How about some eggs and biscuits? I can scramble the eggs and fix some homemade biscuits if you have the ingredients," Everly said to the two men in the kitchen with her.

"How about these?" Drew asked, holding up the can of biscuits.

"That will do, but you guys need to stock up with more ingredients. To make some good homemade food. But I will say that I'm ready to try some New York cuisine."

"Sweetheart, you've come to the city where you can get whatever food you desire. You name it and we'll go." Blake was suddenly by her side, helping her put up the groceries and telling her all about the restaurants she should try. The only thing Drew could do was stand there and shake his head.

"I say we have some breakfast and then go play outside in the snow. It's been so long since I've done that. What about you, Drew?"

"Sounds good to me. I'm waiting on Peyton to call. She said something about a play or show this afternoon that she had tickets to see. But I'm up for a good snowball fight," he said.

"Everly, just let me show you how to make a good snowball. Drew sucks at it!"

"No, I don't. If I remember correctly, the last time we had a decent snowfall, I got you good in the face. You had a black eye that took over a week to heal."

"You just got lucky, that's all."

Everly sat, watching the two men as they bantered back and forth about the quality of snowballs while she started making breakfast. But, before eating, she quietly walked over to the window and looked out. It was a winter wonderland, like nothing she'd had ever seen before, except in pictures.

It was just yesterday I was in shorts and flip-flops, she laughed as she thought to herself. But as she continued to watch the scene below, Everly couldn't wait to get outside.

16

"Remember what I showed you, right?" Drew asked, looking at the snow mound in Everly's hand.

"I got it. Just watch." Everly let the snowball fly and it hit Blake squarely in the shoulder.

"Score!" she said out loud, raising her arms high above her head. "I'm better at this than I thought."

"It's because you had a great teacher," Drew said, shoulders puffed out.

"Well, this isn't fair. Two against one," Blake said.

"Then let's make it two against two." Everly turned as she instantly recognized Peyton's voice. It felt like this dark shadow had come over the fun the three of them were having.

"Hey, babe." Drew walked to Peyton and gave her a quick kiss. "We were just showing Everly the art of making and throwing a snowball. This is her first time seeing or being in snow. You want to join the fun?"

"I think I'll pass." The tone of her voice spoke volumes. "As much fun as this looks, it's too cold for me. Besides, we have theater tickets this afternoon, courtesy of my father." As she finished her sentence, she glanced over at Everly and gave her a courteous smile.

"I need to go and get changed," Drew said. "Everly, use what I taught you and pummel him. He needs someone to knock him down a peg or two." With that, Drew turned and Peyton wrapped her arm in his as they walked toward the building.

Everly watched as the couple walked inside. "I don't think she likes me," Everly said to Blake as he came towards her.

"Peyton? I don't think Peyton likes anyone but Peyton," Blake said.

"That's kinda mean, don't you think?"

"I've been around her a lot longer than you. Just wait. You'll see what I mean. But for now, I say that we go to Rockefeller Center and go ice-skating. The snow is letting up and the Christmas tree is still up. Hopefully, it won't be that busy, but if it is, it won't matter. Think you could stand the cold a little longer?" Blake asked her.

Everly was beyond excited. "Are you serious? I know I can! Just let me put on some more clothing and I'll be ready to go."

She practically ran into the building, hearing Blake's laugh behind her. Everly didn't care if she looked or acted like a tourist. She thought she'd be exploring on her own today, but Blake wanted to show her around, which was fine with her. He was fun to talk to, and she liked the fact that he asked all about her hometown, her likes and dislikes. He even made her laugh. Instead of being a bit homesick, she wasn't. Everly was on an adventure and she was most assuredly liking her new friend.

It didn't take long before Blake and Everly were standing in front of the huge tree with the ice skating rink in front of it. It was as beautiful as Everly had imagined all these years. The photos she had seen did not do it justice. Even though the sun was just beginning to set and the snow had stopped falling, the dark, cloudy skies made the large Christmas tree look stunning, with its glittering lights. The ice rink had its share of visitors, but not so many that it made Everly not want to venture out and at least try the shoes with silver blades attached. She'd never been that good at roller-skating and she was sure ice skating would be more difficult, but Everly didn't care. As far as she was concerned, this was part of the New York experience, something she was going to do.

"So, I'm assuming you've never ice skated before?" Blake asked as they sat side by side, lacing up their skates. It seemed as though Everly had only begun to put her skates on and Blake was finished, ready to step on to the ice.

"No. I mean, yesterday was my first time ever seeing snow. This is so different from my world. Where I come from, we ski, scuba dive, snorkel, and free dive. We go to the water or beach almost every day, and live in flip-flops. That's what I grew up on."

"Now, to me, that sounds much more fun that trying to stand on ice and not fall and bust your ass."

Everly started laughing. "That's because this is nothing new to you. One day, you'll have to visit the Keys and get a taste of my hometown."

"As long as you'd be willing to show me around, I would come, for sure," Blake replied, giving her yet another wink before standing. "Are you ready to give this a go?"

Everly looked down at the skates on her feet. It was now or never, as Blake extended a hand to her to help her up. As she stood, her ankles began furiously rocking back and forth and before she knew it, she had grabbed onto both of Blake's arms for support. She looked up at him to say she was sorry, but not before noticing the taut muscles that were hidden underneath the coat.

"Whoa, there!" Blake expertly caught her before she fell. "Now, just take your time and when you're ready, we'll head to the rink."

"I'm ready. Let's go," Everly said, holding onto Blake's arm as though it were a lifeline to a raft. She watched him step onto the ice as though he was an expert skater, and quickly she was having second thoughts. She hesitated, wondering how she would look if she fell. No, *when* she fell.

"You can do it. Just hold my hand. I'll skate backwards and help you stand up. You're going to do fine." Blake must have read the hesitation on her face.

Everly placed one foot on the ice, and then the other. To her credit, her ankles seemed to steady themselves, but she was taking no chances. She latched onto each of Blake's outstretched hands and found the needed support.

"Now, I'm going to start moving. You fine so far?" Blake asked, giving her a look of encouragement.

"Let's go," Everly said excitedly.

Before she knew it, Everly was slowly gliding around the ice rink with Blake as her guide. She was ice skating in New York City! And, once again, those pesky tears formed at the corners of her eyes and gently fell down her cheeks.

"Are you okay?" Blake asked quickly, seeing the wet drops on her face.

"I'm perfect. This is something I've thought about for I don't know how long, and I'm here. I'm skating. I'm in New York. You have no idea what this means to me," Everly said softly. "Thanks, Blake, for bringing me here. I was sure I'd be exploring today by myself, but it's fun to have someone to share it with."

"No problem. I don't have to go back to work 'til next week, so, if you'd like, I'll be your official New York tour guide for the next few days. In fact, I'd like to ask you something."

Everly looked at him, perplexed. "What?"

"I know we only met each other yesterday, but would you be my date for New Year's Eve? This will be a 'friend' date. We'll go to Times Square to watch the ball drop, eat some food from the street vendors, and make sure we buy some outrageous hat or something that signals the incoming year. What do you say?" Blake asked.

Everly smiled back at the man who still was responsible for her staying upright on the ice. He was like a beam of sunshine, his infectious personality so fun. She liked being around him. How could she say no?

"It's a date. I'm sorry—a 'friend' date."

"Awesome. Now, let's see if we can go just a little bit faster," Blake said. Everly held on for dear life, laughing the whole time as she watched the ice pass beneath her feet, then looked at the happy skaters around her.

■ ■ ■

Drew sat in the stiff chair next to Peyton, who was beside her parents. The play was good, but not keeping his attention at all. In his mind, all he could think about was what Blake and Everly were doing. The snowball fight had been fun, and he'd forgotten how simple pleasures like that brought him joy. He hadn't realized 'til he formed about the third snowball that he had become a little hard around the edges. All work, no play. At least, not enjoying being in the moment. Now, Everly and Blake were off to see the big Christmas tree and go skating, something that sounded much more enjoyable than sitting in a stuffy theater.

"Are you going to let me out?" Peyton asked curtly.

"What? I'm sorry. Of course," Drew replied, coming back to the present moment to realize they were at an intermission. "I'll walk with you to the lobby."

"That's fine. Not sure where you are today, but it would be nice to have my boyfriend with me instead of some far-off place."

"Just have a lot on my mind."

"Does it have to do with Everly?"

Not again, Drew thought as he shook his head. "No, it's work. I don't have to go back 'til next week, but still have three stories to turn in when I get back. I feel like I should probably be home, working on them. But then, I wanted to be with you this afternoon," Drew said, kissing her cheek. "As for Everly, I just want to make sure she gets adjusted to city life. If that really such a bad thing?"

Peyton continued to stare at him, as though she was trying to decide whether she believed him or not.

"Go ahead to the restroom and I'll wait for you here." He watched as Peyton strode off, then took a deep breath.

He had just lied to her. Yes, the articles were due, but his thoughts were certainly not on the work he had to do. He was thinking about Everly and hoping that Blake was treating her well. He'd never questioned Blake's reputation with women, even though he thought that Blake was a little callous with their feelings. Drew just stayed out of it. But he wasn't about to allow Blake to hurt Everly. He would step in if that became apparent.

"So, are you enjoying the play?" Drew turned around to see Mr. Compton, Peyton's dad, standing beside him.

"Yes, sir," Drew said. "Thanks for inviting us. I know these are hard tickets to get."

"No problem. It's really all about who you know. Plus, I knew that Peyton and her mother really wanted to see this."

"Well, thanks again." Drew liked Peyton's father, but also found him intimidating, especially since he owned the paper where Drew worked. That added a little more pressure to the relationship between him and Peyton.

"You two are coming to the New Year's Eve party, right?"

"We are. Peyton gave me all the details just the other day. It sounds like it will be nice."

"Drew, how many times do I have to tell you to call me Nolan?"

"Sorry, Nolan. But yes, we plan to be there. The place you picked is a great spot to watch all the festivities and the ball drop."

"Pulled a few strings here and there. It's going to be a great night, right?" Nolan said, nudging Drew's arm slightly.

Was he missing something here? Peyton's father was acting like Drew should know something, like he was out of the loop on some secret. But he had no idea. Hopefully he was just reading this man's expression wrong.

"There you are," a woman said as she came up to Nolan and gave him a kiss on the cheek. "Almost didn't find you two in this sea of people." It was Peyton's mom, Georgia Compton. When she and Peyton stood side by side, they almost looked like sisters instead of mother and daughter.

"Well, there go the lights. I think it's time to find our seats." Georgia took her husband's arm and they headed back into the theater.

"So, you were talking to my Dad?" Peyton asked.

"Yes. He asked if we were coming to the party and I told him yes."

"That's all?" Peyton asked, rubbing up against him with a sly smile.

"Is there something going on I should know about?" Drew asked, his curiosity getting the best of him.

"Not really. We better go take our seats."

What is going on? Drew knew something was amiss, or had he completely misread the signals? That was always a distinct possibility with Peyton.

As the play resumed, Drew, couldn't concentrate again, but this time, it wasn't about Everly or Blake. He couldn't help but wonder when his relationship with Peyton had taken a different turn.

He went over again how they had met and how they had gotten to this point. Covering that fashion show was a big deal for Drew, since fashion was such a big part of this city. But when he met Peyton, he remembered that it was like a breath of fresh air. They began to talk and soon were sitting at a little diner, having cheesecake and coffee. It seemed like they sat there for hours, and Drew felt so at home with this girl. She seemed to be down-to-earth, working hard to be a model, but also expressed the desire to design her own fashions.

From that day forward, they seemed to talk every day, either by phone or in person. She kept busy with photo shoots and art classes while he continued to work his way through the journalist maze. They dated, but each time he offered to pick her up at her place, she declined. And when he offered to make her dinner at his place, there was always an excuse. But at the time, he didn't care. He was in love.

To Drew, Peyton was the perfect New York girl. He had dated other women since arriving in New York, and his first serious girlfriend, Sonia, had made him wonder if women in the city could be trusted. Drew found out after they broke up that Sonia had been dating other men while they were together. After that, Drew was more reserved. He wasn't a ladies' man, but women seemed to be drawn to him. His sister always said that he didn't know how to have a relationship, but now, he was proving her wrong by what he had with Peyton.

But they had almost called it quits, too. When Peyton finally let him pick her up from her apartment, Drew found out she was living in a beautiful two-bedroom apartment close to the center of town. She even had a doorman to her building. When he arrived and Peyton opened the door, she had a drink in hand and said she had some things to tell him.

That's when Drew learned that Peyton wasn't just some model barely making it from week to week. She came from a wealthy family. Her parents owned several businesses and were currently paying for her apartment 'til she could land on her feet, so to speak. Peyton still confirmed she was a model and she was designing her own clothing line, but with a little help from her father.

Drew remembered how he felt that night. She hadn't been honest with him, but then again, she hadn't lied. He didn't understand why she had kept this part of her life from him, but then she told him the age-old story: she wanted to make sure he liked her for her and not for her money. Coming from the mountains of North Carolina, Drew had heard that line before, but only in a movie. He had fallen in love with the girl, so he didn't know how to respond at first. And that night was the first disagreement they ever had. Drew walked out and didn't take Peyton's calls for two weeks, only texting her, telling Peyton to give him a bit of time to think. Since Peyton had never come to his apartment, she had no way of finding him. But, she did know where he worked.

Peyton showed up several times at his office, and each time, they ended up outside on the sidewalk in a heated argument. Peyton apologizing and Drew just telling her to give him time. This was the first time Drew saw that when Peyton wanted something, she didn't give up. And he liked that. Well, at least, he used to.

Drew knew he had true feelings for this woman, feelings that he had never felt before. Soon, they were spending more time together, and it wasn't long before Drew was offered employment at his current newspaper, one owned by Peyton's father. At first, he hesitated to take the offer, but it came with a much larger salary, more story opportunities, and a huge discount on an apartment in downtown Manhattan instead of across the river in New Jersey.

Drew also thought that it would be the perfect way to show Peyton's parents what a hard worker he was. He wanted them to get to know him, not just through their daughter. Drew was already starting to think that this girl could be the one he could spend his life with.

He had made the big move, job and apartment, less than a year ago, and everything was fine 'til he went to the Florida Keys for Abbey's wedding. Being there for almost three weeks had changed a part of him, something that he was still trying to understand. Since he had been back in New York, everything felt different. His job. His relationship with Peyton. His friends. The city he loved so much. Not knowing why he felt so different was maddening.

Then, yesterday, when he saw Everly in the airport, he felt himself smile inside for the first time in weeks. She reminded him of the tropical island and the relaxed atmosphere he had enjoyed the entire time he was there. That had to be what it was. New York was fast-paced and full of work. People everywhere, serious and stressed. In the Keys, people just enjoyed the moment. A sunset. A walk on the beach. Sitting outside under an umbrella, enjoying some trop rock music. Sand between toes.

Then, maybe it was Everly. She always seemed so positive, even though she had faced some difficulties. Drew knew she wanted to be here more than anything but he hoped she didn't lose that island quality he saw with everyone who lived in the Keys. They were different, and he loved how he felt when he was around them. He could even see a difference in Abbey, his sister, in just the short time she had lived there.

"Hello there. Drew, where are you?" Peyton asked.

Drew hadn't noticed that the play had ended and he was just sitting, staring straight ahead toward the stage. He knew he had clapped when he was supposed to and laughed at the appropriate times, but he had been analyzing his life. His relationship with Peyton. Remembering and wondering.

"Sorry. I...."

"Have so much on your mind. Yeah, that's what I heard an hour ago," Peyton said, rushing by him.

"Hey, wait a minute." Drew gently touched her shoulder and she slowed down and turned to him. "I have a lot going on. I'm sorry about this afternoon. I probably should have told you I couldn't come."

"So you could go with Blake and Everly?" Peyton looked at him with eyebrows raised.

"No, so I could have stayed home and worked," Drew said, but he thought that Peyton's suggestion was probably more correct.

"Well, Mom and Dad would like to get dinner. Shall we go with them or have our own dinner somewhere else?"

"We can have dinner with your parents. That sounds good. But then, I should get back home and work."

"I have some sketches that are due tomorrow, so I need to work, too. Can you work over at my place?"

"Can't tonight, but maybe tomorrow, okay?" Drew asked, hoping this would satisfy Peyton.

"That would be nice, but I do have to work the next two days. Believe it or not, I have a spring photo shoot, but at least it takes place all indoors. I think it's going to be two very long days. After that, I have the next two days off for the holiday. I'm really looking forward to that." Peyton smiled broadly and traced her finger around the buttons on his shirt. "Maybe, we could make this a totally indoor holiday. I know there are a lot of things we could do."

"Now, that sounds interesting," Drew said, taking her in his arms and kissing her lips gently.

"I love you, Drew."

"I love you, too."

17

"I think I'm finally warm," Everly said, her teeth no longer chattering. She sat on the sofa, bundled up in the two blankets Blake had put around her.

"The hot chocolate is great. What's the trick?"

"What trick?" Blake asked with a laugh.

"I've never tasted anything like this. It's completely different than those packets you just dump in hot water."

"Because I make it the old-fashioned way. It's the one thing I do cook around here. Something my Mom taught me a long time ago. Dark chocolate, milk, cream, sugar, vanilla. Top that off with good old marshmallows- except my Mom would use whip cream."

"Sounds like your Mom is an excellent cook." Everly took another sip of the delicious cocoa that was truly warming her body all the way to her toes.

"She was. She died a while back," Blake said.

"I'm sorry."

"It's no problem. My Mom was sick for a very long time. We just didn't know it at the time."

“She hid her illness from you? My Dad has Multiple Sclerosis and was sick for such a long time. That’s one reason I didn’t move ‘til now. He began doing so much better once we found a good doctor. Plus, my mom and I helped him make the necessary lifestyle changes to complement the medicine he has to take.”

“Mom didn’t tell us anything. But she was suffering on the inside. She committed suicide by overdosing on pills.”

“Oh, Blake, I’m so sorry I said anything.”

“It’s okay. I can talk about it more now, since time has passed. But at first, it was hard. We knew that Mom was depressed off and on, but had no idea she was that bad. She hid it so well. She was an excellent cook and loved music. She played the piano like no one I’ve seen before. After her death, the doctors told us that she had come to them and had been on so many different medications for manic depression and bi-polar.

“I always thought she was just moody, and that was my Mom. But she didn’t talk to anyone, not even the therapist she had seen over the years. The biggest regret we’ve had, especially my Dad, is that we didn’t see the signs. My Mom was the consummate actress. One thing I know is that she isn’t suffering anymore. But, that’s enough of that.” Blake stood to get more hot chocolate, leaving Everly on the couch, wondering what to say next.

“So, your Dad is doing okay now?” Blake asked.

“He is better. He just has a strict regimen he has to follow. It seems that the disease has halted, or at least, slowed down dramatically. Enough that I felt comfortable to move here.”

"That's good. I'm sure they are happy for you."

"I just got through sending them the pictures we took today. And the first text I get back is 'who is the guy?'" Everly laughed.

"I hope you said it's some wonderful man that has the makings of becoming a great friend," Blake said.

"Yeah, something along those lines," she laughed. "They're just excited for me. Plus, I had to send some pics to Abbey."

"Drew's sister. Yet to meet her."

"Probably won't for a while, since she and Zach haven't been married that long. I think they're still setting up house, or at least, Abbey is. Zach just lets her decorate the house however she wants. They're so good together." Talking about Abbey made Everly feel, for the first time, an ever-so-tiny bit of homesickness. But it didn't last for long, since the door to the apartment suddenly opened and Drew came in.

"Shit, it's cold outside," Drew said, taking off his jacket and tossing it on the back of the chair. "Hope you guys had more fun than me."

"I told you those plays will put you to sleep," Blake laughed.

"I want to see a play, any play," Everly said enthusiastically. "What did you see?"

"I honestly don't remember. Had too many other things on my mind. Then, we went to dinner. One of those places where an entrée is the size of a baby appetizer."

"Let's have Chinese tonight, since we had pizza yesterday. You do like Chinese, right?" Blake focused his eyes on Everly, waiting for an answer.

"Sure!"

"So, I take it that you're still hungry, too, right, Drew?" Blake asked as he got his phone out to call for dinner delivery.

"Starving. Let's get the usual and then watch a movie. Need some down time, unless you guys had something else planned." At the words, Drew hoped that Everly wasn't going anywhere else with Blake. He still didn't trust him with her.

"Nope. We went ice skating. Then, I got to see the tree at Rockefeller Center, St. Patrick's Cathedral, and Times Square, where we'll be on the 31st to ring in the New Year," Everly said, looking at Blake. "You want to come with us? Maybe you and Peyton? I know you said something about a party, but I wanted to let you know you're included."

"Sounds like you did a lot on your first full day here," Drew said.

"We did. In fact, so much that I felt like I was losing feeling in my feet from walking and the cold weather. I happily paid for a taxi back here. Then, Blake made me some of his wonderful hot chocolate. Sorry your day didn't go as well."

"It's okay. And thanks for the invitation, but we're already committed to the party. Maybe we can all do something New Year's Day." Drew was thinking about how much fun it would be to celebrate the New Year outside in the freezing cold, instead of a stuffy room full of people he hardly knew. If only he could convince Peyton to ditch the party.

Damn, why did she have to be so adorable? So *Everly*? "We're going to have to teach you about the subway system, so you can save some of that hard-saved money of yours," Drew said. "It's really not that hard to get around. Just have to be careful of people and watch your surroundings."

Everly laughed.

"What's that for?" Drew asked.

"Because you sound like my parents, now. I think I sat with them, one on each side, watching video after video of how to be safe as a single girl, then about safety in New York."

"Well, I made a promise to Abbey that I would make sure you were taken care of. I don't want to get on my sister's bad side."

"Drew, I promise, I can take care of myself. But thanks for being my protector."

"You have two protectors now. Probably three, once Donald gets back. He's the one we're going to have to protect you from." Blake was smiling at her and she could feel the goose bumps along her arms. Everly had enjoyed such a wonderful day with him today, a feeling she wasn't expecting and now was very much looking forward to New Year's Eve. But in the next few days, she needed to check on her apartment and find some furniture for it, like a bed and desk. That was all she needed right now.

"The food will be here in about forty-five minutes," Blake said, disconnecting the call.

"Then, if it's okay with you two, I'm going to take a shower and get a bit more comfortable. I'm not use to wearing all this clothing." Once the words were out of Everly's mouth, she cringed. "Oh, that didn't come out right."

Both men were laughing, but so was she. "You know I'm used to island clothes. I feel like I have on every article of clothing I brought with me just to stay warm today. So, no making fun of the new girl," Everly laughed as she walked to her room and shut the door.

"Sounds like you two had a good day. Thanks for showing her around. Tomorrow, I'm going to take her to her apartment and show her the buildings where she has interviews next week," Drew said.

"I don't mind taking her if you need to work. I'm off, so I can do it. And I have to say, you're right," Blake remarked, glancing over at Drew from the TV. "She's special. Very different from the women here."

Drew could feel a sense of dread come over him. He had never seen Blake take any woman seriously in the time he'd known him. He always seemed to have a different girl on his arm each week. Drew didn't want Everly getting stuck in his web.

"Blake, don't mess with Everly."

"Man, talk about protective. I think she can make her own decisions."

"Blake, every time Donald or I see you, it's with a different woman. So, you can imagine why I worry about Everly when she's with you."

Blake leaned forward, looking at Drew. "So, are you her protector or do you like this girl?"

"Of course, I like her. She's been a great friend to me. We've been through this before," Drew said sharply.

"Oh, hell, Drew, you know what I mean. The way I see it, you like her more than just some friend. I've never seen you like this with any woman. Even with Peyton."

"That's not true and you know it. Anyway, Peyton is the one for me. I already told you that."

"I know that's what you said, but you sure aren't acting like it. Let Everly live her life. We had a good time today. And we have a date for New Year's Eve. I promise, I'll be on my best behavior. I won't do anything to upset her. Promise."

18

The hot shower water felt good on her skin. Everly didn't know how tired she was 'til she finally felt her muscles relax in the warm water running over her body. But, it was a happy tired. She finally got to experience some of the sights of New York today that she'd been dreaming about for years. And with the snow that had accumulated over night, it was stunningly beautiful, but cold.

She put on a long-sleeved shirt, a pair of sweatpants, and fuzzy socks to keep her warm. Even though the heat was turned on in the apartment, she was still shivering. Everly was sure her body would acclimate to the weather, hopefully soon. *If not, I'll just wear double the clothes everywhere I go,* Everly thought as she smiled to herself.

After she pulled her wet hair back into a long ponytail, she quickly made her way back to her temporary room. For a minute, she sat on the bed and flipped through the pictures she had taken today. Skating. Rockefeller Center. The Cathedral. Times Square. The row of shops. The food carts. The snow.

Every single picture made her smile, and she couldn't wait to make a digital scrapbook page on her computer of her first day. Plus, she now had plenty of new pictures that gave her ideas for her digital art. Her iPad Pro was certainly going to get a workout here, in the city. She might even try an actual sketch book and pen. Everly loved to draw; it was the one sure thing that helped her relax.

If the guys hadn't mentioned the movie, Everly loved the idea of coming back here to her room, turning on some relaxing music, and sketching. But then again, watching a movie, bundled up in her soft blanket didn't sound bad either on this cold night.

She heard Drew announce that dinner had arrived. Everly looked in the mirror to make sure she was presentable, then made her way into the kitchen. The smell that met her was wonderful. The sight of the many Chinese take-out boxes amused her. It looked like they were feeding an army! But then again, they were used to ordering food for three grown men. All she could think of was that there would be plenty of leftovers.

"So, I was going to take you around town tomorrow to show you the apartment building and the places you're going for your interviews. Sound okay?" Drew asked Everly as they all sat cross-legged around the coffee table.

"Sounds perfect to me. I'll just make sure to bundle up good." Everly took a bite of her sweet and sour chicken and moaned. "This is fantastic!"

Drew laughed. "It is one of our favorite places to order from. Now tomorrow, it's supposed to warm up a little bit, but not enough to melt the snow."

"Ugh, that means dirty, nasty slush," Blake said. "I can tell you now that it's not as pretty as what you saw today."

"I don't care. I think I love it all."

"Ha! Just wait till you have to go through a garbage strike in the middle of the summer heat. I want to hear you repeat those words then!"

"That bad?" Everly said.

"Very bad," Drew added as he grabbed a box and proceeded to a second helping of food.

"Well, if you boys don't mind, I'm going to call it a night instead of watching a movie. I'm more tired than I thought, and I want to get on the computer for a little while. Make sure I have all my information downloaded to my phone and iPad for tomorrow. Drew, are you sure you're free tomorrow? Blake said he would help me."

Drew looked at Blake, who grinned widely. "No, it's fine. Peyton is on a photo shoot for the next two days."

"Okay. Goodnight, you two," Everly said, and walked slowly to her room and shut the door.

■ ■ ■

"This is it?" Everly looked at the building that housed her apartment. It wasn't anything like she'd imagined from the pictures on the Internet. Not that it was terrible, but it wasn't as clean as she thought. Or maybe, she was used to Drew's apartment in a better part of the city.

"It's not that bad. I checked. The neighborhood is safe. I think you'll like it here." Drew secretly wished she would be living closer, but wanted to give her encouragement.

Everly took a deep breath as she looked at the building again. "Then, I guess it's time to meet my roommates."

The apartment was on the second floor, so they both took the short flight of steps. As she stood in front of the door marked "2A," she was suddenly nervous. It was one thing to be staying with someone she knew, and another to be moving into a place with total strangers.

Everly cautiously knocked on the door, then heard the soft fall of footsteps. She looked at Drew for one last bit of support and his smile helped to booster her confidence.

The small girl that answered the door didn't look like she was even out of high school, but Everly vaguely recognized her from the Skype call they'd done a few weeks ago. This had to be Tisha.

"Are you Tisha? I'm Everly, your new roommate," Everly said, and extended her hand to the young girl.

"They didn't call you?" Tisha stood at the door with a strange look on her face.

"Call me?"

"Those idiots. They don't do anything right. Come on in," Tisha answered, ushering Everly and Drew into the small space.

Everly looked in every direction and was trying to figure out where the rooms were. The place was very small; the couch was practically in the kitchen area. But she knew this before she came, right? She looked back at Drew, who seemed to have a concerned look on his face as he surveyed the living space.

"The landlord was supposed to call you. The room isn't available anymore. Some guy moved in last week. Can't remember his name yet." Tisha was at the stove, cooking something. Apparently, they had arrived in the middle of her meal.

"Not available? But I already put down a deposit. The woman I spoke to, Miss...." Everly's head was rapidly becoming fuzzy as she tried to process what Tisha had told her. This wasn't part of the plan. Everly had everything mapped out. The room was available. She had put the deposit down the end of November.

"I don't know who you're talking about, but the room is taken. You'll have to call them back. And I don't know anything about a deposit." Tisha kept cooking, as though what was happening was no big deal. *Was this how it was in New York?* Everly thought in a panic.

"Everly, I'm sure there's some mistake. Let's call and find out. It will be okay," Drew reassured her as he gently put his hand on her shoulder.

"But-" was all Everly could say before Drew interrupted her.

"Thanks, Tisha. We'll let you know what we find out," Drew guided Everly toward the door because she seemed to be stuck in place where she stood.

"Good luck," the young girl said as Drew shut the door.

"I just talked to her a few weeks ago. She didn't say anything about this. She had to have known. Or maybe, Gilly knew instead."

"Gilly?" Drew asked looking puzzled.

"Gilly, my other supposed roommate. They both seemed so nice. Tisha just acted like it wasn't any of her business. You'd think she would try to at least help me." Everly was hurt and frustrated, even angry. This wasn't supposed to happen.

"It seems like the landlord found someone else who could move in sooner, or was willing to pay a higher rent. The big thing is trying to get your deposit back. Do you have all your paperwork?"

"Yes, but can they do that?" Everly asked, her heart now beating fast with anxiety.

"Not supposed to, but yes, I've heard of it happening. New York is a busy place and people want to keep their apartments filled. Did you sign a lease?" Drew asked.

"I signed a rental agreement. It was month-to-month, but I thought that would be a good idea in case this place wasn't what I saw on the Internet." Everly felt defeated. She was looking forward to seeing her new room, talking to her roommates, and making some friendly connections.

"Well, most reputable places would have you sign at least a six-month agreement or lease. Maybe, that's some indication of the people you were going to rent from."

"Now, I have to start my search all over. I have no place to go! I set aside money for a hotel, but that would only last about a week. I don't want to use any of my other money I've allocated for other things."

"Boy, you did plan this all out, didn't you?" Drew asked, grinning at her.

"Why are you smiling? I'm homeless!" Everly now stood outside the building, in the cold, shaking her head, trying to figure out what she was going to do.

"You aren't homeless. Do you really think that we'd have you out on the street? Remember, Donald doesn't come home 'til next week, so you're covered there. We'll help you find a place. Between me and Blake, we have some connections, and I'm sure we can find you something."

"Yeah, but will it be something I can afford? I put back nine months of rent in case the job didn't work out and I had to search for a new one. I can't go over that amount."

"Everly, I promise, you will find an apartment. There are plenty of places in the city. Just take a few moments to breathe. Let's go get some coffee," Drew said, pointing to a little diner on the street corner. Everly nodded and they quickly crossed the street.

Once seated in the booth, Everly took out her iPad, looking up the information on the apartment. She read the fine print and saw nothing out of the ordinary, and certainly nothing that said they could rent the place out from under her, but they did. Now, to get her deposit back. She quickly took out her phone and made a call, only to be met with an answering machine. Everly left a polite message, but in a frustrated voice.

"Wow, you were pretty nice for what just happened. Any other New Yorker would have been leaving a few choice words with that message," Drew said.

"Well I'm hoping that old saying, 'Honey attracts more bees than vinegar' holds true. I guess it's not in my nature. I'm upset, but there's got to be another place. I just wish I didn't have to go through the process of finding one again. Just to find that one," Everly remarked with a sigh, glancing across the street at the building," was a chore. I really thought I had researched everything I needed to know."

"Sometimes, things just happen, and not how we've laid it all out. When I moved here, I was across the river, in Jersey. Wasn't my first choice and my roommates weren't the best, but I got by 'til I could find a new place. I didn't worry about so much, just kinda went with the flow. I can tell you, it's less stressful that way." Drew gave her that knowing look and Everly wished she could adopt Drew's positive attitude.

"Okay, since I can't do anything else about my living arrangements 'til we get back to your place, I guess the next stop is to let you show me where I need to go for my interviews next week. On my map, they're within walking distance of each other."

"Sounds like a plan and this is the perfect time to teach you about the subway." Drew signaled the waitress for their check so they could leave while Everly gathered her tote.

"Perfect! I've been so excited about this," Everly said, grateful to take her mind off the apartment situation. She would figure out something, as long as it didn't involve her going back to the Keys.

19

The subway station was only one block away. Even though, in the back of Everly's mind, she was still aware that she now had no place to live, she was excited about her next New York experience. The Subway. She knew before coming here that this was going to be her best mode of transportation. She had wanted to bring her bike, but was warned against it by several people, including Drew. Though biking in Key West was as natural to her as walking, New York was a different beast altogether. It could be dangerous, and only those very experienced bikers that could deal with loads of traffic took advantage of riding. So, since she didn't have a car and she was being as frugal as possible, this would be her best bet.

As Everly and Drew descended the stairs into the subway area, she was smiling from ear to ear. Yes, it might be dirty and there were a few people that made her wary, but she was loving every minute of it. Drew took the time to explain the subway map and show her how to get a Metro Card, which she downloaded a large dollar amount onto. Drew gave her a lecture on not standing too close to the platform edge, and not showing or taking out any valuables while in the station or on the train. And if she was by someone that made her feel uncomfortable, to move away. She needed to use her instincts and she would be just fine.

Before coming, her parent's biggest worry was her getting from place to place in such a large city. They didn't worry about her in Key West because she had grown up there and it was a small island town. Both of her parents had been to New York before she was born and knew to some degree where she was going. And they were her parents. Again, it was another lecture on safety which she dutifully sat through. She knew they were only making sure that their only little girl would be safe, but she wished she could reassure them that she would be fine. This evening, when she got home, she would call them and tell them about her day, but would leave out the part that their daughter was now homeless. Once she found a place, she would tell them the whole story.

They took the subway to Midtown, where all four places she was being interviewed for jobs were located. She and Drew went to all the buildings, Everly making notes on how to get back to each one next week. Just seeing the buildings made her nervous. She already had a good start because Lance knew each of the owners of these firms, but now, it was up to her to land the job. If not, she could always fall back on her little online web design business, but that's not what she came here to do.

She wanted to work in a larger design firm, learning other techniques and showing what she could do. Maybe, one day, she'd own her own graphic design and web business. But, that was just a thought. Right now, she just wanted to prove that she could get a job, provide for herself, and live in the city that she had dreamed about since she was a little child. As for her long-term goals, she was still deciding what she wanted to do.

"This is where we get off. Only a short walk and we're back home," Drew said as the train came to a complete stop. They exited the train and began the ascent up the stairs.

"You mean, *you're* home." Everly's excitement of the last few hours was not fading as she remembered how her morning had begun.

"I told you, when we get back, we'll start searching for an apartment. We'll find you something," Drew said. "As for tonight, I think it's time we go out to dinner. Take-out two days in a row is a bit sad for a house guest. Tonight, we're going to my favorite burger place, just a few blocks away. We can walk there. You're going to love it."

"What about Peyton?" Everly asked tentatively.

"Remember? She's on a shoot and I won't see her 'til she's finished, which will be tomorrow night. And even then, it's usually the next day. She goes home and rests, or so she says."

"Wow, that sounded like you don't trust her."

"It's not that. Kinda hard to explain. Maybe, we can talk about it tonight over a delicious hamburger and the best fries you've ever had. That is, if you want to listen to my love life stories. I could probably use the advice."

Everly looked at him. He wanted relationship advice from her? *She* wanted to be with him. At least, she thought she did once. Spending the day with Blake yesterday opened her up to different possibilities. She'd had a wonderful day with him, and a small part of her could see herself spending more time with Blake. But Drew still held a special place in her heart, even if he was unavailable.

"I don't mind listening, but I'm certainly not an expert on love. But if Blake decides to go with us, maybe we can save that conversation for another time. Maybe tomorrow?"

"Are we asking Blake to come along?" Drew asked.

"I thought it might be better, especially if Peyton finds out you went with me to dinner. From a woman's perspective, that would be considered a date, even though those two people are just friends. And I can tell that Peyton isn't too fond of me. Plus, sometimes when friends are together, things can happen that they don't mean to." Everly cringed inside. Her words had come out all wrong. "I didn't mean that anything would happen between the two of us. You've made that perfectly clear. Crap! I'm not explaining myself at all!" Everly gazed toward the sky for a second trying to collect her thoughts.

Drew just smiled. This girl didn't know how simply adorable she was. "Everly, I knew what you meant. And yes, people can put themselves in compromising situations. But we know where we stand, and I think Peyton understands our friendship, too." *At least, I hope so,* Drew thought. "If Blake wants to come, that's fine with me. I know he likes the burgers there as much as I do." *But if he stays home, that's fine, too,* Drew thought quickly. This girl was doing something to him, and he couldn't grasp what it was.

"So, how did you like the apartment?" asked Blake, walking out of the bathroom wearing only a pair of sweatpants, and no shirt. Everly was speechless for just a moment. If Blake didn't work out regularly, she'd be shocked. He was built; it seemed like every muscle was well-defined, but not like a body builder. Just a handsome, rugged man. Looking at him sent small jolts of electricity through Everly's body, something she didn't expect.

"It was okay, but that doesn't matter. As of right now, I'm homeless. The landlord rented the apartment to someone else without notifying me. Now, I have no place to go and I don't know if I'll get my deposit back." Everly was glad she found her voice. Talking about her situation brought her attention away from the six-pack abs she'd been staring at.

"You got to be kidding!" Blake said, pulling a t-shirt over his head.

"Nope. So now, I have to hunt for a new place before your other roommate gets back." Everly instantly felt weary at just the thought of trying to find another apartment.

"We can help," Blake said. "I heard there was a vacancy downstairs with the girls, but not positive. I can ask."

"The girls?" Everly looked at him with a wrinkled brow.

"Friends downstairs. I only know Shari, but she said that Whylen moved out. Maybe, they're looking for another roommate. There's only three rooms, so I don't know what your rent would be, but I can check."

"I'm sure there's no way I can afford what you guys are paying here. I had my rent money saved based on the place I was supposed to be moving to next week." Everly seemed to sink deeper into the sofa, thinking about her situation, forgetting that she hadn't even taken off her winter wardrobe.

"Don't worry. I'll ask, and you can go from there. Okay?"

"Thanks, Blake. And Drew? Don't say anything to Abbey if she should call. I don't want her to worry, or worse yet, tell my parents. I have a feeling they're keeping tabs on me through her. I know they mean well. Right now, I think I'm going to go do some apartment hunting online. Let me know when you want to leave for dinner."

"Dinner? What are we doing for dinner?" Blake asked.

"Everly and I are going to get some hamburgers," Drew said.

"Wanna come?" Everly asked before Drew could say another word.

"Of course! I know exactly where he's taking you. Only the best burgers in the city. And the French fries – hmmm," Blake said excitedly. "That was where I was going to take you on New Year's Eve, but we'll go somewhere else now."

"It's all new to me, so everything sounds good. As long as I'm not paying fifty dollars a plate," Everly said with a giggle. "Off to the internet I go."

"What are you thinking?" Drew asked the question, staring straight at Blake as soon as he knew Everly's door was shut.

"About what?"

"The downstairs apartment. You know Peyton's Dad owns this building. And we both know Peyton isn't warming up to Everly like I thought, or at least, not yet. Plus, I don't think she can afford it. She doesn't even have a job yet."

"You have a better idea? You knew where you were taking her wasn't the best place, but you took her anyway."

"I can't stop her from looking at an apartment, but at least I'll know where she is in case she needs help."

"Drew, you act as if she's an invalid. If you haven't noticed, Everly is a big girl. She's a stunning woman who can take care of herself. I don't know why you are acting so Captain America, unless you're falling for her."

"Not this again!"

"Then you won't mind if I start dating her."

"Hell, Blake, she just moved here. Give her a chance to meet people. Get her footing. She doesn't need some guy right now."

"Damn, you sound jealous."

"That's enough, Blake. Back off."

"Okay, okay. Just be careful. You don't want to mess up what you have with Peyton. She's a winning ticket."

"And Everly's not?"

"Drew, you know exactly what I mean. Money. Prestige. Family name. Everything that can make your dreams come true, and more. You have the girl all us guys would love to have. Don't mess it up, dude." Blake started walking to his room. "So, what time are we leaving for dinner?"

"In an hour or two." With that, Drew heard Blake's door shut and he was all alone in the living room.

What are you doing, Drew? he asked himself quietly. He couldn't even concentrate- on anything! The moment Everly entered New York City, his life had been turned upside down.

20

"You weren't kidding about these burgers," Everly said, her mouth full as she tried to speak, which made her laugh.

"We can tell you like them." Drew looked at her sandwich, which was almost gone. Then it reminded him of their dinner at Margaritaville in Key West where she had taken him for a burger.

"If I lived where you guys do, I think I'd be here every day. There's a café back in Key West that I went to all the time. I loved it. Whether it was to get some breakfast, conch chowder, key lime pie, or just coffee, it was and still is one of my favorite places. I have a feeling this spot might be my New York haven."

"Well, you've only just arrived. There are so many things to show you and places to eat. Sometimes, it's a good thing most of us New Yorkers walk everywhere, to burn the calories off from the food we eat," Blake said. He was sitting beside her in the booth. Everly could look out and enjoy the bustling New York sidewalk, with skies that looked like they were threatening to snow again.

Drew sat across from the couple. *A couple,* he thought. He just couldn't see Blake and Everly together. Blake was a player, always with a different woman. Why was he so interested in Everly? Drew wished he could read his mind and figure out exactly how this man felt about his friend. He wasn't going to let her get hurt. Not again.

"So, I found a few places on my internet search this afternoon. Again, I don't know the town like you two, so I need some help." Everly finished the last of her French fries then pulled out her iPad to give them the information about the apartments she had found.

"I don't mind," they said in unison, both men looking at each other as if they were wondering who she'd choose to help her.

"It doesn't matter to me. I know you both had other things planned before I popped up on your door step."

"Why don't we all go tomorrow?" Blake suggested. "We can get some food while we are out and maybe even catch another New York sight or two."

"That's fine, but tomorrow night, I want to eat at home. I'm not used to this much dining out. I'm ready for some home-cooked food. If you have the pots and pans, I'll do the cooking. How about some chili sprinkled with cheddar cheese, crackers on the side, and my famous homemade Florida Keys specialty: key lime pie? I know that doesn't exactly go with chili, but soup sounds wonderful with this cold weather, and the Key Lime pie just sounds good. At home, I have a piece every week." Homesickness came over her for a brief moment. There were some little things she was missing about the Keys, but Everly knew she could have them here with her if she just tried.

"I'm not turning that down," Blake answered, looking at her with a smile.

"Sounds good to me, too. I know we have cookware, but you'll have to check it out when we get home. Then, whatever you need for dinner, we'll pick it up tomorrow while we're out. Sounds like we have a plan." Drew peered over to Everly giving her another big smile.

"I put in a call to Shari about the room downstairs. If they do have a space, you might not need to go apartment hunting, after all."

"As much as I love your building, I'm sure I can't afford it. Not after looking at other places today that were in my price range. But, it can't hurt to check. Would be nice to be in a place where I already know some of my neighbors," Everly said, casting a sideways glance at Blake.

"I think I'd like that, too." Blake was looking directly into her eyes and Everly felt giddy inside. She never expected to meet such an appealing man as soon as she had arrived in New York.

Drew watched the whole exchange and felt sick to his stomach. But why? Whatever this was had to go away. His world had made sense at one point. Now, it was totally haywire. The ring of his phone brought his thoughts back to the table and one look at his cell phone screen told him it was Peyton.

"I'm going outside to take this. Be right back." Drew rose from the table noticing that neither Blake nor Everly heard a word he said. They were off in their own conversation, Everly laughing and Blake smiling at her as if she was the only girl in the world. It made him sick.

"Hi, there," Drew said as he stepped outside in the cold weather. "How has your day been?"

"Long and tiring. I'm working for a photographer that thinks he's God's gift to the world of fashion. Nothing any of us did today was right. So, we start from scratch tomorrow. Another long day. But then, it's just me and you for two days. What have you been up to?"

"Eating dinner with Blake and Everly. Everly's apartment fell through and she has nowhere to go."

"So, how long is she staying with you?" Peyton asked in an irritated voice.

"We're hoping to find something tomorrow. Plus, Blake knows someone who might have a place. We're checking on it now."

There was silence on the other end of the line. Drew rubbed his forehead, feeling the tension of the conversation settling there. This was Peyton being, well, Peyton. So he tried to lighten the mood. "Hey, you aren't jealous, are you?" he asked playfully.

"What do I have to be jealous of?" Her voice was now harsher than before.

"I was just joking."

"I know I have a lot more to offer you than she does. She's just some girl from a little Florida town." Peyton said the words now in a playful, girlish tone, but Drew knew the underlying meaning.

"Peyton, you do know I love you for you, not for your family or anything else. Just like you are. Remember when we first met? Why can't we go back to being those two people?"

"I'm sorry. I'll admit a little jealousy has crept in, but I know how you feel. It's just that you seemed a bit obsessed with this girl. She can take care of herself, you know," Peyton said.

"I know, but we've been over this time and again. I don't want to rehash an old argument. I just want to talk to my girlfriend." Drew could hear a slight laugh on the phone.

"You're right, sweetheart. I just get a little nutty sometimes where you're concerned. I'm really sorry, okay?" Peyton now sounded like the girl he had met that day on the photo shoot.

"It's okay. Why don't you go take a long hot shower and go to bed. You want to be rested for tomorrow."

"You know what would make it better? If you came and took that shower with me," Peyton said, once again her voice transforming into a husky, sexy tone.

"If I came over, you definitely wouldn't get any sleep," Drew said teasingly.

"It would be worth it."

"I love you. Good night," Drew said softly.

"Good night." And with that, Peyton clicked the phone off.

Drew stood outside for a second, replaying the conversation he had just had. Peyton's moods could change on a dime and there was a time that didn't bother him. But now it was beginning to create stress he didn't need. Slowly the tension he was feeling lessened 'til he looked through the diner window at Everly.

She looked so happy, sitting there with Blake. And for once, he was acting like a decent guy. Maybe he really did like Everly in a way Drew had never seen before. It wasn't his place to police their budding friendship, but he knew one thing. If Blake hurt her, there would be hell to pay.

■ ■ ■

The next day, the trio went from one apartment to another, looking for the best place for Everly to live. Every building or room seemed to have something that just didn't feel right to Everly, and she was beginning to get depressed. What if she didn't find something? What if she just had to settle on something that really wasn't that good? If it meant staying in New York to make this work, that's what she would do. She didn't want to go back to Key West and admit that the city had defeated her. Everly knew in her heart that she would be successful. She would make this work somehow.

"Okay, this is where we stand. This apartment and that one were okay and the rent was good. Just wasn't too crazy about the building or that this one," Everly said, pointing to a spot on the map, "was over a bar. Doesn't feel safe. One thing I do know is that I'm tired. Just want to get some groceries and go home. I can think about all these places while I cook. I need something to take my mind off this mess."

"You're going to find something. It might take some time, but it'll work out." Blake grasped her hand, giving it a squeeze. Everly liked the gentle encouragement he was displaying. Was this a man she could see herself with? *Maybe,* she instantly thought to herself.

"So, where is the grocery store?"

When they got to the small store, Everly went through each aisle, finding everything she needed, including the key lime juice. She wasn't sure if she'd find it in New York, but there it was, sitting on the shelf. Just the sight of it made her smile, and suddenly, she couldn't wait to have a piece of the pie. As for the chili, she was using her grandmother's recipe, which she loved. Her family only made the delicious soup during the winter time, when the temperatures would get cool. For the people of south Florida, the upper fifties and lower sixties were cool and deemed "sweater weather." For her, it was chili-making time.

As she walked back to the apartment with Blake, Drew, and their groceries, she knew this was the perfect weather for her dinner tonight. She also knew that cooking would help her sort through the problem she had on hand. Having a place to live was the one thing she wasn't worried about the day she boarded the plane to come here. Now, besides acing her interviews, it was her biggest challenge.

Everly had found out that the guys had plenty of pots and pans when she looked the night before, and had them waiting on the counter. After putting up the other groceries that weren't necessary for tonight's culinary delight, she got to work. Even though Drew and Blake came to talk to her occasionally, she had her mind on other things. After going through the facts in her head, she knew that she had to pick one of the places she had seen today. They were all available next week so it was just a matter of choosing which one.

"So, how would you like some great news?" Blake asked, coming to stand beside her in the kitchen just as she put the pie in the oven.

"I would love it. You have no idea."

"The room on the second floor is available. Shari said you can come and see it anytime. Even this evening, if you want to."

"Really?" Everly said excitedly, but the feeling was short-lived.

"What's wrong?" Blake could see the excitement leave her face as quickly as it had come.

"Blake, I know I can't afford the rent here. I don't even have a job yet!"

"But you're interviewing next week, and like you told me, you're probably a shoe-in because of your boss in Key West. At least, go look and find out."

Everly stood there, stirring the soup while she was thinking. It couldn't hurt to look, but she didn't want to get her hopes up. But what did she have to lose?

"Okay, I'll go. But let me wait 'til I put the pie in the fridge, and then we can walk down. Did you tell Drew?"

"No, I came straight to you. I'll go with you," Blake said.

"Go where?" Drew came around the corner just in time to overhear the end of the conversation.

"It seems the apartment downstairs has an available room for rent. I'm going to go look at it in just a bit."

"And I'm going to take her, since I know Shari." Blake looked at Drew as if to say "back off."

"If it works out, that would be good. You're already starting to become familiar with this area." Drew wanted to say more, but he would let Blake handle this. He knew he had to back away and let Everly handle her own life. But it just didn't feel right to do so.

"I'll call Shari and tell her we'll be there around five o'clock. Sound okay?"

"Perfect!"

Everly went to change back into her nicer clothes, since she could be meeting her potential roommates. Then, she stuck the pie in the refrigerator to cool off and, with Blake by her side, went to the see the apartment. She could tell that Drew had wanted to come, but stayed behind. She wanted him there, too, but knew his life was different from hers. She couldn't rely on him every second. She had to make it on her own. And that was what she was doing.

21

"Hi, Blake! Aren't you looking good?" the woman said that answered the door. "I haven't seen you in quite a while. How are you doing?"

"Good. Taking the next few months off to go strictly to school, get this damn master's degree off my back and finished. Then, on to work full-time." Blake then turned to Everly.

"Shari, this is Everly Meyers."

"Nice to meet you. So, I hear you're from Key West. What in the hell are you doing up here, in all this damn snow? I'd have my ass sitting somewhere under a palm tree with a beer in my hand."

"I was born and raised there, so it was time for a change. My parents are still there, so I'm sure I'll go back for plenty of visits. Thanks for letting me come to see the place." Even though Shari was a bit colorful with her language, Everly liked her. She was a bit shorter than Everly, with cropped black hair and porcelain skin. She had an outgoing personality, which Everly loved. If they didn't become roommates, she could see herself as friends with this woman.

"Well, when it suddenly became empty, London and I were wondering what we were going to do. Can't afford this place with just the two of us." She led them down a very small hall to a room that wasn't much bigger than a walk-in closet. Everly was trying to imagine how she would even fit anything in here: bed, desk, clothes. The closet was tiny, too, but the room did have a window, even if it overlooked an alley.

"How much is the rent each month?" Everly asked, knowing this was the biggest question of the day.

"We split the rent three ways even though the rooms are different sizes. It would be eight hundred per month, and we split the utilities, which usually is about eighty to a hundred."

Everly didn't gasp out loud, but in her mind, she did. $900 a month? She had been prepared for a maximum of $700. She could use the money she had saved, but the room was so little. She might be able to fit a twin bed, a tiny desk, and maybe, a crate for a night stand. The rooms she had seen earlier in the day had been much larger, but also in areas that she didn't feel good about.

Everly felt like her head was overloaded. She didn't want to decide right now, but she didn't want to lose the opportunity for the space, either. "Can I let you know tomorrow? I just need to go back and look over my finances. I've saved money, but I don't interview for jobs 'til next week. I just need to make sure I can do this. How long is the lease and what is the deposit?"

Shari gave her all the necessary information as Blake stood beside her, gently putting his hand on the small of her back. This gave her a bit of comfort, with him there for support.

Blake was fast becoming a friend in the few short days she had known him.

"Thanks, Shari, I really appreciate it. I'll let you know something. Right now, I have a dinner to finish cooking."

"You cook homemade meals? Then I know you have to move in, please. I don't think I've had a good meal that didn't come from a take-out box in so long," Shari said with a laugh.

"Thanks again."

"Well, what do you think?" Blake asked as soon as they were in the elevator.

"The room is so small. I was trying to imagine what it would look like with my stuff. It felt more like a closet than a room, except it did have a window, which I liked. But the rent and utilities weren't at all what I was expecting. Then, compared to what we saw today and how quick I need to move, I might not have a choice."

"It would be nice for you to be in the same building as me. I mean, as us," Blake remarked, trying to act casual.

Everly knew her face had turned a bit red at his words. Yes, she was beginning to like this man.

"So, how did it go?" Drew asked the minute the door to the apartment swung open.

As Everly finished preparing dinner and pulled out plates from the cabinet, she told him all the details.

"At least you would be in the same building as me. I mean, us," Drew said, quickly.

Everly couldn't help but laugh.

"What's so funny?"

"That's exactly what Blake said when we were heading back up here," she said with a smile. "I'm beginning to feel like I have two big brothers. And I like it." She dished out the soup into bowls. She surrounded the bowl with saltine crackers, then sprinkled tiny bits of cheddar cheese across the chili.

"Now, this is my grandma's chili recipe. If you don't like it, you're crazy." After giving each man a plate, Everly took her seat between them at the bar in the kitchen.

"You can cook anytime you want," Blake exclaimed after just one bite of soup. Drew had to agree. It was wonderful and reminded him of his mother's cooking. It had been so long that they'd had a decent home-cooked meal. But what made the meal was the key lime pie. It was perfection as far as Drew was concerned. And it reminded him of his trip to the Florida Keys.

"I know I cooked this, but I have to say, the pie is wonderful. It's a little bit of home for me."

"I think I'm going to have to visit the Keys. Remember, you already promised to be my tour guide." Blake grinned at her and she could tell that smile was beginning to melt her heart. He had been so nice, and she was certainly growing fond of him. She had Drew and now Blake. Even though the apartment had been a bust, she was meeting people and making some friends- well, except for Peyton.

"I think I might take that apartment downstairs. It's more expensive than I had planned and smaller, but I'm afraid I won't find something before next week," Everly said.

"We aren't going to just kick you out if you don't have a place by then," Drew said. "I want to make sure you find the right place for you."

"Downstairs isn't bad, just not what I expected. But I think I can make anything work. Plus, I would only be signing a six-month lease. That would give me time to get my job and look for another place that's more reasonable- and hopefully, a bit bigger."

"That sounds like a great plan," Blake said as he reached to get another piece of pie.

The sound of keys in the door made them all turn their heads at once. When the door opened, Peyton walked in, loaded with two bags of take-out food and a small suitcase.

"Peyton, what are you doing here?" Drew asked abruptly, getting up to walk toward her.

"That wasn't quite the welcome I expected, but happy to see you, too." Peyton sat the bags on the counter, almost sliding Everly's key lime pie onto the floor.

"I brought dinner and a few things so I could stay the night. Since tomorrow is New Year's Eve and I have the next few days off, I thought I would just stay here tonight instead of going back home," she said, draping herself around Drew. She kissed him a little longer than normal, which made Everly uncomfortable.

"Thanks for the dinner, but Everly fixed us a home-cooked meal. Chili and key lime pie."

"You're welcome to some. We have plenty left over," Everly said, trying her best to be nice to this woman who clearly didn't like her.

"Oh, how sweet. So, you like to cook." Peyton looked at Everly with a false smile once again.

"Love to. I was getting a bit tired of eating out, so I insisted on making dinner. Plus, the pie reminded me of home."

"Well, thanks for the offer, but I brought salad and sushi. I think that will be a bit kinder to my waistline, since I picked up another photo shoot next week." Peyton proceeded to unload the boxes of food, paying no attention to what was already on the counter. Drew came quickly to her side, helping with the bags.

As Everly watched the couple while she continued to eat, she could tell that Drew was a different person when Peyton was around. He was suddenly anxious, like everything had to be perfect for this girl. She wondered if he was truly in love with Peyton, or if it was something else.

They continued to eat, now a foursome, with Peyton dominating the conversation, giving them minute details about the last two days. Everything from the wardrobe she was forced to wear to the photographer that, in her opinion, was an idiot. Everly glanced over at Blake once to see him widen his eyes and grin like he wanted to laugh. She almost giggled but held it in. They had been having such a wonderful evening 'til Peyton showed up.

After Everly put the food away, Black and Drew washed and put away the dishes. She didn't have any time to talk to Drew or Blake about the apartment downstairs. She had wanted to ask them if it made them uncomfortable if she took it, but at this point, she really couldn't see any other way to have a place by next week.

"I'm going to call it a night," Everly announced to the trio. "I'm a bit tired after our jaunt around the city today, and I have a few things I want to do."

"Rest up, because we have a big night planned tomorrow," Blake said to her with a smile.

"Jaunt around the city?" Peyton asked, looking at all three of them.

"Drew and Blake went with me to look for an apartment." She really didn't want to give any more details and hoped Peyton wouldn't ask, but Everly wasn't that lucky.

"That's right. Drew said that your place fell through yesterday," Peyton said.

"It did, but I think I have a new apartment. I promise, I won't be here much longer." She knew what Peyton was thinking. Everly could tell by the tone of Peyton's voice and the way she looked at Drew. She wanted Everly out, and the sooner, the better. "Good night, everyone." And Everly went to her borrowed room.

She laid across the bed and sighed. This had been a stressful but good day. There were changes to her supposedly concrete plan. She knew she had to let go of that perfectionist side of herself, but it was hard when she had waited so long for this. Today, she loved being with Drew and Blake. They made the day fun, kidding her about each place they visited. Their rides on the subway, lunch with a street vendor, and more. They had showed her Radio City Music Hall, the New York Public Library, the NBC Studios and they even found the M&M's World. Everly had brought home a large stash of the chocolate treats. Then, dinner tonight had been so relaxing, and it felt good to eat leisurely.

But then, there was Peyton. Everly knew why she was staying the night. If only Peyton felt secure in knowing that Drew had eyes only for her. Everly wished she could tell her, but there was no way she was getting involved in their relationship.

Peyton wasn't the type of friend Everly was used to, and she knew that in her circle, Everly would only be an acquaintance, if that. And if it wasn't for Drew, Everly was positive she would have never met her.

Everly took out her notebook, along with her iPhone to use the calculator function and began crunching some numbers. She could take the room on the second floor. She had saved enough money, but for some reason she felt uncomfortable. This threw her off. But, if she was going to live in this city, she had already learned that she had to be more flexible. This wasn't Key West, where she had a very normal, everyday routine. But Everly knew eventually this city would become her home, just like Key West was. It was just going to take time.

So, tomorrow, New Year's Eve, she would put a deposit down on her new home and then spend the evening with Blake, along with thousands of other people, as they brought in the New Year. Just the thought of everything going on in her life right now made it hard to go to sleep.

She quickly changed clothes, crawled under the covers for more warmth, and tried to continue reading a book on her iPad that she had started on the plane ride here. But, it was no use. All Everly could think about was tomorrow night's celebration, and the fact that she would be with Blake. Now, there's something that wasn't in her original plan, and it made her smile.

22

As she handed the money over and signed the lease, Everly couldn't help but feel elation. The landlord told her that she could move in any time after the first, but Shari had told her this morning that she could move in today, if she wanted. Everly told her that she would wait till January 2nd, so she didn't spoil any holiday festivities. The timing would be perfect. She could get moved in and still have two days before her interviews. Everly already knew where to go, and living here was going to have her even closer to her potential employers.

After she sealed the deal on her living space, she had to get a bed of some sort. The easiest thing was an air mattress, for now. She had to have something quick. So, she and Blake, who offered to be her guide again, went shopping.

Everly was really beginning to like Blake. His charismatic personality was infectious and she enjoyed being around him. He made her laugh, forget some of the anxiety she had been feeling, and was taking her tonight to one of the biggest celebrations in the world.

She quickly found an airbed, linens, a lap desk for working, and a crate to put beside her bed as a temporary nightstand. Everly also found a three-drawer plastic container large enough to fit some of her clothes in, and purchased hangers for the rest. Next, she found a little lamp that would be bright enough to illuminate the room. That would be enough to get her started. Hopefully, when it warmed up, she would be able to go to some of the local flea markets and find some furniture that was in her price range.

"You did pretty good. I wouldn't have thought of some of the things you bought to get by. You should have measured the room so you could've bought furniture. That way, you wouldn't be sleeping on the floor," Blake remarked as they unloaded her purchases from the trunk of the taxi.

"Well, I won't be truly on the floor. The bed is raised, just not a normal bed, like what I imagined. But, this is just fine 'til I can find something I can afford. Plus, weather permitting, I plan to be out and about as much as possible. There's so much to see and do that staying home doesn't even sound appealing. At least, right now. I'm sure once the newness wears off, I'll be thinking quite differently," Everly said as they took her stuff to Blake's apartment.

As they entered, Peyton was in the kitchen, making coffee dressed only in a man's t-shirt while Drew stood at the refrigerator, shirtless, with only pajama bottoms. Everly's breath caught in her throat, seeing him that way again. It brought back memories of the two of them in Key West, on the beach.

"Are you okay?" Blake asked. He couldn't help but notice Everly's hesitation upon entering the apartment so he walked over to help her with her packages.

"Sure. I just remembered something that I didn't get, that's all," Everly said, covering up her open display of shock.

"Good morning," Peyton cooed as she stood next to Drew. "Or, I guess I should say, 'good afternoon.' Oh and happy New Year's Eve."

"Yes, Peyton, it's lunch time." Blake's sarcastic tone almost made Everly laugh. She turned around to see Blake putting the rest of her bags in the corner of the room. "We've already been to the realtor's office and went shopping for Everly's room downstairs. Think we have her all set up."

"Downstairs?" Peyton said, her eyes swinging first to Drew, then Blake, and finally, Everly.

"Yes, I was able to rent a room in the apartment on the second floor. It's not what I planned, but I needed a place quickly. It's only for a few months while I get settled in." Everly had been dreading Peyton finding out where she was going to live.

"How nice."

"Now, if she needs anything, we're just upstairs," Blake said, coming to stand so close to Everly that she could feel the heat emanating from his body. That also had her head spinning. Why was she reacting to two different guys in two different ways? She had never experienced an attraction to two men at the same time. What was wrong with her?

"Everly seems like a big girl. I think she will do just fine on her own."

"Thanks, Peyton, for that vote of confidence. These guys act as though we can't think for ourselves. But I have to admit, I'm glad they're here." Hopefully, that would win her some brownie points with this woman.

"I couldn't agree more."

"I may sound like a little kid, but I'm going to go take a nap. I want to be rested and ready to go for the evening." Everly then turned to Blake. "Thanks again for all your help this morning. I know I could have done it myself, but the extra hands were needed with all these bags, and I enjoyed the company." She then looked at Peyton and Drew. "Enjoy your party tonight."

"We will." Peyton watched Everly disappear, with Blake following behind.

"So, when were you going to tell me about her living here?"

"When she decided to move in. Last night, she didn't know, and as you know, we just got up. I didn't know she and Blake had left this morning. So, I found out the same time you did." Drew was telling the truth. Why didn't Everly ask him to go with her?

Because Peyton is here, you idiot, he thought, closing his eyes and sighing. This had to stop. He felt like he was on some merry-go-round between two women, and none of it made sense to him.

"I'm going to take a shower," Peyton said softly in his ear. "You want to join me again?"

"Why don't we wait 'til we are at your place," Drew said, not fully in the mood for sex.

"That does sound better." She kissed him on the cheek, then nibbled slightly at his ear. It sent vibrations through his body, but he still had mixed emotions flowing through his mind. He watched Peyton walk off, then slowly leaned back against the counter. He needed to talk to someone, but who?

He thought he could talk to Everly, but not for the next few days because he was spending them with Peyton.

Everly had been such a good friend in Key West. Maybe she could help him sort out his feelings for Peyton. He thought about talking to his sister, but he knew she couldn't be unbiased. Peyton wasn't on her list of friends.

■ ■ ■

Everly groggily opened her eyes. She wasn't sure how long she had slept until she glanced at her phone. It was almost five o'clock. She had slept for three hours! She sat and stretched, wondering what time they needed to leave for Times Square. Then, she heard a soft knock at her door.

"Hey, there." Everly opened the door to see Blake standing there and he appeared as though he was ready to walk out the door for the evening.

"Sorry if I woke you, but I think we need to leave shortly. I'm sure the square is already filling up and there are a lot of streets closed," Blake said.

"You should have woken me earlier. Sorry I slept so late."

"You needed the rest. Tonight is going to be busy and fun. Dress warmly. Looks like it is going to be in the lower thirties, with a bit of wind. Except with so many people around, we might not feel it."

Everly looked at the man at her door and couldn't help but smile.

"What?" Blake said.

"Nothing. Just excited about tonight," Everly said quickly.

"Can you be ready in thirty minutes?"

"Yep."

"Oh, and don't bring anything with you. They search bags and stuff. I've got some cash so we can get something to eat and drink. It'll have to be water because they don't allow alcohol. We can celebrate with some champagne when we get back here. Sound good?"

"Sounds perfect. Now go, so I can hurry," Everly said teasingly. She turned and went through her suitcase, still on the floor. She took out her thermal leggings and shirt, two pair of socks, her new coat, and a hat and scarf that she would be wearing for the first time. A scarf. A winter scarf! She couldn't help but grin because she was finally able to wear a winter scarf, something that never happened down in the Keys.

Everly entered the big room with her hat, scarf and coat in her arms, then saw Drew and Peyton getting ready to leave, also. Except they weren't dressed for an evening to be spent outside.

Peyton's dress was a beautiful deep red that was low cut, showing the sides of her breasts. The hemline was shorter than something Everly would have chosen, but she admitted it looked good. Peyton's dark hair was curled and swept to one side, with sparkling diamond earrings that slightly dangled from her ears. Drew was dressed in a tuxedo, looking more dashing than she had ever seen him, even at his sister's wedding.

As for her date, Blake looked sexy and handsome, all rolled into one. He, too, had his coat nearby, and was dressed in a shirt, sweater and blue jeans. And even with the amount of clothing he had on, he looked rugged and manly. Everly was more smitten by this man as each minute passed.

"Peyton, your dress is gorgeous," Everly said. "And Drew, a tuxedo? Wait 'til I tell Abbey you wore one here and not at her wedding."

"Hey, Abbey didn't say we had to. Remember, it was more laid back. This is a party and work function."

"Well, you both look great. I hope I have enough clothing on to keep warm. My body is still adjusting to the cold, so I've layered on a bunch of clothes."

"You look perfect," Blake said, not taking his eyes off Everly.

"I think it's time to go, Drew," Peyton said, not even acknowledging Everly's compliment. "Hope you two have a great time." She walked out the door.

Drew looked directly at Everly now. "Be careful and have fun. Your first Times Square celebration. I have to say, I wish I was going with you guys."

"You'll have fun. Enjoy, and Happy New Year!" Everly responded, smiling at him. She watched as he closed the door behind him.

"Blake, do you think Drew is happy?" Everly asked.

"Yeah, I think so. Peyton just has a way of getting what Peyton wants. But Drew seems okay with that."

"I hope so. He's such a great guy not to have someone that really cares for him."

Everly began putting on the layers of clothing that would help keep her warm: a sweater, coat, scarf, hat and gloves.

"Okay, I think I'm ready, but now, I have to go to the bathroom," she said, laughing. "Be right back."

Blake just shook his head. It was going to be an interesting evening, one he was looking forward to.

They took the subway to the closest station to Times Square that was available. From there, they walked. It was chilly outside, but so far, the clothes she had layered were keeping her warm. Plus, swarms of people were already filling up the streets that had been blocked off for the festivities.

They ducked inside a small restaurant and grabbed some French fries and a drink, then went back out into the cold.

"So, where is the best viewing spot?" Everly asked. The further they walked, the thicker the crowd became.

"We're going to get as close to the ball drop area as we can," Blake said.

"The what area?" Everly asked with a puzzled look.

"Where they drop the ball. That's at One Times Square. Of course, that's where everyone is heading. Here," and he reached for her. "Take my hand so we don't get separated."

Immediately, Everly took Blake's hand and he pulled her as close to him as he could. Everly liked the feeling. It made it feel like a real date. She hoped that he reached for her not for security, but out of wanting to have her hand in his. Wanting to be with her as more than just a friend. She knew they had only known each other for five days, but they had spent pretty much all day and all night together since she arrived in New York. She already knew some of his intricacies, foods he liked, TV shows he adored. He loved to kid with her, talk to her, and treated her so sweetly. Even Drew's warning about him being a womanizer just didn't seem like the Blake she had come to know over the last few days. She was beginning to think she might like this man.

"What do you think about this spot?" Blake asked as he came to a standstill.

Everly looked around and could see they were standing near a sidewalk, but not on it. They were surrounded by people. She didn't think they could move even an inch. Then, she looked up and was mesmerized. There it was. The ball. The actual ball that she had watched so many times on TV. She was going to see it in person. She starting giggling like a little girl.

"What's so funny?" Blake asked, smiling with her, though he didn't know why.

"It's not funny, but exciting. I can't believe I'm really here. I mean, this is unbelievable. I've got to try to call my parents." Everly unzipped her coat pocket and reached for her phone. She quickly pressed the FaceTime logo and before she knew it, her mom was looking back at her. But with the crowd noise, Everly couldn't hear her.

"Hey Mom! Where's Dad? I can't hear you, but just wanted to show you something. I'm at Times Square, getting ready to watch the ball drop. We have a few hours, but it's so exciting." Everly then saw her father on the phone, and turned the view around so she could show them where she was. Everly raised the phone above her head and panned it around in a circle, hoping she was catching a glimpse of everything for her parents.

"I'm sorry I can't hear you, but I love you guys. Happy New Year!" Everly looked to see them both blowing kisses to her and waving goodbye. As the phone clicked off, she realized that she had a tear falling from her eye.

"Are you okay?" Blake asked.

"Yeah, just seeing my parents was a bit rougher than I thought. This is my first holiday away from them."

"I understand. When I moved here, I was a little homesick, but not a lot. I missed my Dad, but was also ready to move away from all the memories. I do remember watching the ball drop with my Mom. She loved it."

Everly looked up at him and he looked so gentle. And then, she felt his arm encircle her shoulders, and she couldn't help but move closer to his side. She took in all the sights and sounds of everything around her. She talked to the family standing in front of them that had traveled all the way from Texas. The people behind them had come from Canada for vacation and decided to stay one more day just to witness this. When the family in front of them brought out their Happy New Year's hats, Everly wished she and Blake had remembered to bring something to wear. But it didn't matter. She was here.

"I have to get some pictures, if you don't mind taking some of me. I'll have to do a giant blog post tomorrow, welcoming in the New Year and posting about my move so far."

"You have a website?"

"I guess you could say, a personal blog. But I advertise my web services on there. That's how I make a little money on the side. I love working on websites and Lance was so great about letting me," Everly said.

"Who's Lance?" Blake asked.

"My boss in Key West. He was, or should I say, *is*, like a second father to me. He let me start working for his firm when I was seventeen. I guess I pestered him enough to let me try. He didn't realize how good I was 'til I got in there. He's the one helping me find a job here. Or, at least, he helped me set up some interviews for next week. Just hope I can continue my little side job while I'm here. I love working with smaller companies as they start a new site."

"Maybe, one day, I'll have to get you to help with mine. It is awful right now, but I was waiting 'til I graduated in May to even look at it again. Come next week, I'm going to have my hands full with school and my internship. Plus, helping at Mr. Compton's office when I can. Hopefully, all that will land me the job I've been working for all this time."

"Sounds like we both have a busy plan ahead of us."

"It does, but it's also refreshing to meet a woman that is down-to-earth and likes what she does. Most women I've met, and I don't mean this meanly, seem to come here to be an actress, singer, or model. Then, they complain when they have to wait on tables to get by. Not that there's anything wrong with that, but you have to work twice as hard to get where you want, at first. Then, you can sit back, and maybe, it all works out. You can't complain. You have to just keep putting one foot in front of the other."

"Wow, you sound like a motivational speaker. But thanks for the compliment. I was always the nerd back home, but I'm hoping I'll fit in just fine up here."

"I know you will." Blake said as he softly squeezed her shoulder just a bit tighter. "We only have fifteen minutes to go. Get ready to count down and watch the confetti fly."

"I had forgotten about the confetti. I have to get more pictures," Everly said.

"I think your phone is going to be out of storage by the time we get back home, from the number of pictures you've already taken," Blake laughed.

"Not funny. This is my first time here and I'm excited. You have to cut me some slack."

"Okay, no more teasing. It's just that I can't help it. You're just too cute."

"I like that compliment much better." Everly knew her cheeks were red from the cold, but now, it was from his words. Her happiness meter was high right now, and she couldn't think of a better date to have by her side. Well, maybe one person, but she wouldn't think about that right now.

"There it goes." Blake pointed to the glistening ball high in the sky. The crowd was excited, cheering and counting. Blake and Everly joined the countdown.

5, 4, 3, 2, 1 – "Happy New Year!" shouted the crowd around her, seeming like one giant voice. Then, the confetti came raining down on them. It was nothing like Everly had ever experienced in her life. It was exhilarating, even though she was cold.

But when she looked at Blake, he placed one of his hands on each side of her face and gently brought his lips to hers. The kiss was magical. A warmth spread through her entire body, and she no longer felt the cold. She only felt his soft lips and his body pressed against hers.

"Happy New Year, Everly," he said, only inches from her face.

"Happy New Year to you," were the only words that would come to her shocked mind. He had her speechless, and so happy. And then, she kissed him back, as gently as he had kissed her.

23

Drew watched the crowd below. He sipped on his glass of wine and wondered where they were. Somewhere down there, Blake was with Everly, and he hoped that she was safe. He couldn't stop thinking about how Blake could hurt her emotionally, and he wanted to protect her.

"It's only a few minutes before the New Year. Can you get us some champagne? I'll hold our spot so we can watch the ball drop and bring in the New Year together," Peyton said sweetly as she came to stand beside Drew.

"Sure. I'll be right back." Drew walked away and Peyton's dad appeared next to her.

"Glad you decided to come to the party. So much better than standing in that sea of people below. How is Drew doing? Haven't been able to talk to either of you this evening. Do you think he's still going to pop the question tonight?" Mr. Compton asked.

"I think so," Peyton said with confidence, though inside, she wasn't so sure. At first, she had been positive that on Christmas Day, he would ask her to marry him, but when he didn't, she didn't say anything. So, it had to be tonight. He had been hinting around too much, asking her questions about their future. They were the perfect match. He worked for her father's paper with the potential, in Peyton's mind, to one day take over her father's business. They were the power couple that everyone wanted to be.

Peyton knew her friends thought so. They seemed to remind her of it every day. But when she shared with them that she was getting engaged on Christmas and that didn't come about, they didn't say anything and just avoided the subject.

"He hasn't come to me to ask for your hand," Mr. Compton said.

"Dad, that's old-fashioned. He wouldn't do that. We're adults and shouldn't have to ask for permission." Peyton suddenly put her hand on her father's arm. "I should have asked you to get a glass for Dad, too," she said, letting her father know that Drew was right behind him.

"Sorry, Nolan. Just a minute and I'll be right back," Drew said quickly, and started to walk back to the bar.

"No, Drew, that's fine. I think I've already had my share of drinks for the evening."

"But Dad, you have to have one when the clock strikes midnight," Peyton said sweetly.

"That's for you young people," Nolan said, turning to Drew. "I've been hearing some great things about your articles. Plus, your work is going viral on the internet."

"Thank you. I love what I do. Thanks for inviting us tonight. It's beautiful up here. Never seen the ball drop anywhere but down there." He gestured to the crowd below.

"Yes, I've done that a few times, when I was much younger. Now, it's nice to see it from an aerial view, and a warm one, at that." Nolan laughed a little and hugged his daughter. "Enjoy yourselves," he said and walked away.

"I really like your Dad," Drew said. "He's made a name for himself all on his own. That's to be admired."

"Well, I know he loves you. He always praises your work, and both my parents always ask about you. I think it might be nice if we visit them a bit more often. What do you think? Maybe more family dinners?" Peyton asked, hoping that Drew would ask her that important question as they rang in the New Year.

"That might be nice. And what would be special to me is for you to come and meet my parents in North Carolina. It would be a fun trip."

Peyton couldn't see herself in the mountains, hiking and walking through tourist attractions. But maybe, this is what was holding Drew back from asking her to marry him.

"You know, I think that might be a great idea. Did you have a date in mind?"

"You mean, you would go?" Drew asked excitedly.

Peyton immediately saw how important this was, and knew this had to be the ticket to getting that ring on her finger. "I think I could manage it. Just need to work it into my schedule. I've been offered a few more photo shoots and I'm going to be working with a few fashion designers on an internship again."

"Another one? I thought that your Dad was going to help you finance your clothing line after you finished your current internship. What happened?"

But Drew didn't get an immediate answer. Everyone was suddenly crowding around them, counting down as the ball descended the pole. Peyton had joined the crowd, yelling out the numbers, and before he knew it, everyone was wishing each other "Happy New Year."

"Happy New Year, sweetheart." Peyton turned Drew toward her and he didn't have a chance to say anything before she pressed her lips to his.

"Happy New Year," he said when they came up for air. He still had the conversation in the back of his mind about her clothing line, the trip to meet his family, and more. But Drew felt like she wasn't telling him everything. Something just didn't feel right. But this wasn't the time or place to bring that up. Maybe, they would get a chance to talk tomorrow.

At the thought of talking, he remembered what was going through his mind earlier: wanting to talk to Everly. He hoped that she might help him make sense of what he was feeling. As he watched the crowd below disperse quickly from the square, Drew wondered once more where she and Blake were.

■ ■ ■

They got off the subway at their stop and he reached for her hand, which she gladly gave. Everly and Blake walked up the steps hand in hand. She didn't want this moment to end. There were still people milling about in the streets, celebrating, but now that they were closer to home, the amount of people seemed like a normal night, as far as she knew. Then, Everly smiled. This was her home, now.

Blake unlocked the door and Everly rushed in. The warmth of the room felt good, and she started shedding the layers of clothing she had on. But before she had completely taken off her winter coat, Blake had his arms around her waist and pulled her into another kiss, this one a bit steamier than the first. Everly found herself reaching up to wrap her arms around his neck, while his hands drifted down her back. He kissed her, one after another, 'til she almost couldn't catch her breath, so she suddenly backed away.

"What's wrong?" Blake said.

"Nothing. Things are happening a bit fast."

"I don't think so. We have practically been together for the last five days nonstop, and I've loved every minute of it."

"I have too, but I just like taking things a bit slower. I want to get to know you better, Blake. Spend more time with you. If that's what you want."

"I do, but it's a rare occasion that I have an apartment all by myself. Or should I say, *we* have it all to ourselves."

Everly couldn't believe her ears. "You mean, this is all about having sex tonight? The kiss at Times Square? Holding my hand, walking home?"

"No, I'm sorry. That didn't come out right. That's not what I meant," Blake said. "But I will admit, I find you irresistible. I won't apologize for that."

"You are kinda cute yourself," Everly said, "but I'm not ready for that just yet. I guess you can call me an old-fashioned girl. I like to get to know someone on a deeper level. I've been hurt before, and I don't want to go down that path again. I hope you understand. I won't change who I am just because I've moved out on my own."

"Everly, you're adorable," he said as he came up to her and pulled her into another embrace. "I think I like this old-fashioned thing. Is this what people used to call 'courting?'"

She laughed at him, even though the lightning bolts that were passing between them sent a warmth through her that she couldn't deny. "Now, that's carrying the old-fashioned thing a bit too far. Let's just call it 'enjoying each other before we rush into something we might regret.'"

"I can tell you, without a doubt, I wouldn't regret it." Blake kissed her tenderly once more. "But we'll take our time. Besides, it might be nice to just spend time with each other. I will admit, though, that this is new to me, so you have to be patient, okay?"

"Since you're giving me the same courtesy, I will do it for you. I really had a wonderful time tonight. Thanks for making my first New York New Year's celebration wonderful." Everly kissed him again, and then, before she went into her bedroom, she looked back at him and smiled.

24

For the second day in a row, she woke up with a smile. Everly realized she was beginning a brand-new year in a brand-new city, but that was only part of the reason for the smile. Right now, she was remembering the evening she shared with Blake last night. It had been magical to her, but she had almost given in to the feelings that Blake had brought to life in her body. He made it so easy to forget the promises she had made to herself, but she was glad she had regained her senses in time. And also, that Blake was enough of a gentleman to honor her wishes.

So, they were going to get to know each other better. Did that mean they were dating? Were they exclusive? *There's no way,* she thought. They hadn't known each other long enough, and she wasn't going to fool herself by thinking otherwise. When it came to affairs of the heart, Everly didn't have much experience after her one failed attempt at love. Being cheated on had hurt her much more than she wanted to admit, but she had survived. Along the way, she had learned some valuable lessons. Everly was glad that she hadn't crossed that line last night, but she couldn't promise that she would be able to resist in the future. She knew it would help both her and Blake once she moved into the apartment downstairs.

She smelled the scent of coffee again and knew that Blake was up. Maybe, they could fix breakfast together. That sounded romantic, and a perfect way to start the day.

"Good morning," she said, coming into the kitchen, wrapped up in her sweatshirt with her pajamas still on. "I smelled the coffee."

"Good morning to you, too, and Happy New Year, again," Blake said, coming over to give her a kiss. "You hungry?"

"Starving, actually. So, what do New Yorkers do on New Year's Day?" Everly asked, staring up into his hazel eyes.

"Most of the time, we sleep in because we've been up all night," Blake said with a smile. "But I had a bit of distraction this morning, so I was up earlier than usual."

"What was the distraction?"

"I think you know exactly what I meant." He kissed her again.

"How about we fix some breakfast together?" Everly asked, once the tingling of her lips receded. Walking to the refrigerator, she opened it and surveyed the contents. There were eggs, cheese, butter, and milk. "Do you have any flour? Or maybe, some bread?"

"I doubt we have flour since we don't cook that much, but we do have bread."

"Then, how about cheese omelets and toast?" Everly asked.

"Sounds great to me. I think I could get used to this. Are you going to cook like this after you move downstairs?" Blake asked, nodding.

Everly couldn't help but laugh. "I plan to. Maybe, you can be my guinea pig for some new recipes. I used to cook all the time in Key West." As she started taking the food staples out and putting them on the counter, Everly remembered all the fun times she had cooking with her mom.

"Do you miss it yet?" Blake asked.

Everly didn't say anything, at first. There were a few things that she longed for, but overall, these first few days had seemed like a dream come true. This was something she had worked to accomplish for so long.

"I don't know how to explain it, but I do and I don't. I have to say, the warm weather is great, but then, I loved our snowball fight the other day. I miss my flip-flops, but I finally get to wear boots. I guess it's a trade-off."

Blake walked up next to her putting his arm on her waist. "I'm sure glad you are here. And maybe one day you can take me to Key West. I've never been past Disney World as far as Florida is concerned except to fly into Miami for a cruise."

"We'll just have to see." Everly gave him a quick kiss on the cheek. Then, she began fixing breakfast, giving Blake instructions. They were laughing and having such a good time as they mixed ingredients, joking around, that they didn't hear the door open.

Drew just watched as Everly and Blake started cooking, and he noticed how close they were. But when Blake kissed Everly, he felt a heat rising to his cheeks.

"Hi, guys," Drew said as he shut the door. Both Everly and Blake turned quickly, separating like they had been caught red-handed doing something they shouldn't.

"So, how was your evening? Survived the crowds of Times Square?" Even though Drew was talking to both of them, he was looking directly at Everly as she was trying to fix an omelet.

"We had a fantastic time. Well, at least, I did," she answered back.

"I did, too. We had the perfect spot to watch all the festivities and we dressed warm enough that we didn't freeze. But then, all those bodies together can help with the wind," Blake said, smiling broadly at Drew. "How was the party?"

"Nice. The usual for a holiday work party. All the same people, well mostly, from Peyton's Dad's businesses."

"I thought you and Peyton were spending today together," Everly said. "Is she with you? We're making omelets, if you want to join us." Drew loved her sincerity and wanted to stay with them. The breakfast sounded good, and he was sure that the kitchen hadn't seen this much activity in a long time.

"We are. I just came by to get a few things. We're going out to Peyton's parent's country house. I should be back sometime tomorrow."

"Blake is going to help me move in downstairs tomorrow. I'll be officially out of your way. Then, I need to practice my interview skills. I've never interviewed for a job before. I've only worked one place."

"There's no doubt that you're going to do just fine. We can work on that over the next few days, too. I've interviewed dozens of times for just about everything, so I think I'll be able to help you there, too," Blake said, putting his arm around her waist.

Drew could tell that something had transpired between the two people in front of him. They were getting close. He didn't know what had happened last night, but whatever it was, Drew hoped that Blake had been nice. It wasn't his place to tell Everly what to do, but if he could, he would tell her to stay away from Blake. But it looked like that was too late, now.

As Drew packed a few things for another night away, he could feel tension throughout his body. What was happening between Everly and Blake before his eyes wasn't sitting well with him. He should have been the one to help Everly get the things she needed for her apartment. He should have been the one to take her to Times Square last night. He should be the one making....

Stop! he practically yelled to himself. He was just feeling guilty for not keeping his promise to Abbey, that's all. As long as Everly was fine, he was going to go enjoy a stay at the country house. It might do him some good to get away from everyone. The apartment did seem to be getting a little smaller each day, and he could feel the tension.

"Drew, have a good time. Tell Peyton I said 'hi,'" Everly said before he could walk out the door.

"I will." Drew took one more look at the couple, then headed toward the elevator.

"Do you think he was okay?" Everly asked Blake, who was already eating his food.

"He's fine. Probably in a tiff with Peyton again."

"Do they fight that often?"

"I wouldn't really call it a fight. Just, Peyton seems to rule the relationship, in a way."

"Yeah, I could see that. She's assertive and confident." Everly wanted to use other words that came to mind, like "bitchy" and "mean," but didn't want to sound like that herself.

"So, what are we going to do today?" Blake asked. "They're calling for snow again, with a high of thirty degrees. Feel like going out to sightsee?"

"I say we go to the grocery store to pick up a few more things you guys need around here, and maybe, some movie snacks. Then, watch TV all day and have pizza tonight. What we got the other day was wonderful and sounds so good, even if I'm eating brunch with you right now."

"You're definitely my kind of girl. TV and pizza."

"Now, if you were in my town, we would be getting sandwiches from the deli, then spending the day at the beach or biking around town. Maybe, even go have drinks at the pier. Then, at sunset, we would be watching the sun go down over the ocean at Mallory Square. At least, for your first visit there."

"New Year's Day on the beach – love that idea. And you in a swimsuit? That sounds even better." Blake gave her a sexy glance as he raised his head from his breakfast plate.

"Behave," Everly teased him as she finished her meal then started cleaning up the dishes. "Let's go back to the grocery store in a bit. It won't take me long to get dressed. But what kind of movies do you like?"

"You get to pick since you're the guest here."

"I like chick flicks and sci-fi. Either of those interest you?"

"Seriously, anything you chose is fine with me as long as we get to spend the day together." Blake shot her another sweet look and Everly felt like melting inside. This man was suddenly sweeping her off her feet and she couldn't help but go with it, even though she had promised herself to spend these first few months by herself, just learning who she was with her newfound independence. But Blake had put a kink in that part of her plan. And Everly had to admit, she liked it.

25

Everly looked around the room once more to make sure that she had everything. All her things were stuffed in the suitcases, just like the day she had arrived. The excitement of moving her stuff downstairs was almost more than she could bear. Her own place – finally!

"You about ready to start this move?" Blake was suddenly standing at her bedroom door and she couldn't help but smile.

"I think so. Feels like the day I packed to move to New York, even though I'm only going down two flights of stairs."

"I'm glad you won't be that far away. It'll make this courting thing much easier," he said, giving her a hug as she stood up.

"You like that word, don't you?" Everly teased him.

"Yeah, it sounds really cool."

"I'm ready. I have a lot of unpacking to do, then tomorrow, I have to start preparing for my interview on Tuesday. Actually, two interviews! I almost forgot!"

"Let's take one thing at a time." Blake gave her a reassuring kiss on the forehead. That little gesture reminded her of their day together yesterday. They shopped, cooked, watched movies, and ate pizza, just like they planned. But they also couldn't get enough of being so close to each other. Everly had snuggled into Blake's arms as they watched movies, and it felt like she just belonged there.

"Everly, are you ready?"

Blake's voice brought her attention back to the present. She would have to thank Donald for the use of his room, once she finally got to meet him. It was certainly bigger than where she was heading now, but at least her new place had a window, even if it was small. It would let in a bit of natural light, something that she craved from living in the Keys for so long.

"You got your key?" Blake asked, taking the handle of one of her rolling suitcases from her.

"Right here." She produced the shiny object on a ring that had a little flip-flop on it.

"I guess this is from home," he said as he looked at the little pink shoe next to the key.

"Just a little reminder of Key West."

"Well, my island babe, let's get you moved into your new space." Blake expertly handled one suitcase and several bags of the items she purchased the other day. They would have to make two trips to get everything, but that wasn't much, considering she was moving into a new apartment.

Everly stood at the door of her place – apartment 2B - and took a deep breath. She almost felt as though she should knock, since she didn't know who would be home.

"Do I just walk on in?" she asked, turning to Blake.

"I would. You live here now, too. Shari already knows, and I'm sure she told London."

Everly put the key in the door and opened it. "Hello?"

"Hi," said a male voice. "You must be Everly." And older gentleman was walking toward her and Blake with a huge smile. "I'm Eugene, London's friend, or should I say, her assistant, too. Shari left about thirty minutes ago, and said you would probably be here this morning. It's so nice to meet you."

"Thanks." Everly shook the man's outstretched hand. He seemed sweet and friendly, a broad smile gracing his face. He also shook Blake's hand quickly, then turned to quickly go back to his laptop.

"London is in the shower. She's getting ready to go to Paris for a few weeks. She has a couple of photo shoots and is meeting some designers to discuss the Spring Fashion Week. But I'm sure she wants to meet you before we leave."

"That would be great." Everly looked to Blake for some reassurance and got a sly wink.

Everly walked back to the tiny room she was shown the other day and opened the door. This was her place, now. She had a place to call her own in New York City. Another milestone on this dream journey of hers. She had tears running down her face, but they were of joy, not sorrow.

"I've never seen a girl cry so much when she's happy," Blake said as he wiped away the tear on her cheek.

"I know. Kinda weird, huh?"

"No, I think it's kinda sweet. Just shows me what a kind heart you have."

Suddenly, the door behind them swung open widely, and a tall woman with a body shape that left Everly speechless walked through the door, completely naked!

"You must be Everly," the woman said, reaching back to get a towel as though it was no big deal she was unclothed in front of two strangers. The woman wrapped her body, then reached out to shake both of their hands.

"And you must be London," Everly said as calmly as she could. "It's nice to meet you. This is my friend, Blake."

"Hi, there." To Everly, it seemed like Blake was mesmerized by the woman, but then again, she was naked at first, nothing hidden in any way. And she was a model.

"I see you met Eugene. We're getting ready to go to Paris. When I get back, we'll have to go to lunch or something. I here you're from the Florida Keys. I love it down there. Did a magazine shoot there a couple of years ago, and now, having you here makes me want to go back for a small vacation."

"It's a great place," Everly said, still trying to take in what had just happened.

"Make yourself at home," London said before closing the door to her bedroom.

"Did that just really happen?" Blake whispered in Everly's ear.

"If you're referring to the nude woman that looks like a goddess, then yes," Everly said.

"Never knew Shari lived with a supermodel. Why would she be living here?" Blake wondered out loud as they made the trip upstairs for the rest of her stuff.

"As soon as I find out, I'll let you know," Everly said. "But it sounds like she isn't here that much. Wouldn't it be great to travel like that?"

"Of course!"

By the time they got the rest of Everly's things and went back downstairs, London and Eugene were making their way out the door.

"Have a great time," Everly said as she watched them walk toward the door.

"It's just Paris. And it's work. Your Key West is more my style," Eugene said.

"See you in a few weeks," London stated nonchalantly, and then, they were gone.

"I guess I have the place to myself 'til Shari shows up. Maybe, I can get everything set up. Blake, you don't have to help me. I'm fine from here. Need some girl time to fix up my space. But tomorrow, are we still on for some interview training?"

"Yeah, sounds good." Blake suddenly sounded a bit distant.

"What time? Maybe, I can come up for breakfast again, since you now have more food in the cabinet and the fridge. Maybe, even make homemade biscuits, another one of my specialties."

"That sounds good. I'll see you then, but if you need anything, just let me know." Blake kissed Everly on the lips, but the feeling that she experienced yesterday and earlier today seemed to be missing.

"Are you sure you're okay?" Everly asked.

"Positive. Just have some work to do that I forgot about. I guess I'll be doing that while you're fixing up your room. Remember, I'm just upstairs or a phone call away."

"Got it." Everly heard the door shut, then looked around. This was her new space. And, while she was by herself, she had to talk to Abbey.

26

"Hello." It was Abbey, alright. Everly turned the camera on her phone to show off her new apartment.

"Abbey, I'm moved in. Well, almost. My room is a wreck, but I've got a space in Drew's building."

"How did you do that? I thought we found you a place across town?"

"It's a long story, but the landlord rented the other room out to someone else. Trying to get my deposit back now, but it's not looking hopeful, unless I want to hire an attorney. That would cost me more than my deposit. So what do you think?" Everly panned her camera around the area.

"It's beautiful. What about your room?" Abbey asked.

"You mean, my closet?" Everly laughed. "It's a bit on the small side, but it will do, for now. I didn't have a place to go and this room opened up a few weeks ago. Kinda glad it's in Drew's building. He and Blake are just upstairs."

"Blake? I don't think I met him, but it's been a while since I was there. Is he nice?"

"All I will say is that we spent New Year's Eve together at Times Square. It was wonderful and he kissed me. We even spent New Year's Day watching TV and eating pizza because it was snowing outside. Snowing, Abbey! I've never seen snow, and I've already had a snowball fight." Everly finally turned the camera around so the two girls could talk face to face.

"Everly, don't take this wrong, but you've only been there a week and there's already a man in the picture? I thought you were taking this time for you. 'No strings,' if I remember your words correctly," Abbey said softly to her friend.

"I know, but he's sweet, nice, and good looking. He's fun to be with and a gentleman, which is a breath of fresh air. I didn't see it coming, either, but it's nice."

"What does Drew think? I mean, I know it's none of his business, but just wondering."

"I don't know because I haven't seen him much these last few days. He's been away with Peyton. She is definitely, um, *different*."

"You're being nice, you know, but then, I expect that from you. I've only met her once and I hate to say this, but that was enough for me. I can't see her and Drew together at all. But you've seen them interact. What do you think?"

"I don't know. I mean, Drew seems to love her, but I get the feeling that he's a bit unsettled. Not sure if that's the right word to use, but he just doesn't seem like the guy I met in Key West that was so carefree and happy. I mean, he *is* happy. Abbey, I'm sorry. I'm not helping things, am I?" Everly said.

"You're fine. I've noticed that Drew hasn't been his usual self when we talk on the phone. I kinda figured that Peyton might be the reason. I think Drew has gotten himself into a situation that's a bit sticky."

"What do you mean?"

"I'm probably just being the over-protective sister. Anyway, this phone call is about you. So, now that you are moved in, it's time for your interviews, right?"

"On Tuesday. Blake is going to coach me a bit tomorrow. I've never interviewed for a job. I've only worked for Lance, and I just bugged him 'til he gave me a job. Then, he realized what he'd been missing with my expert skills," Everly laughed. "Speaking of, how is everyone?" She almost didn't want to know, afraid a feeling of homesickness would wash over her, but deep inside, she wanted to make sure that everyone was doing okay.

"It's the same old thing here. Work has been a bit busy without you here. Lance is trying like crazy to find someone to replace you, but it's been a struggle. But I think he settled on a guy today. Now, I'll be the only woman at work. That's going to be weird."

"I bet it will," Everly said, realizing that she no longer had a place to go to if she ever did go back to Key West. But that wasn't her plan, so she wasn't going to let this small piece of news upset her. Her trips back to visit the islands would be for pleasure only. New York was her home, now.

"Well, you show them who's boss, then," Everly said. "Please, tell everyone I said 'hi.' I better get back to work. Not that it will take a long time, but I have an air bed to blow up and clothes to hang up."

"An air bed?"

"Yep, I had to get something quick and I didn't want to settle on just any piece of furniture. This will do until I can find something used. I hear they have some great flea markets in the spring. Hopefully, by then, I'll be able to find a place with a bigger room. Oh, but I forgot to tell you this. One of my roommates is a model. She just left for Paris for two weeks. Too bad I couldn't have her room. It's plenty big enough, and she isn't even here!"

"Maybe, when she gets back, you can talk her out of her room. I would certainly give it a try," Abbey said.

"That's not a bad idea. Maybe I should run it by Shari, first."

"Shari?"

"Oh, that's my other roommate. She's nice, but she's out right now so I have the place to myself, which is kinda nice. I haven't had this since I moved here."

"Go enjoy your alone time. Everyone needs some, and I'm sure in a crowded city like New York, you need it worse than if you were here."

Everly laughed. "Abbey, it isn't that bad."

"I know. But how I miss you. We all miss you."

"I miss you, too. Like I said, please tell everyone I said 'hi.'"

"I will." Everly hit the disconnect button, and suddenly, she was alone. There was silence throughout the apartment, except for the occasional sound of a horn or siren coming from the city streets. But it didn't bother Everly.

She inflated the bed and slid it against the wall. After putting her linens on the bed and covering them with a new blanket and the one she brought from home, Everly put the wooden crate next to the free side of her bed. She placed the lamp and her charging station for her electronics on top, and filled the bottom of the wooden box with her books. She put her lap desk against the case, where she could easily grab it.

The plastic drawer space was quickly filled with clothes, and then, she hung up what was left. The one thing she didn't remember to get was some type of curtain for the window. Though it looked out into an alley and there were no windows on the building across from hers, she still felt exposed by not having a covering. She went into the hall and found a closet full of towels and took one that she could use for a temporary cover. Then, she remembered another item to put on her shopping list: towels, along with the curtain.

Once everything seemed to be in its place, Everly laid across the air bed and took in the silence around her. It felt like the first real time she could rest and think about everything she had been through so far. Living with the guys. Times Square kiss. No apartment, then new apartment. Drew and Peyton. Blake.

Everly couldn't help but smile every time she thought of Blake. And laying on her new bed, she reached out her hand, wondering what it would be like to share it with him. To share with any man. At twenty-six years old, she was still a virgin, which was probably a rarity here. Even in her relationship that went south, she had never had sex with her boyfriend. And when she found out that he had been cheating on her the whole time, she was thankful that she had never taken that step with him. It would have been disastrous for her, both emotionally and physically. But now, things just felt different. She was older and a bit wiser.

Everly heard the door to the apartment open and then shut. Hopefully, it was Shari, because she had probably forgotten to lock the front door, something she wasn't used to.

"Shari?" Everly, very tentatively, walked into the hallway, studying everything around her.

"Everly, is that you?" came the voice.

Everly sighed with relief. "It's me. I know I'm supposed to lock the door when I come in, but I keep forgetting. I didn't do it at home unless we were in for the night, so this is new for me. But I promise, I'll get the hang of it," Everly told the woman, who was now putting a few groceries up in the cabinet.

"No big deal, but I always keep the door locked when I'm at home. So, are you all moved in?" Shari continued.

"I am. There wasn't much, just some simple furniture and my clothes. But I would like to get some groceries. Any kitchen rules I need to know about?" Everly asked.

"Just clean your dishes, and whatever you put in the cabinets and refrigerator, make sure you mark with your name. That way, we know whose food belongs to who," Shari said. Everly felt like she was welcoming and decided that, even though the room was a bit small, maybe, this was where she was supposed to be for right now.

"I love to cook. Do I need to get pots and pans?"

"We have plenty here, but they don't get much use. As you can probably tell, London is gone a lot of the time and I'm working every chance I get."

"What do you do?"

"I'm in the process of writing a play, taking acting lessons, and waiting tables. That keeps me busy enough that I'm usually here just long enough to take a shower, change clothes, and sleep. The only reason I can afford this place is from an inheritance from a great aunt of mine. She was on Broadway and left me a good sum of money to pursue my writing and acting goals. But so far, things haven't quite panned out like I hoped. I have enough money for about another year. If that doesn't work, then I'll be heading home," Shari said as she stuffed her tote with clothes, a water bottle, and a few snacks from the refrigerator.

"Where is home?" Everly asked.

"Austin, Texas," Shari said. "The home of beef, cowboys, and weather that's hot as hell. But I must admit that last summer here was brutal, especially when you have to walk everywhere. Hope you're prepared."

"Remember, I'm from Key West. Gets pretty warm there, too."

"Not much of a breeze here, though. But we're talking about the summer, and right now, we have snow on the ground. Everly, welcome to New York. And I have to be leaving again or I'm going to be late for my shift at work. I should be home later, but it might be pretty late. Just lock up when you go to bed. Have my keys with me. See ya later." Shari put her tote on her back and rushed out of the apartment.

It's time for a bit of studying, Everly thought. She had to ace these interviews, not only to secure a job, but also to show Lance that his recommendations weren't wasted. He had faith in her and she didn't want him to think it had been misplaced. But then she heard the rumble of her stomach.

Everly looked at the food in the cabinets and, just like with Drew and Blake, there wasn't much. The refrigerator was just as bad. Before she watched some videos on interviewing skills, it was time to go somewhere on her own. She knew where the grocery store was by now, and thank goodness, it wasn't far away. But carrying back loads of bags wouldn't be a good idea. She was going to need a tote of some kind, and she quickly added that to her ever-growing shopping list. Today, she would just pick up some basics; only a few bags would be easy to carry. But this made her realize there was still so much to learn about living in this big city.

27

She quickly dressed for the weather after looking outside to see that snow had begun to fall again. Everly loved it and, though the holidays were officially over, it still felt cozy watching the little flakes fall to the ground below while she was tucked away in her new home. She emptied her backpack and took only her driver's license and debit card with her. Until she could get a rolling cart for groceries, the pack on her back would be the best way to carry things.

As she stepped out of the door and onto the sidewalk, the wind was a bit brisk. Everly tightened the scarf around her neck and pulled the hat down around her ears. The walk didn't take long, but once inside the store, she panicked. She couldn't feel her toes, something she had never experienced before. So, she grabbed a basket and quickly went through the aisles, picking up only a few things 'til she could shop more thoroughly. Maybe, Blake would come back and help her get more items. Maybe, they could even make a date out of it. She smiled to herself.

Once the items were paid for, Everly realized the feeling was back in her toes. It was the cold! She laughed to herself, then looked around to make sure no one saw her. Her groceries fit easily inside the backpack. Once she bundled up, with the pack on her back, she went back outside into the cold.

Everly walked back slowly. Yes, she was cold, but this was the first time she was officially by herself. Here, on the streets of New York. Even though the skies were grey, the buildings and street looked lovely as the snow fell all around. She looked everywhere as she walked and reveled in the feeling. She was loving every second of it. And, even though her experience so far wasn't without its few little bumps, it was all she imagined.

"Hi there, stranger." Everly looked away from her front door to see Drew. It seemed like forever since she had seen him.

"You look like you're about to go on a hike," he teased her.

"You're finally home. How was the country?" she asked as she took the backpack off and unlocked the door to her apartment.

"It was nice, but cold. Did a little skiing, and mostly sitting around. How about you? Looks like you're moved in?" Drew asked.

"I am, and I also just went to get groceries all on my own," Everly said proudly.

"You're making progress. But you can get your groceries delivered, you know."

"That would be no fun. This way, I got to go out in the snow again." She laughed. "But I did get a little scared when I got to the store and couldn't feel my toes. Never had that happen before."

Drew snickered. This was his Everly. *His?* he thought. *Yes, his little sister,* he quickly told himself.

"Want to come in and see my little closet, or shall I say, bedroom?"

"Sure."

"Where's Peyton?"

"Just dropped her off at her place. I need to work on a few articles before I go back to work tomorrow. Hey, you have your interviews in a few days, don't you?" Drew asked.

"Yes, so I'm in study mode once I get these groceries put away. I even bought some snacks to munch on while I work. Reminds me of Key West, for some reason. Blake is supposed to help me with interview questions tomorrow."

"I can help you right now, if you want," Drew said quickly.

"You just said you need to work on your articles, and it's getting late, though I wouldn't mind the extra help," Everly said.

"I can spare an hour."

"Then I accept your offer, but look here, first." Everly showed Drew her little room and Drew had to admit that, though it was tiny, it was homey. It looked and felt like Everly. The colors of the linens on her bed to the little turtle on the top of the wooden crate by her bed. Everything looked bright and cheery - just like this Key West girl.

"Let me take my stuff to the apartment and I'll be back. Have you had dinner?"

"I was going to make some soup in a bit."

"Let's just order sandwiches from the deli. They deliver."

"Who doesn't deliver in this city?" Everly asked as she shook her head.

"Not many, but there are a few. Just thought that if we ordered in, then we'd have more time together to work on those interview questions."

Everly looked at him and smiled. He had helped her so much and she loved that they had become such friends. There was still that little piece of her that was attracted to this man, but she held it in check. They were only friends, but who said they couldn't be *best* friends?

"I think I could eat a good turkey club sandwich right now, with some chips. But I know it won't be as good as the deli in Key West. They're the best!" she said.

"I'll be right back."

Everly put up the groceries and, true to his word, Drew was back in a flash. He had changed clothes into a sweatshirt and sweatpants, looking comfortable and very sexy. He hadn't shaved in a few days and the dark stubble was in stark contrast to his blonde hair. When she saw him like this, she understood why Peyton was like she was. She was just being protective of this man, making sure he didn't wander to anyone else. Everly thought that Drew just wasn't that kind of guy, though even his own sister had warned her how the women seemed to flock to him. But Everly saw a different side of Drew. She was sure that the guy Abbey described wasn't the one with her right now. Everly also knew, somehow, that Drew wasn't the man that Peyton needed in her life. She just wanted to take care of a friend whom she loved.

Wait – loved? *What am I thinking?* Everly thought to herself. That was just an errant thought. She had Blake in her life, now. He was the one that made her feel special. She couldn't say she loved him, but she enjoyed spending time with him. Blake was special and had been so helpful since the day she arrived.

"Boy, you look like you're thinking about something mighty hard," Drew said, placing his keys on the counter. "You okay?"

Everly composed herself. "Yeah, just trying to figure out how to practice for an interview. I've watched YouTube videos with tips, read articles, and more. But I'm so nervous."

"Well, let's order our dinner first, then we'll get started. You are going to do just fine." Drew could sense her anxiety, but had a feeling that a job interview wasn't the only thing that had her feeling on edge. He hoped he hadn't said or done anything to upset her. Or worse, that Blake was the cause of the tension.

"I'm surprised you and Blake aren't practicing tonight," Drew said, fishing for more information.

"He said he had some work to do," Everly said casually.

"He wasn't at home when I was upstairs."

"I don't know, then. Drew, are you positive you're okay? You seem, I don't know, nervous."

"Looks like we're a bit alike tonight because I thought the same thing about you. I promise, I'm okay. Just hungry," Drew said.

"And I'm fine, too. So, where shall we start on this interviewing thing?" Everly asked quickly, to send the direction of the conversation somewhere else.

It wasn't long before they were eating sandwiches, telling some of their funniest stories about growing up, laughing the whole time. Not one interview question was discussed.

It's just so easy to talk to him, Everly thought as she finished the last bite of her sandwich. Being here with him brought back more memories of their fun times in the Keys. He was certainly complicating her feelings.

"Can I ask you something? Maybe some advice?" Drew asked. "I know I'm supposed to be helping you but I'm hoping you can help me."

"What's wrong?"

"It's about Peyton."

"Okay."

"I-" Drew hesitated. How could he ask Everly questions about his love life when she had once thought he had feelings for her? Or, did he have feelings for her, now? Drew felt so confused.

"Drew, it's okay. Just ask."

"I love Peyton. I've been thinking about asking her to marry me. But every time I get ready to pop the question, I hesitate. I stumble. What's wrong with me?" Drew leaned back on the sofa, where they had been eating.

"Oh, wow. I didn't see that coming," Everly said. "Not that it's a bad thing, but I'm not sure I'm the person to ask. Don't you know someone who's married that could help you? Maybe, Abbey?"

"I talked to her when I was in Florida. Believe me, it wasn't much help. I had planned to ask Peyton on Christmas day. I even bought a ring." Drew let his head fall back on the couch and stared at the ceiling. "But when it came time to ask, the words just wouldn't come out. So, then, I was going to ask her New Year's Eve, or right after midnight. But still, no go. The crazy thing is that I love her. I really do."

"Are you afraid to commit? I mean, you can love her, but maybe, the thought of being with her for the rest of your life is making you nervous. I'm just guessing out loud. I've only had one serious relationship and that didn't turn out well at all. Even now, dating Blake is a bit scary for me, and fun too."

"You and Blake are dating? I mean, like really dating?" Drew asked, his heart pounding.

"I think so. Well, we're spending a lot of time together and I'm really enjoying being with him. He's been helping me, and-" Everly paused, not sure if she wanted to share so much information.

"And, what? Come on. I told you my secret. I promise, whatever it is, it won't go out of this room. And that goes the same for me."

"You promised. Okay – Blake and I kissed on New Year's Eve, right after midnight, and it's been pretty special since then," Everly said shyly.

"Well, the other day, when I came home to get some clothes, I walked in to see you two kissing in the kitchen."

"Oh, I didn't know that," Everly said. "He's nice and I think I really like him."

He's doing it again, that little shit, was all Drew could think. He was using Everly, he was sure of it, but he couldn't say anything. Not yet. Suddenly, he wondered if they had slept together. Ugh!

"Blake's a nice guy, but he's had a few girlfriends since we've known each other. Just be careful, okay?"

"Drew, I can take care of myself. I've been bad at the relationship thing, but I promised myself I'd let go of some of those hard feelings once I moved here. To give people a chance. I actually have you to thank for introducing us."

Drew's stomach churned. This wasn't how he was supposed to feel. *I'm in love, remember?* he told himself. But the thoughts of Everly and Blake together didn't sit well with him.

"But back to Peyton. I'm going to ask a question that might sound harsh, so don't get mad. Promise?" Everly said, moving to sit right beside Drew.

"Promise," he answered back.

"Do you really love her? I mean, that love that every time you see her, your heart skips a beat? And you want to be with her every minute, but can't. So, when you get together, the time is even more special?"

"You sound like a greeting card!" Drew laughed, but looked at Everly to see she was very serious.

"So? What is it? Does any of that ring a bell with you?"

Drew sat and thought for a few seconds. He felt utterly confused. The woman he professed to love didn't make him feel that way, but the girl sitting beside him did. Why couldn't he just tell her that? Why couldn't he just admit that?

"Sometimes, she does. I mean, Peyton can be a bit bossy, but I like that in her. She knows what she wants and she goes for it. Like I do."

"But does that make for a good relationship? Especially a long-term one? I always saw love as a compromise, but in a good way. One where you want to be with someone so bad that if they want pizza and you want Chinese, you settle for pizza because it will make them happy. And you know, without any doubt in your mind, that the other person will do the same thing for you. Maybe that sounds too over-the-top romantic, but I feel there's someone out there just like that who is only for me. Do you feel like Peyton is that one for you?"

The knock on the door brought them both out of the deep conversation. "Hold that thought," Everly said. She answered the door to find Blake standing there, flowers in hand.

"Hi, there!" Everly stood back so Blake could walk in. "Drew and I just finished dinner, and he was getting ready to help me with some mock interviews. The flowers are beautiful." Everly took them and put them in the biggest glass she could find 'til she could ask Shari for a vase.

"I thought I saw your stuff upstairs. How was the trip?"

"Fine. Everly said you were working tonight. A school thing?" Drew asked, knowing that his excuse was just that: an excuse.

"I had a meeting with the guy handling my internship and I got through early. Thought I would surprise Everly with dinner, but it seems you two have eaten."

The two men sat across from each other, staring, without saying another word. The tension was palpable when Everly came back to the couch. "Is everything okay?"

"Of course," Drew said. "Hey, thanks for the advice, and good luck with the interviewing skills. I'm going back to work a day early, or at least for a half-day, so I have a few things to do. If you need anything, let me know."

"I will," Everly said, giving Drew a hug. "We'll talk more later," she whispered in his ear.

"Well, this is a nice surprise" Everly stood on her tiptoes and gave Blake a kiss on the cheek. But he wanted more. He kissed her hungrily. The kiss sent her senses reeling, but was it from the guy who held her in his arms, or from the guy who had just left? Everly was confused right now. Drew was acting funny. Then, it seemed like Blake and Drew were not so friendly when she was in the room. She felt like her senses were on overload.

"Are we still getting together tomorrow? Breakfast, so you can have some of my homemade biscuits?"

"Sounds wonderful to me. If you want, you could just come and stay the night. Then, you wouldn't have to worry about coming up in the morning," Blake said softly in her ear.

"This is my first night in my new place, so I'll take a rain check for another time, okay?" Everly said, her heart beating so fast she was sure it would burst. This attractive and very attentive man wanted her, to help her, to take care of her.

But she couldn't reconcile the emotions going through her mind. It seemed like Blake made her blood boil. But every time she was around Drew, those feelings that Everly had when he was in Key West were growing again. As much as she wanted to say they didn't exist, they were there. And Everly couldn't deny it anymore. But he was beyond reach. He wanted to marry Peyton and she had to accept that. And she had Blake, who had his arms around her right now. Why not accept what she had right in front of her instead of pining for someone she couldn't have?

27

"Will they really ask me that question?" Everly sighed, tired of trying to make sure she said the correct thing to every question Blake asked. Finally she just laid her head on the table.

"They could. I'm just throwing some things at you that I've encountered in my numerous interviews."

"I'm calling it quits. I'm just going to go tomorrow and be myself. If they don't like me, they don't like me. My work should speak for itself. I'm beginning to feel, though, that these firms want someone who is a workaholic. I love designing and coding, but I don't want to work eighty hours a week in some cubicle. I want to get out and enjoy the city. Maybe, even take my laptop to Central Park and work. Of course, when it's a bit warmer."

Blake walked around the table and took her in his arms. "I think you're going to do just fine." He kissed her forehead, then each cheek, before landing on her lips. That sizzling sensation went through Everly and she couldn't resist his charms. But she was also keenly aware that she was in Drew's home, too.

Just like they had planned, Everly had come up for breakfast and the two had fun making biscuits together. Blake helped her mix the dough, dusted her with flour, and she got back at him by making him taste the raw dough. The whole time was filled with laughter and Everly loved every second of it.

The whole time they had been in the kitchen, Drew had not appeared once. Everly assumed that he was working, so didn't bother him to see if he wanted to eat breakfast with them. Or maybe he had already left for work. She also remembered the stressful atmosphere yesterday afternoon between the two men.

"I need to clean the dishes and put away the biscuits. You guys have plenty for several days, but I'd like to take a few home with me."

"I should keep them here so you have to come up here and stay with me." Blake constantly had his hands on her, and even though she liked the attention, something was beginning to feel a bit over-the-top. Or was she just nervous?

"And who is this?" The strange voice came from the living room. Everly looked over to see a man a little older than Blake and Drew standing there with luggage in tow.

"You're back! Donald, this is Everly Myers from Key West."

This was the man whose room she had used. "Hi, it's so nice to meet you." Everly extended her hand to the man and he quickly shook it. "Drew and Blake promised me that you said it was okay to stay in your room, so I was careful not to move anything. And I made sure everything was clean before I moved out."

"You're already gone? We didn't even get a chance to talk."

Everly knew immediately that she liked Donald. It was something about his eyes. They just sparkled, and he looked like he was genuinely a happy person.

"Well, then you're in luck. She took a room downstairs when her apartment didn't turn out like she hoped," Blake said, coming to stand beside her, putting his arm on her shoulder.

"I just moved in yesterday and so far, so good."

"How do you like New York? This place sure is much different than your island paradise. I love it there," Donald commented. "Looks like Blake is taking good care of you." He gestured to Blake's arm that was protectively around her.

"Drew and Blake both have helped more than I could have hoped for. I have my own place and start my interviews tomorrow."

"That should be fun. Well, right now I need to get unpacked and start working on a project I got over the weekend." Donald grabbed the handle of his suitcase and he moved toward his room. "Everly, I think you and I do the same thing. Coding and web design, right?"

"Yes!" Everly said excitedly.

"Then we'll have to sit down and talk more later. Good luck with your interviews."

"Thanks. Who do you work for?" Everly asked, but Donald had already shut the door to his room.

"He works for himself," Blake said. "Has a pretty strong business he's building up. I'm surprised he's still renting here, but some of his contract work is for Mr. Compton, so he gets a reduced rent rate."

"Peyton's Dad?" Everly asked.

"Yep. It seems everyone in this apartment is attached to that family in one way or another."

"I've noticed that." Everly started thinking about the conversation she had with Drew yesterday. Did Drew feel like he owed Mr. Compton something? Is that why he was dating Peyton? Or was he dating her to climb the corporate ladder?

"Where are you, my love?" Blake asked, bringing Everly back to the present.

"My head is swimming with everything I have to do. I really need to go. There are a few things that have to be done before tomorrow. Will I see you later?"

"I hope so. Dinner tonight?"

"What about dinner here, with Drew and Donald? Sounds like fun."

"I was thinking about something more intimate," Blake said, meeting her at the door.

"Well, then we'll have to make plans for the weekend. I have a job to find and that's my focus. Not that you're a distraction – well, you really are," and Everly reached up and gave him another kiss. "- a very nice distraction. I'll see you tonight, and tell the guys. I'll let you three plan dinner."

Safe behind the door of her apartment, she took a deep breath. There were too many facts floating through her mind, like giant puzzle pieces she couldn't quite put together. Peyton. Blake. Drew. Donald. The building. Marriage. Complicated love. Feelings she shouldn't have, but did. And for the wrong person. Or was he the right person?

Everly finally made it to her little bed and laid down, spreading the blanket all around her. She had come to New York to get away and start fresh. But she had only been here a short while, and her life felt more complicated than it had ever felt living in the Keys.

"I'm not thinking about it anymore," she said out loud. "Getting a job is the only thing I'm going to focus on. No guys. No relationships. Just me and work." Though she was talking to air, the words came back to her loud and clear. She had let herself get swept away in emotion and she had thrown caution to the wind. Right now, she was tired of thinking, and quietly fell to sleep.

■ ■ ■

As she stood before the building once more, Everly's anxiety was increasing. Her body felt jittery. When she looked up at the twenty-story building, it was the first time that she wished she was standing back on Duval Street, in front of the art gallery where her beloved office was housed. She suddenly remembered her desk in front of the window, looking down on the street below that was usually full of tourists.

Everly had desperately wanted to move, but this was the part of making her giant leap into independence of which she had been most afraid. This is where her people skills were lacking, and she could only hope that her work and Lance's recommendation would help her land a job in the city. Though she had a nice savings account, it would run out eventually, and she needed the work.

With a deep breath, she went inside. When she had come with Drew and Blake last week, they hadn't walked inside the building. They had only shown her where it was. She had two interviews here today, two hours apart. Then, two tomorrow in another building, two blocks away. Those were her only prospects, and one had to work.

Everly quickly found the first office, which was located on the tenth floor. As the elevator doors opened, a flood of people rushed in and she was swept along for the ride. She glanced at the row of numbers by the side of the door to see if the appropriate floor button was pushed, and laughed to herself because almost every button was lit up. And, with the amount of people that were in the elevator, she could understand the reason why.

As Everly walked out onto the tenth floor, she surveyed her surroundings. It was an older building with marble floors and ornate wood lining the walls. When she looked to her left, she saw the office of Gold Key Digital, LLC. She found herself walking slowly, hesitant to take this next step.

Once inside the office, Everly walked to the receptionist, gave her name, and took a seat in the waiting room. She could see the row of cubicles through the open doorway. It was so different from what she was used to. She felt like she was having a panic attack, but then she heard her name.

"Everly Meyers?" the woman said.

"That's me."

"Follow me, please," she said with half a smile.

Everly found herself walking down the aisle she was just spying on. She saw person after person, all men, in a tiny box-like area, with computer screens around them. Each person had two screens on a large desk and just enough room to move their chair from side to side. The air felt stuffy, and all she heard was fingers clicking on computer keyboards. There were no pictures on the walls, no boards to show projects in the works, nothing like what she was used to.

"Mr. Salten will see you in here. He will be back in just a moment."

"Thank you." Everly took a seat in a room in front of a big, vintage desk that had a brand-new iMac computer placed on the corner. She longed to go around and look at it, but didn't dare. She had always wanted one, but settled on a MacBook so she would always be portable. She would be able to go anywhere and work. She ran her hand down the back of the computer, looking at all the details.

"Love that computer," the man said as he entered the room. Everly was so startled, she quickly jerked her hand away and sat back straight in the chair.

"I'm so sorry. I was just looking at it. I've always wanted one, but opted for the laptop. More portable."

"I completely understand. So, you must be Everly Meyers. I'm Eric Salten. It's nice to finally meet you." He was looking at papers in front of him, and Everly could see from where she was sitting that it was her resume and the letter from Lance.

"You come with a very glowing recommendation. Lance is a good friend. Still jealous that he's in Key West and I'm stuck up here. Which brings me to this question: why did you move to New York?"

This was an interview question? Everly thought to herself. If it was, it was an easy one. "I was born and raised in Key West. While I do love it there, I wanted to have an adventure of my own. I've always loved New York City, even if I was only here once as a child. So, when I decided to strike out on my own, New York was my city of choice."

Mr. Salten just continued to stare down at the papers, going from one to another. "Well, my idea of places to go and yours are totally different, but then again, I wasn't raised in those islands. But I sure like visiting them. Lance is always a gracious host every time we go down there. By now, I'm thinking that you don't remember me."

Everly sat there, trying to remember the man sitting in front of her. He looked a bit familiar, but she couldn't remember.

"I'm really sorry, but I don't."

"It's okay, but I do remember you. It was about four years ago. I was at Lance's place for the weekend and we stopped in the office, the one above his wife's art gallery right there on... what's that street name?" Mr. Salten asked.

"Duval Street," Everly answered politely.

"Yeah, the one that's always so busy. Anyway, we got there and you were very eager to show Lance the project you had finished. We both sat there as you went over every detail, then left the office. Lance told me then that no one else had been able to do that project until he had given it to you. He told me that, even though you were young, you were the best. I'm thinking, right about now, he wishes that you were back in Key West."

Everly felt flushed by the compliment. "My friend Abbey did tell me that he was having a bit of a time replacing me, but that shouldn't be hard in the Keys. So many people want to move there."

"I can see why. Don't think I haven't given it a thought or two, but my wife would have a fit. She loves the city life, even on days when we freeze our asses off up here. Anyway, I've looked over your resume and, though you've only worked at one place, it happened to be one of the best in the business. I do have a position open. Basic coding, minimal web design right now. But it would be a start. I could start you off at this salary." He pushed a piece of paper across the desk. "Raises are based on work evaluations that we do every six months. For most companies, it's once a year, but with the way technology changes, we do them more frequently. The only hitch is that I have to know something by five o'clock today. I held the spot open for you, but I have three other applicants that are qualified, just not as much. I also would need you to start tomorrow. We just had a large project come in at the first of the year, and it's going to take a team of about four people. Someone with your experience would be a perfect fit."

Everly stared at the paper. It wasn't the amount she was hoping for, given her new rent, but she did have her savings. Then, she could always do side jobs.

"I have a quick question. I did this even when I worked for Lance, and he was fine with it. I like building websites for small businesses like personal bloggers and solopreneurs. Do you have any rules against that?"

"To tell you the truth, I'm not fond of the idea, but as long as they're not connected to any of the jobs in our system, I would be fine with that. But if they became a conflict of interest, you would have to let it go."

"I understand. It's just, the salary you're offering is a bit lower than I expected, but I don't want to sound greedy." Everly couldn't believe the words had just flowed from her mouth. She was going to lose the job before she could even say yes.

"You're the same as you were four years ago," Mr. Salten said with a laugh. "You spoke your mind then, and I see you still have that trait, but in a charming way. This is what I will do. You work for me one month. If your work is as good as I think, I will give you a five thousand dollar raise on your annual salary."

Everly quickly did the figures in her head and realized that would help with the increase in her rent. "I will let you know in a few hours, but it sounds great." She stood up and extended her hand. "Thank you, Mr. Salten."

"Please, call me Eric. We go by first names around here."

"Then, thanks, Eric. Oh, and one more question. Do you have any office space with a window?"

"Now, you're getting a bit picky. Remember, you'll be the newbie around here, so no windows. If you need a breath of fresh air, you'll have to walk outside on a break."

"Just thought it couldn't hurt to ask. Thanks again."

"Five o'clock," Eric said as she walked out the door.

Once Everly was in the hallway, she felt her whole body relax. She didn't realize how tense every muscle in her body was, and soon, she was back to breathing normally again. So, that was an interview? It wasn't as hard as she imagined. And Eric reminded her just a bit of Lance. But to give him an answer today? What about her interviews tomorrow? What if they offered her more money? This is where she lacked skills because of only working for one person since she had become part of the work force.

Her next interview was on the seventh floor in one hour, and she decided to still go check it out. She felt elated that she technically already had a job, even though she wasn't sure of the pay. Or the office. Or the jobs they did. That was one question she forgot to ask. She wished she could have met some of the other employees. But maybe, that wasn't how this was done.

Everly made her way down to the seventh floor and located the office. It was similar to where she had just come from, but a little smaller. Everly felt confident now, after talking to Eric. Maybe, this would be a better fit for her. And more money, something she could use.

As before, she was called back to a room for an interview, and this one was a bit more polished. From the looks of the pictures on the desk, she thought this could be a woman's office. And she was right.

A woman with long red hair came in and sat down, not acknowledging Everly at all. She sat at the desk, took out papers that Everly immediately recognized as her resume, and began flipping through them.

"Everly Meyers?"

"Yes ma'am."

"I'm Constance Yates. I own this firm and do all the hiring. And firing. I see that you were an employee of Lance Peterson. Nice guy. You have good experience and his reference was a good report of your work. So, why are you here in New York?"

Everly's immediate impression of this woman was that she was cold and unfeeling. She brought her own type of winter into the room. Her whole body was easy to read: unapproachable.

"I was born and raised in Key West, Florida. I had dreamed of moving here since I was a little girl. So, once I was able to, I did. I learned coding and web design at an early age and did very well with it. I worked with Lance for the last eight years, starting with him while I was in my senior year of high school."

"So, he was your only employer?"

"Yes, ma'am. Except, I do side jobs helping small businesses and bloggers set up basic websites that they can maintain on their own."

"Well, here, there are no side jobs, only the work we do. If someone approaches you to do some work, it comes through me. That is, if you are hired."

Ms. Yates read a few more things, and the silence in the room was deafening. Everly wanted to jump up and run out of the room.

They discussed more work-related issues, Ms. Yates asking Everly what she would do in this or that situation. A few times, Everly got flustered, drawing a complete blank for an answer. She knew this was not going well.

"Miss Meyers, though your work seems to be above reproach, I don't think you would be a good fit for our company.

Thank you for applying for the job, and I wish you luck." Ms. Yates stood up and Everly knew she was being dismissed. But she had one more thing to say.

"Ms. Yates – I know that I wasn't the type of person you wanted today, but I don't understand why you asked me such weird questions. I'm one of the best coders around and I can build a website that will make a company shine. I'm not being boastful, just stating facts and reciting compliments I received from many people I have worked with since I was just a teenager. I know you wished me luck and I truly wish the same for you. Thank you for allowing me to apply and letting me know what an interview is truly like."

Everly was upset, but tried to keep her calm. She wanted to tell this lady just what she thought, but that wasn't her. She needed to stay calm and realize that everyone was different. But here, the island vibe she was so used to didn't seem to come with the job territory. So, she turned around, headed out of the office, and into the hall.

Once again, Everly found herself trying to relax all the tense muscles throughout her body, but from frustration this time. She took several deep breaths and saw a bench at the end of the hall. She went and sat down, letting her tote sink down beside her. When she thought about the second interview, Everly was flustered but also couldn't believe that she had told the woman how she felt before leaving her office. Everly usually kept her anger to herself but she couldn't help but respond to Ms. Yates. She was the type of person Everly had dreaded to meet when she moved to New York.

But now, Everly had a big decision to make and she felt confused. When she looked at the clock, she saw that she now only had forty-five minutes to let Eric know what she was going to do.

Everly pulled out her phone and started to dial the familiar number. Lance would be able to give her some guidance. This was his territory. The people he knew. She could rely on him for help.

But she slowly sat the phone on her lap and turned it off. If she was going to live in the city and be independent, then she had to make her own decisions. And live with the consequences. The more she thought of Gold Key Designs, and Eric, she did feel like it was a place she could work and, hopefully, make friends. But she could be giving up money by not taking the interviews tomorrow.

As Everly tried to decide, she could feel the tension and anxiety building up inside her again. She had to decide, and quickly. She picked up her tote bag and phone, then headed to the elevator doors.

"You're back," Eric said, seeing Everly standing in the reception area. "I hope that you have accepted the offer?"

"I have. I will be here tomorrow. What time?"

"We work from eight-thirty 'til five o'clock. We've been known to work over some, especially if we're finishing a big project, but for the most part, we work hard and go home. I'm a big believer in people having a life outside this job. But while they're here, they work."

Just hearing those words from Eric let Everly know that she had made the right choice. He was beginning to sound like Lance, and most certainly not like the woman on the floor below.

"Welcome to the gold mine, Ms. Meyers," Eric said.

"The gold mine?"

"Just a nickname we gave ourselves a while back. You know –

Gold Key, gold mine? Just a play on words. I wonder sometimes if I should have named this place Gold Mine Designs. Sounds like a positive incentive to me," Eric said with a laugh.

"I'll see you tomorrow morning." Everly walked out, feeling happy. She had a job! And on her first interview ever. She couldn't wait to share the news with Drew. *And Blake,* she added quickly.

As she walked to the subway station, she couldn't help but smile. Though it was still cold, the sky above was clear between the stunning skyscrapers that were surrounding her. Good things were happening and everything seemed to be working out for the best. Even riding on the train made her happy, now. She knew to be careful, but right now, she was ecstatic. She was going to work tomorrow morning!

28

"I'm so happy for you," Blake said, picking her up and spinning her in his arms. "That's pretty good, that you nailed your first interview and walked out with a job. And you didn't think you could do it. Sounds like you didn't need any coaching from me."

"Or Drew!"

"When did Drew help you?" Blake asked in a monotonous voice.

"Day before last. I told you, remember? The night you brought me flowers. I will say, you asked tougher questions, so I appreciate that. But anyway – I have a job in New York City! You know everyone at home didn't think I would be able to do this. But I think I'm doing really well," Everly said with a smile. But she noticed a slight difference in Blake's demeanor.

"What's wrong?"

"Nothing, why?"

"I don't know. It seemed like, suddenly, you had this look on your face, like you were upset."

"No. Just didn't know that Drew was over the whole afternoon."

"It wasn't the whole afternoon. He came by to say hi and talk a bit. I showed him my new place, he helped me with a few questions and we talked. Then, you came. What's the problem?" Everly couldn't understand why this would bother him. Blake almost sounded like he was jealous, even a bit mad. But they weren't even in a committed relationship. Everly suddenly felt tiny warning signs flash in her mind.

"There's no problem. I was just asking," Blake said sweetly, and gave her another hug. "I'm really excited for you. I wonder if Donald knows the firm where you will be working?"

"Is he here? I'll go ask him," Everly said, quickly starting to move toward the familiar room. But she hadn't moved hardly an inch before Blake took hold of her arm.

"He has a rule that no one disturbs him when the sign is on the door."

"The sign?"

"Well, it's made of a bunch of Post-It notes, but we know to leave him alone when they're on the door. Means he's working and not to be disturbed. I'll show you."

Sure enough, the door to the room she had once called home had a mash-up of blue, pink, yellow, and green squares taped to the door. Everly just giggled.

"That's probably a good system," Everly said quietly. "I know when I would work on a big project back home, I would sometimes put in ear plugs or a big headset with soft music to be able to work. And everyone knew if they wanted my attention, they had to put a hand on the desk. Though,

Roger was famous for just poking me in the arm and scaring me."

"Roger?" Blake asked warily.

"Roger was my coworker back in Key West. He's a sweetheart and we worked together so well. I'm hoping I find someone like that here. But from what I saw today, I'm not sure. There were so many people, all in cubicles. And they were all men. I'm used to three people, and an open-air office that looked over a tourist street. But I guess I'll find out tomorrow, right?" She wrapped her arms around Blake's neck and gave him a passionate kiss.

The couple made their way back toward the living room, but it was with one kiss after another. Blake's hand traveled up and down Everly's back, then caressed her neck. He kissed her lips, then her ear lobes, sending feelings through her she had never known.

Everly found herself responding to the man that had enveloped her in his arms. She touched his face and slid her hands through his hair. Her senses were reeling. Before she knew it, they were both lying on the sofa, and Blake's hand was traveling down her chest. The sensation felt so good, but anxiety reared up inside her. Everly quickly sat up, almost hitting Blake in the head.

"What's wrong?" Blake asked, panting heavily.

"This is what's wrong. I want to celebrate, but not like this. And not here," Everly said. "Donald could walk in any minute, and so could Drew."

"Then, let's go to your place," Blake said, sliding up to her and kissing her cheek.

"Blake, I think we may have a misunderstanding." Everly turned towards him. "I like you. I really do. You're funny, sweet, and caring. I love being around you, but I'm not ready for *that* just yet. We've only known each other a short time. Like I told you before, I want to get to know you, and I hope you want the same thing. Can't we move just a bit slower?"

"I'm sorry. I really am. I just got caught up in the moment. We were celebrating, right?" Blake laughed, but Everly saw a tinge of disappointment in his eyes.

"Please don't be mad. I really do want to be with you, but I don't want just a physical relationship. I need some more time."

"I guess I need to look up those courting rules, huh?" Blake said.

"I had forgotten about that," Everly laughed.

"I had, too," Blake said, but there was no hint of laughter in his words.

"Listen, I'm going downstairs. I have a few things to do before tomorrow, and I need to make some phone calls. Want to get dinner tonight, since last night, we had company?" Dinner the previous evening had been so much fun with Donald, Drew, and Blake. She had laughed more than she could remember over Donald's jokes, and had decided he reminded her of Roger. He was sweet and knew all the work that she did. They were like kindred spirits. Drew had been nice, but quiet the entire evening. And Blake was just his normal self.

"I'm actually going out with friends tonight. Something we already had planned. But we'll catch up tomorrow, okay? I will want to hear all about your first day on the job."

"Sounds good," Everly said. She gave him a quick kiss on the cheek, waved 'bye,' and headed to her place, downstairs.

She couldn't help but notice Blake's change in body language and tone after she asked that they slow down. Even the way he answered her about plans tonight. The feeling in her gut didn't give her any reassurance. Something wasn't right, but she couldn't figure it out. Or, she was just overthinking things, which, with everything happening, she tended to do.

But for now, she had phone calls to make. And the first one had to be to Drew.

■ ■ ■

Drew looked at the vibrating phone on his desk. He was right in the middle of writing his article, but when he saw who it was, he immediately answered.

"How did the interviews go?" he asked excitedly.

"Wow, how about a 'hello?'" Everly giggled.

"Sorry, just wondering how it all went."

"I have some news, but wanted to see if you want to celebrate with me by having dinner at my place. I want to have pizza again."

"You're going to turn into one giant pizza at the rate you've been eating them," Drew said, smiling to himself.

"I love them. Anyway, can you come?"

"I would love to, but I promised Peyton dinner downtown. But, did I hear the word 'celebrate' in there?"

"Yes, you did," Everly said, "and no one wants to have dinner with me. I got a job!"

"Way to go! What about the interviews tomorrow?"

Everly proceeded to excitedly tell Drew all the details. "I'm getting ready to cancel those. I just hope I made the right decision. It was so hard not to call Lance before I said yes."

"Lance?"

"Remember, my boss in Key West? I like to call him my second dad?"

"That's right. Abbey loves him. Why didn't you?" Drew asked.

"I figured if I'm going to be living on my own, I need to make my own decisions. If I mess up, I'll learn. Or, I might just make the right decision and be okay."

"Love the confidence. You sound like a New Yorker, already."

"What are you talking about? I am a New Yorker, now," she squealed into the phone. "I'll let you go. I know you're busy and I've taken up a lot of your time. But I couldn't wait to tell you."

"Why aren't you celebrating with Blake tonight?" Drew asked tentatively.

"He said he had plans tonight with some friends. But he was happy for me," Everly answered. *Maybe, a bit too happy,* she thought, but didn't say anything to Drew.

"If I get home early enough, I'll stop by. I'll text you to see if you're up."

"That sounds great. Have a nice evening and enjoy your dinner. Tell Peyton I said 'hi.'"

"Will do," Drew said and clicked the phone off.

Yes, I'm hoping for a nice dinner, and no, I'm not telling her you said "hi," Drew thought to himself. He knew, without Peyton saying a word, that she didn't like Everly. He couldn't figure out why, but he would let time take care of that. Hopefully, they would be friends, especially if Drew and Peyton got married. He considered Everly a close friend, and it would be hard if his wife couldn't accept their friendship. But he was getting way ahead of himself. He still hadn't proposed, but he felt it would be soon, for sure.

29

Everly stood in front of the large mirror in the lobby of the building of her new office. She made sure she looked dressed for work. The clothes she had on were so much more different than those she had worn to the office in Key West. Everything had been so relaxed there, but New York was different.

Yesterday, before she left the office, she forgot to see how others were dressed. So, she did her best, searching through her clothes to come up with something appropriate. She had called her parents last night to give them the good news, and asked for their opinion of her attire. Then, she called Abbey again, asking for her advice.

Since Abbey had once worked in a more corporate setting, she helped Everly pick out just the right outfit for today. *Thank goodness for FaceTime calls,* Everly thought.

Everyone she talked to last night had been so excited for her, making Everly promise that she would call today to let them know how the day went. She only hoped that she had nothing but positive notes to share tonight.

She had also had a quick visit from Drew. It was a bit late, but Everly didn't care. Drew was the one person she really wanted to see yesterday, which confused her. Her feelings for Drew seemed to be bouncing back and forth, like a tennis ball in the middle of a game. She desperately wanted to make sense of all the men in her life right now, but there was no time for that. She gave herself one more look in the mirror before heading up to her new place of employment.

This time, when she walked into the office, it was different. Everyone was talking, drinking coffee, and getting ready to start their day. She only saw two women, who were in the back of the room with papers in their hands. She recognized one of them as the receptionist from yesterday. Everly stood there for a moment, feeling like she was frozen, and wanted to bolt back out of the door. But then, a familiar face caught her attention.

"So, you're here- and early, I might add. I like that," Eric said. "Welcome. Let me show you to your desk."

Thanks," Everly replied weakly, clearing her throat. She followed Eric through the maze of men as they made a path for her and Eric. Then, she was at a small little space, where a grey table with drawers sat. It was as long as the cubicle was wide, housing two computer monitors. The keyboard was on the desk, along with a cordless phone. The rolling chair looked a bit worn, but she was sure it would work just fine.

"This is your workspace. No window, but you're welcome to decorate it how you want. Just nothing lewd, political, or religious. Try to keep those things off the table for conversations in the workspace. Find a good family or puppy picture.

Hell, you probably have some beach pictures that would do us all some good." Eric laughed. "Anyway, welcome, Everly. Looking forward to working with you. But now, I think I need to introduce you to the staff. Just remember that you don't have to remember everyone's names at first. Get to know your team. I think you're going to fit in well with them. But, I want to warn you that you'll be working with all men. Do you have a problem with that?"

"No, but should I?" Everly asked with some concern.

"No, but some women that have worked here before did. It's not that I just hire men. I hire the person who is best for the job. And you were the best candidate to fill the opening I had, so I'm glad you said 'yes' yesterday. We have a strict policy, as do most businesses, about any inappropriate behavior, so let me know if anything occurs. But I've seen your work, so don't bruise their egos too badly."

"I'll do my best." Now she was worried about what she had gotten into. Would she be able to work with them? She had no trouble in Florida, but they were like a little family there. She was feeling edgy as she looked at the faces before her.

"Hey, everyone, let me have your attention. We have a new employee. I would like you to meet Everly Meyers, straight from the beautiful islands of the Florida Keys. Actually, you're from Key West, right?" Eric asked, looking over at her.

"Yes." That was the only word she could say because her mouth had suddenly become dry.

"Please welcome Everly. I told her that she could come to any of you if she had a question, just like you did when you first started working here. So, let's get to work." Eric walked to her. "Now, yesterday, we didn't get this far when we talked, but we work in teams of four or five here. When a project comes in, the people of each team are divided up between who would be better at the task. This helps us produce a website faster, and good sites, at that. On your computer, you'll have all the necessary software and login information to be able to work on different platforms. I like to provide two monitors for each computer. That way, you have more to work with when putting these, what I call 'puzzle pieces,' together to make the site run smoothly.

"We also like to name the teams around here, and you're with team Alpha. These guys have been here the longest, but you shouldn't have any problem. Your background makes you a great fit with them, even if they think they know more than you. If you have any problem, like I said earlier, just come to me." Eric motioned for her to follow him to the space right next to hers.

"Everly, I would like you to meet Jones." Eric introduced her to a tall African American man who had one of the friendliest smiles. "Jones is my only employee that actually started with me over twenty years ago, when websites were babies. Jones, Everly."

"Nice to meet you. Eric let me read your resume, and I have to say, it's impressive. I have to ask, and I mean no disrespect, but were you a nerd in school, like me?" Jones smiled.

The ice had been broken and Everly felt relieved. "Definitely. I'm still considered the nerd amongst my friends back in the Keys. Hoping to make a better impression here, in New York."

"Welcome. You're just in time. We have a big project that's getting the best of some of us, and we could use some fresh eyes on it. Let me go get Danny and Trey. Be right back."

As Jones walked off, Eric turned to Everly. "You know where to find me. Take today to settle in, get your passwords from Jones, and ask any questions. Okay?"

"Sounds great. Thanks, Mr. Salten."

"We go by first names around here, remember? Call me Eric."

"Thanks, Eric."

Just as Eric walked away, Jones came back with two men at his side. They looked like they couldn't be much older than her, but had clearly worked here for a while. This was the oldest working team in the office.

"This is Trey," Jones said, nodding his head toward a gorgeous dark-haired man with ice-blue eyes, who just seemed to glower at Everly. "And this is Danny." This time Jones motioned to a man who was a little shorter than the other two, and a bit heavier. But he had a happy smile on his face and immediately shook Everly's hand.

"Let's all go to the conference room and catch Everly up to speed on this project. Let's see what we can do about this hiccup." They all started walking quickly, leaving Everly just enough time to stash her tote under her desk, grab her iPad, and follow them.

They went into a workroom filled with large white boards. Each board was labeled with a team name, and now, Everly saw where they did their brainstorming. This was familiar to her place back home.

"Everly, this is Project Pain. We are putting together a website for a large manufacturing plant. They had a website that was lacking, and came to us to completely revamp the site. We need to make it more user-friendly and to attract more customers to their products. They also want to develop customer forums for people to be able to help each other."

"It's been a rather big project, because the previous website was useless. But just when we get something fixed, they want to make a change or suddenly something goes awry with the coding. Eric wants us to finish it and hand it off to their in-house web team that'll be handling daily maintenance. We were hoping to do that before Christmas, but that was a joke. Now, our goal is the end of January. And here are the problems."

Everly listened and took notes, just like she had at home. It was a mess. As she looked at the list of problems, she didn't know what she would be able to do without looking at the site.

"Today, just look around the site. See if you see something we might have missed."

Everly heard a snicker and looked over at the man named Trey. He sneered at her like there was no way she could be smart enough to even be in the same room as they were.

"I can't wait."

Since she couldn't write down the problems fast enough, she took pictures with her iPad of the problems listed on the board and hurried back to her desk. She noticed that all four of their desk spaces were right in a row, which would make it easier for them to work together. But if she had her way, the four of them would have no walls separating them, so they could work together better as a team. But there was no way she was mentioning that today.

Everly looked at the list from the photos she had taken and, using the passwords and information that Jones gave her, quickly signed into the computer and started checking things. It felt good to be back at work, though she really thought that it would be longer before a job would pan out.

"You aren't going to be able to figure it out." There was a voice behind her and Everly knew without looking who it was. She turned around to see Trey propped against her cubicle wall. "Me, Danny, and Jones are the best in this office, and we can't even figure out the problem. At least, not yet. So, don't try to be some hero that comes marching in with your tight pants and sexy shirts. That doesn't work around here." He shook his head and walked off.

Everly had been here less than two hours and she already had some guy thinking that she was no good? What about giving someone a chance? She didn't know what to say or think. This was her first day and she was going to do what she could. If the problem couldn't be solved, there was usually a workaround. She had done that so many times. And tight pants and sexy shirts? She wasn't dressed that way. She had on nice dress pants, a button-up shirt, and a cardigan over it because her body still wasn't use to the cold, icy New York weather. She didn't know what Trey's problem was, but she would steer clear of him the best she could, even though they were supposed to be working together.

By lunch, she had looked at each problem that had been on the list. But now, she just needed a break. "Jones," Everly said as she approached his desk. "How does lunchtime work around here? Or breaks, for that matter?"

"We usually take lunch from twelve to twelve-thirty. Most of us eat at our desks because it's not enough time to go anywhere. Did you bring something to eat?"

"I did because I wasn't sure what was around here to eat."

"Haven't been here long, have you?"

"That obvious?"

"So you are a newbie New Yorker," Jones said with a smile. "There are plenty of little places, but really, it's just best to bring your own. Save yourself some money. But I have to admit, I sneak out every now and then just to get some fresh air. But with the weather today, I'm staying inside. Not sure why you left sunny tropical islands, but I hope you're having fun so far."

"It's been an experience, but I'm happy. I've met some interesting people. I'm a bit shocked that I got a job so quickly. Still trying to take it all in."

"New York is a fabulous city, but honestly, it isn't for everyone. I hope you're finding what you wanted, and I sure am glad to have you on my team. But let's keep that between you and me, okay? Don't want to damage some egos, if you know what I mean."

"No problem there. But I've looked at the problems. After lunch, I think I might be able to take care of one. What should I do?"

"Go in there and fix it, girl. That's what you're getting paid for. Just let me know what you're working on before you start, okay?"

"Thanks, Jones."

"You're welcome."

Everly looked around and saw that everyone was sitting in groups or paired up as they ate lunch. She suddenly felt all alone, but decided to read on her iPad as she ate the salad and sandwich she had brought from home. She wasn't sure about bringing her lunch at first. Those around her might think she was weird, but she felt glad that she made the right decision.

Thirty minutes came and went so fast that she hardly had time to finish eating. This was very different from Key West. They took one-hour lunches and didn't rush. Lance only told them that the work had to be done and by what date, and they worked together to get it done. They had been like a well-oiled machine, especially when Abbey came to work with them.

Everly let Jones know of the problem and began to work. Within three hours, the situation was solved and she showed Jones what she did.

"Well, I'll be damned," Jones said. "We should have thought of that. It was so easy. Well, not the coding, but the answer. Good job. At least, we can take that off the list."

"Going to look at something else, now," Everly said as she turned back to the computer monitors illuminating her small area.

"You go right ahead. Just keep me in the loop."

"Will do."

Everly loved it. Solving these problems was like candy to her, even if it could be frustrating. She seemed to get lost in the computer screen. She knew she should probably socialize a bit, but being back at work almost felt like her normal routine. What she used to do in Key West.

"See you were able to fix the issue. I say it's beginner's luck. Plus, you chose the simplest thing on that list. Trying to earn brownie points on your first day here?" Trey was standing at her cubicle with a smug look on his face.

"Honestly, I was only trying to help and be part of the team." Everly didn't know what else to say to this man, who clearly felt his territory invaded by some stranger. She hadn't even talked to Trey for him to have already formed an opinion of her, good or bad. *What is his problem?* she thought.

Trey gave her a stony look and walked away. Everly took a deep breath and looked at her phone. It was five o'clock. That's why she heard the chatter of voices. People were getting ready to go home. She had become so engrossed in her work that she had lost track of time.

"Nice work today." This time is was the friendly voice of her new boss behind her as she packed her tote.

"Thank you."

"Was your first day okay?"

"It was great. It feels good to be working again," Everly said, not daring to tell Eric the truth of how she felt upset about Trey. It was only her first day, and there was no way she was going there.

"See you tomorrow, Key West girl." He turned to walk away.

So, she was the "Key West girl?" A new nickname, and one she would accept. Everly loved her hometown, and by earning a nickname today, she felt like she might just belong to this new group of co-workers.

30

Between the cold weather, the subway trip home, the walk to her building, and her first day on the job, Everly was tired. *But it's a good kind of tired,* she told herself.

She let herself into the apartment and saw a huge note on the refrigerator from Shari. She wouldn't be home tonight, and that was fine with Everly. At this point, she only wanted to take a shower, have a bit of dinner, and go to bed. Maybe, read a little, if she could keep her eyes open.

As she sat her stuff down in her room, Everly heard the knock on the door. She knew it could only be Drew or Blake and she walked lazily to the door. As she peeped through the tiny hole, she was shocked to see Donald standing on the other side.

"Hey, Donald. Come in."

"Saw you out the window a while ago, and wanted to come and see how your first day went."

"How did you know I went to work today?" she asked quizzically.

"Drew told me last night, when he got home."

"Thought you might have talked to Blake."

"No, I never saw him last night. He didn't come home. So, how did it go? The reason I ask is that I used to work for Eric."

Everly needed to answer Donald's question, but she was stuck on the fact that Blake never came home.

"Everly?"

"Oh, I'm sorry. Just a bit tired. Not used to this cold weather or the cramped subway cars. As far as walking, I should be used to that, since I rode a bike everywhere at home, but the cold weather is wearing me out," she said.

"So, how was it?" Donald asked insistently.

"I liked it. As a matter of fact, I was able to solve one of the small problems on a website that the guys were having a hard time with."

"Good for you!" Donald said with a huge smile.

"Donald, can I ask you a question? Why are you not working with them anymore?"

Donald's face wasn't as animated anymore, and Everly thought that she might have just brought a bad memory to the surface.

"I helped Eric start that firm. I mean, he brought me on board when he was only a few months into business. He was floundering, to say the least, but between me and one other person, we had that business profitable in about three years, which is pretty damn good in New York City. Eric started hiring all these young kids out of school. He knew he could pay them less and get more work out of them. So, eventually, I just left. I didn't like having to babysit all these kids that thought they knew more than me. That's when I started working on my own."

"Well, I can certainly understand that. My first day and I already had some guy give me a hard time about my work. And, he made a sexist remark about my clothes."

"Did you tell Eric? He'll fix that fast."

"No, I didn't want to say anything just yet. It was only my first day. I will if it keeps up."

"Glad you found a good firm, but if you're as good as Drew says you are, you might just want to work on your own. There's plenty of business out there," Donald said.

"I do some small stuff on the side, but right now, I just want to make sure I have a steady paycheck." Everly smiled at him.

"I understand," Donald replied.

"So, can I ask you a question?" Everly said quickly.

"Sure. Need some technical advice?"

"No, not quite. It's about Blake. You said he didn't come home last night."

"Yeah, he does that, sometimes. He'll leave for days. He just seems to be in and out. Drew, on the other hand, is steady, unless Peyton insists on him staying over at her place. As for me, I'm a slave to my work. But I love it. I have a feeling you like what you do, too."

"I do." Everly didn't want to talk about work. She wanted to find out more about Blake.

The knock at the door took her attention away from the questions swirling in her head. She peeped through the door to see Blake standing on the other side. A broad smile graced her face.

"Hi, there," Everly said as she opened the door. "We were just talking about you."

"Who's 'we?'"

"Me, that's who." Donald stood up and walked toward the door. "I came to see how Everly's first day was at Eric's place."

"Is that where you're working? Gold Key Designs?" Blake asked.

"Wow, it seems everyone knows this place better than I do. I told you yesterday."

"No, you didn't."

"Then, it must have been Drew I told last night."

"You saw Drew last night?"

"Wow, you sure are full of questions." Everly quickly noticed the strained face Blake was wearing.

"I'm sorry. Just been a long day."

"Well, I'm outta here," Donald said. "Everly, if you ever need anything, let me know. I might like to get with you to see if you want to make some money on the side. I could use some help on certain projects. And Drew told me that you are really good at your job."

"We'll certainly get together and talk. Thanks for checking on me." She gave the man a hug that took him by surprise.

She shut the door behind her and turned to Blake. "So, how has your day been?" She really wanted to ask where he had spent the night, but that wasn't her business. They might have shared some kisses and a few great dates, but they had never said they were exclusive.

"Quite busy, actually, but I came here to see how your day went. I thought that maybe we could have pizza."

Everly laughed. "I just had pizza last night. Even though I could probably eat it every day, I'm not feeling it tonight. I had planned to take a shower, grab a sandwich, and go to bed."

"I think that plan sounds awfully nice." Blake walked up to Everly and wrapped his arms around her waist. She felt the pull to be with him, to kiss him, but there was also something that wanted to pull away. But, before she knew it, she was locked in an embrace that was sending her senses reeling once more. Blake's slow kisses, so deep and sensual, sent feelings through her that she had never experienced before.

His hands began exploring parts of her body and she closed her eyes, lost in the sensation. But when his hands traveled to places that were off limits, as far as she was concerned, it was as if an alarm went off in her head.

"I'm sorry," Blake said quickly. "I just get a little carried away with you. There's something about you, Everly, that just has me mesmerized."

What was wrong with her? Was it bad to get lost in the physical pleasure of someone she liked? There was the word that stung her. *Liked.*

When she had sex for the first time, it was going to be with someone she loved. Not liked. But was she falling in love with Blake? She wanted to be with him. He made her laugh. He seemed to care. He checked on her. He seemed to be doing all the right things. And her body did respond to his touch. What was holding her back?

"That's a nice compliment," Everly responded as she slowly disentangled herself from Blake. "But I'm tired after today. Work was stressful, as any first day would be, I'm sure. I had to put up with a guy that feels threatened by me, even though he doesn't know me. All I did was fix a problem they had been working on for a few weeks."

"Ouch! You became a hero on your first day," Blake said as he made himself at home on her couch. "Might need to watch yourself, there."

"What do you mean?" I was just doing my job."

"Yeah, but you're the new girl. It might look as though you're showing off, and you don't want that."

"So, I'm supposed to sit back and just let something go by that I know I can do? That's crazy."

"No, that's called playing by the corporate rules. You've always worked for a small business. Here, it's different. Sometimes, it's like a game. Make this person happy and you get to move this way. Then, you make that person happy and you get to move this way." Blake was gesturing with his hands like someone moving up a ladder.

"But I was just doing my job. I'm not going to hold back just because some guy can't stand for a woman to show that she has brains."

"Whoa, I didn't mean to upset you! I was just trying to tell you how some places work. That's all."

"Sorry, I didn't mean to say it like that. I'm just a bit frustrated. And tired."

Blake scooted over to sit beside her, wrapping her in his arms. "I have to go out of town for the next couple of days. So, let's make plans to go out this Saturday. We'll go somewhere near Central Park and, if the weather cooperates, we'll take a carriage ride. We can take some blankets. If there's snow on the ground, it'll be beautiful. Just like you."

"I think that sounds perfect." She got up slowly, taking his hand and tugging him to the door.

"Are you sure you want me to leave?" Blake leaned on the door, looking sexy as ever.

"No, but I think it's best. I'll see you Saturday. Enjoy your trip."

"It's just a school thing." Blake gave her one more deep kiss before walking toward the elevator. "Can't wait 'til Saturday."

Everly closed the door and felt like every muscle was in desperate need of rest. It had to be from the tension from her day. She needed to just rest. But, as she went to take a bath, another knock came on the door. She walked quietly to peer once more through the tiny hole in the door, and saw Drew standing there. She immediately wanted to open the door, but hesitated. She couldn't do this to herself. She had to let him go. If she let him in tonight, they would stay up talking, which only made her confused feelings even worse. So, she had to take a stand.

Everly watched as he knocked once more, then headed toward the elevator. *This was best,* she told herself. If she could only keep this up for a while, maybe she would be able to figure out what she was feeling for these two men in her life. But for now, Everly just hoped the hot shower she was looking forward to would help her to relax and sleep.

31

It seemed like the next few days were a blur, but she could see a routine developing in her new life. Everly was quiet each morning so she didn't wake Shari, if she happened to be home. Then, she would get dressed, make lunch, and be out the door. The short subway ride and walk felt good, even with the cold weather that she still wasn't used to. At work, she had solved another crisis and garnered more hateful stares from Trey, but she didn't care. Eric and Jones were happy with her work, and she was enjoying what she did.

In the evenings, Drew had come by again, but she didn't answer the door. Everly did text him during the day to say "hi" and apologize that they hadn't had time to spend together, but she just didn't want to see him right now. Well, she did, but hoped that by not seeing him, she would know how to trust her heart.

But when she woke on Saturday, she felt energized. Blake would be home today. Shari was gone for the weekend and London was still in Europe. She had a whole weekend to herself, though she didn't know if Drew would want to come by or not. But she was concentrating on her afternoon and evening with Blake.

She went to the little diner down the street for coffee and a bagel. She sat with her iPad, reading for a while, then walked back home. She received a text from Blake that he was home and that he would pick her up at four o'clock. So, as soon as Everly got home, she took a leisurely bath and got ready for her special date. She had yet to see Central Park and couldn't wait to share it with him.

Just as she was putting on her earrings, the phone rang. Everly smiled. "Well, hello there," she said.

"Hi, there, yourself," Blake said in a sexy voice. "Are you ready for a magical evening?"

"Yes, I am," Everly, answered back softly.

"I'll be there in five minutes."

Eagerly, she got her coat, gloves, and her tote bag with her two blankets, and was at the door when she heard the knock.

"Wow, you look beautiful," Blake said, staring at her. Everly had chosen her outfit carefully, wanting to look her best, but knowing that it was going to be cold outside.

"So, dressy jeans are okay? You didn't tell me where we're going."

"We're going for Italian. Sant Andrea Café, since you have an intense desire for Italian food."

"Just because I love pizza?"

"Did I guess right?"

"Yes, you did."

"Well, your taxi awaits you downstairs."

"No subway or walking? Wow," Everly said.

"Tonight is our first date."

"We've already been out several times, and even made breakfast together." Everly laughed.

"Nope, this is our first *official* date. Those other times were friend dates."

"So, there's a difference? You'll have to explain yourself when we get to the restaurant," Everly said with a smile.

"My pleasure," Blake said as he slid into the taxi beside her.

The little Italian restaurant that Blake took her to was right by Central Park. She could see it right across the street, and even saw a few carriages pass by.

"This is beautiful." Everly felt as though she was in one of her dreams that she had imagined when she thought about living in New York. The park across the street, still lined with snow, was beautiful even as dusk approached. The little restaurant was romantic and the aroma coming from the kitchen smelled delicious. And to top off everything, the handsome man sitting across from her was treating her like a princess.

"I thought you would like this place. It's one of my favorites. They say it has the best pizza around, but I'm sure you probably want to try something else by now," Blake said.

"Definitely! It seems like I've lived on pizza lately, even though I have to admit, it's been very good. So, what do you suggest?" asked Everly.

"For me, it's anything with pasta. I'm having Chicken Parmesan. It's delicious."

"Then, I think I'll have the Fettuccine Alfredo. I do have to say that everything on the menu looks and sounds absolutely delicious," Everly said.

"And so do you," Blake said.

"Thank you sir. You certainly have a way with words," Everly said. She sat there looking at the man sitting across from her. Tonight, he looked sexier than she had ever seen before. And the way he was looking back at her, she could see a hunger in his eyes.

If this was their first official date, could this be the beginning of a relationship? Everly thought. The thought made her nervous, given how she had been hurt before in the past, but she could only hope that things would be better this time. But, there was still that nagging feeling in the back of her head. That feeling about Drew that she just couldn't shake.

It didn't seem like much time had passed before they were eating two delicious plates of wonderful food. They barely talked as they ate, but were still able to share a few tidbits of their life. Everly asked Blake more about his childhood, and he was more open and shared happier memories than last time they discussed it. Everly shared with him more about her life in Key West. And talking about her hometown brought back a little longing for the island life. But overall, New York was turning out to be everything that she planned.

"That food was wonderful!" Everly marveled as Blake helped her with her coat.

"Now, it's time for that carriage ride. It's only about a block away. Do you think you can walk that far in this cold weather?" Blake asked.

"No problem. In fact, it will help me burn some of the calories that I just devoured. I feel completely stuffed, but in a wonderful way," Everly said with a smile on her face. She took Blake's hand and they began walking down the sidewalk.

It wasn't long before they were in front of a beautiful carriage with a stunning horse at the front. Everly wanted to go and pet it, but wasn't sure of the protocol. Blake paid for their carriage ride, and soon, they were sitting side by side, covered in the blankets that Everly had brought with her. Yes, the weather was cold, but the wind was not blowing. As the carriage made its way around Central Park, she couldn't get over the beautiful lights of the city. Everything around them seemed to twinkle. Everly then imagined what the park must look like during the Spring. She couldn't wait 'til she could come here and just lay on a blanket on the grass in the middle of the city.

"Are you warm enough?" Blake moved a bit closer to her, if that was possible, in the carriage seat.

"Most definitely," Everly said as she snuggled against Blake. Before she knew it, Blake leaned over and kissed her on the lips. First, it was soft and gentle, and then turned into a deep, passionate kiss. It felt as though time and space stood still for her. She was still confused about the feelings that she had for Blake. But he was here, now, and was proving to be the gentleman that she had always dreamed of. The combination of the carriage ride, warm blankets, and sensual kisses from Blake made for one of the most romantic dates she had ever experienced.

"That was wonderful," Everly said as they both exited the carriage. She watched the horse as Blake tipped the driver. This time, she reached out and petted the animal. The horse was sweet and gentle, and Everly just smiled.

Then, she backed away and looked up into the night sky around her. The lights of the city were magical, and the man that came to stand beside her was handsome and loving. At that moment, Everly was sure that Blake was stealing her heart.

They found a taxi close by and they scooted in close together, Blake wrapping his arm around Everly's shoulders. The ride back to the apartment was quiet, neither one of them saying a word. They sat as close as they could, stealing a kiss every now and then. Everly still watched out the windows as they drove by the lights of the stores. There was so much more of the city she wanted to explore, and she couldn't wait. Especially when the weather got warmer, she knew she would be a little bit of everywhere. Hopefully, Blake would be by her side.

She unlocked the door to her apartment and they both stumbled in. They took off coats, scarves, sweaters, and hats. Then, she found she still had her gloves on and laughed. "One day, I'll get used to having all of this clothing on. It's still an adjustment for me, because I'm still used to tank tops, shorts, and flip-flops." Everly laughed again.

"I would love to see you wearing that," Blake said. He had already told her how he would love to see her in her own hometown. And in her bathing suit.

"Yes, you've already told me that," Everly responded as she took off the gloves and set them on the counter. "So, now, what would you like to do?" Everly knew it was a loaded question and wasn't sure what would happen next.

Blake slowly walked up to her, cupped his hands around her face, and began a slow exploration of her face with his lips. He started on her forehead, then worked his way down to her nose. She kept her eyes closed the entire time, just feeling the sensations. He kissed each eyelid, and then each earlobe. Then, finally, Blake made his way to her lips.

Everly was lost in the moment. She felt totally consumed by feelings she had never experienced before. It was as if she couldn't think. She was just reacting with her physical being.

Before she knew what was happening, Everly found herself and Blake in her bedroom. She leaned up against the wall, and Blake took off his shirt. She watched him, mesmerized, ignoring the small warning signs that were flashing in her mind.

This was normal, right? She tried to think. Then, Blake slowly looked at her and gently helped her pull her sweater over her head. Everly's head told her to "stop," but her heart was saying "yes" with each touch of Blake's hands. Everly felt almost helpless.

"Are you sure Everly?" Blake asked in a husky voice in her ear.

"I think so," she said as she looked down to see Blake now unbuttoning her shirt. Everly's heart was pounding so hard that she was sure that Blake could feel it beating in her chest.

He lifted her up and placed her on the small bed in her room. Everly was nervous and wanting at the same time, but there was a sensation in her head that gave her pause. But she pushed it away and gave into the feelings that were surrounding her.

■ ■ ■

Everly laid awake and listened to the sound of a soft, light snore in her ear. She felt confused and wondered what had happened. How did she lose her composure? Something that she had dreamed about since she was a teenager had not been anything like what she imagined. She had given into an urge, and now, was lying beside the man, regretting everything that had happened. She liked Blake so much, but she had always promised that she would give herself to someone she loved. And she couldn't say she loved Blake.

She wanted to cry, wanted to talk to someone, but had no one to talk to. Except Drew, and there was no way she would tell him about this. But one thing was for sure: she needed some time alone, to figure out what she was feeling. She could feel the tears welling up inside and she didn't want him to see her cry.

"Hi, there." Blake was now awake and he slowly propped himself up on one hand. "That was wonderful. You are so beautiful, Everly." He dipped his head to hers for another kiss, and his free hand wandered to her abdomen.

"Blake, please don't take this wrong, but would you mind if we call it a night?"

"What's wrong?"

"I just need some time to myself. I'm sorry, but this wasn't supposed to happen. I wasn't ready for this."

"But it was perfect. You were perfect," he said, kissing her hand.

"It shouldn't have happened. We've only just begun dating. You even said this was our first official date."

"But it's been weeks, now."

"Blake, please. Can we talk tomorrow?"

Blake rolled to his back and got out of bed. He quickly got dressed, not saying a word, and Everly looked the other way.

"I'm not sorry it happened, Everly. I really care for you, and it was special."

"Blake, I'm looking for love. And this was meant to be for that man I loved. I thought there was a possibility between us."

"You mean, falling in love? I never promised anything like that."

"But the way you acted toward me. Remember the whole 'courting' thing? Were you just playing with my emotions? Was all of this just for sex?"

"No, it wasn't. But I never said I love you. I never tell a girl that."

Everly felt like she had been slapped in the face. "How many girls?"

"It's not like that. Come on, Everly. You know I like you. We've had a blast being together and going places since you got here. But I'm not a 'fall in love' guy. Maybe one day, and maybe with you, but not right now."

Everly felt as though she would be sick to her stomach. "Please go, Blake. We'll talk tomorrow."

"It'll have to be Wednesday because I'm going out of town tomorrow. Everly," Blake said as he sat on the edge of her bed, "it really was nice. I think you're a great girl."

"Just go, Blake. Just go," Everly said softly, without even getting out of bed. She laid there as she heard him walk into the living room, get his stuff, and then close the door as he left. Only then, did she let the tears fall.

Suddenly, she found herself sobbing, curled up in a ball on her bed. Why had this happened? Why had she allowed it? She suddenly felt so alone, and so dirty. And she had no one to talk to in this big city. This was the place to make her dreams come true, but slowly, things were not what Everly had imagined. For the first time since she stepped foot in New York, she wondered if she had made a mistake by moving to the city.

32

It was already noon on Sunday, and Everly still did not want to get out of bed. She had gotten some breakfast and then quickly crawled back under the covers, trying to hide from the world around her. The phone on the nightstand had rung several times, and she didn't even look to see who was calling. She didn't want to talk to anyone, except one person, and she knew that she couldn't talk about something so personal with him.

The knock on the door to her apartment made her sit up straight. Everly decided that she would just let whoever it was go away. But whoever was on the other side of the door was persistent. Everly finally decided that they were determined to talk to her. She put on her robe and slippers and headed to the front door. Through the little peep hole, she saw Drew standing on the other side.

"Hi, there!" Everly said, trying her best to sound as upbeat as possible. "I think I might have a cold, so I'm not going to open the door. But I'll give you a call later, okay?" She leaned against the front door, hoping he would go away.

"I don't care about catching some cold. Come on, open the door. I want to talk to you for a minute."

It was no use. Everly knew he would stay there, so she slowly opened the door. By the look on Drew's face, she knew that she must look a mess.

"Oh, you do look like you don't feel good," Drew said the minute he saw her. Her eyes were swollen, she had tissues in her hand, and was still dressed in pajamas and a bathrobe. Since the first time he met Everly, he had never seen her like this.

"Do you have a fever?" He quickly put his hand up to her forehead, which felt fine. "Do you have any cold medicine you can take? If not, I'll run down to the store and get you something. Hopefully, it'll make you feel better."

"It's nothing, really," Everly said. "I'll be better in the morning, for sure. Just feel like I need to rest today. So, how has your weekend been?" She was glad he was here. He brought a comforting presence she so desperately needed right now. She only wished she could talk to him about last night. About her confused feelings because she suddenly knew she wished it had been him last night instead of Blake.

"The usual. Time with Peyton. You'll be proud of me. I've set the date for a proposal. Valentine's Day. I'm going to talk to her Dad, and then have a romantic dinner. And, if it's not too cold, take her on a carriage ride at Central Park and pop the question."

Thoughts of the evening Everly just had hit her like a huge wave, and the tears began to fall. She couldn't stop them and she didn't want to.

"What's wrong?"

"I'm not feeling well. I'm sorry for being such a crybaby."

"I'll be right back. I'm sure we have some cold medicine upstairs."

"Drew, I don't need any medicine. I just want to go back to bed, okay?"

"Are you sure?"

"I promise. But congratulations. Peyton is a lucky girl to have you as a husband. And I'm lucky to have you as my best friend," Everly said and gave him a hug.

"I don't like leaving you like this."

"Drew, get out of here. I'm okay. Just being a big baby right now, but I need to rest so I'll be able to go to work tomorrow."

"Well, tomorrow night, it's dinner at my place. I'll see if Blake and Donald want to join us. I'm going to cook. I finished one of my big assignments and I'm celebrating. When I lived at home, my Mom taught me how to make chicken pot pie. Does that sound good to you?"

"Sounds perfect. But you don't have to worry about Blake. He told me yesterday he's going away for a few days."

"So, you guys had a date, huh?" Drew asked, trying to be excited for her, but something inside of him wouldn't let him do it.

"We had a nice time."

"Well, I'll let you go, but if you need anything – anything – you just call, okay?"

"Drew, I promise."

Everly closed the door and the tears came once more. Now, her best friend, the guy she now knew she was in love with, was going to get married. To a woman that didn't let him be his true self. She could only hope he was marrying her for the right reasons. As for Everly, she had said it before, but now, she meant it more than ever. There would be no relationships for her. She needed time for herself, and after what happened last night, she had to make sense of it. She had wanted it to happen, but then, she didn't. She felt so guilty for giving in to a sensation that was so new to her. She felt like her body had betrayed her.

She laid back in bed and shut her eyes, hoping to go to sleep so she could forget about her problems for a while. But sleep eluded her, and all she could do was lay and cry.

■ ■ ■

As the alarm on her phone sounded, Everly sat on the edge of the bed. Even though she wasn't fully rested, she got up, got dressed, and headed for work. She knew that she was only running on adrenaline, at this point. Her mind still replaying the events of Saturday night with Blake and her epiphany about her true feelings for Drew yesterday.

As Everly entered the building to go to work, she looked in the same mirror that she had looked in all last week. She had dark circles under her eyes that she had tried to cover with concealer. It helped, but it didn't do the job completely. She forced herself to smile, but she could see the sadness that was lying there. She only hoped her coworkers wouldn't see it. She was looking forward to getting lost in her work, to try to forget about what happened.

Everly was quickly at her desk and going over notes from last week. Eric called a staff meeting and she sat in the back, away from everyone. He went over generalized items that were part of every type of company meeting, and it reminded her of some of the ones that she had attended while working with Lance in Key West.

At the thought of the Keys, for the first time since she moved to New York, she felt like she wanted to go back home. Some things were what she had always imagined, but others weren't. But she couldn't give up this easily. It had only been almost a month but she was already thinking of going back home. That made her feel like such a failure.

"So, everyone knows our projects for the week?" A unison of voices answered "yes," and everyone went back to their desks. Everly looked at the list of items that still needed to be repaired on the website they were currently working on. She wanted to make sure that she was on track with Jones, Trey, and Danny before she went any further. She knew there were two other items that she could fix very easily, but after what happened last week and Trey's remarks, she didn't want to rock the boat or cause any more stress than what she was already feeling.

"Everly, let's go into the conference room and go over these items again," Jones said as he headed toward the room, once again Trey and Danny following close behind. She picked up her iPad and followed, reaching the room just as everyone sat down.

"So, here's where we stand. We still have four major issues that need to be fixed with this website. Thanks to Everly,"

Jones said, pointing in Everly's direction, "one of the most pressing items is taken care of. Now, who wants to tackle which problems on this list? Eric wants this website to be finished this week."

"Well, since Everly worked her magic last week, why doesn't she just take the whole list?" Trey said, looking at her with his dark, hooded eyes.

"Trey, I don't know what your problem is, but I will not be treated like this. All I did was my job, and I fixed a very simple problem that you should have been able to do very easily," Everly said, anger rising up inside of her. She took a deep breath and sat back down. She could be upset over what had happened this past weekend, but she had to hold it together at work.

"Wow, little Miss Princess has a temper," Trey remarked, looking over at her. "Honestly, I don't know how you did it last week, and it was probably just a fluke that you got it right. But I think you should be given the responsibility to fix the rest of the website, since you seem to have the magic touch."

"Trey, that's enough!" Jones suddenly took control of the situation. "I'm the team manager, and what I say goes. Since everyone is not picking an issue to work on, I will make the assignments. And whatever you do and whomever you have to ask to help you, do it. Eric just told me that this is one of the most important websites, and if we don't get it fixed, he'll find people that will. In other words, we could lose our jobs. Is that enough for you to leave this bickering behind you? Everly has done nothing wrong and has only been here a few days. So,

Trey, whatever your problem is, straighten up your act now or you can get the hell out of this office."

Everly looked over at Trey and could see the redness in his face. She knew she had done nothing wrong, but for some reason, this man did not like her. The only reason she could think of was because she solved something that he couldn't.

"Jones, I'll take problems number one and two. That leaves only two problems left. I think that I can have them finished by the end of tomorrow. If not, I should be finished by Wednesday. Will that be sufficient?"

"Everly, do you really want to tackle two problems right now? You're still new to this project, and I don't want you to overburden yourself. Believe me, there'll be other projects in the future where you'll wish you could run away for a while."

"Yeah, let's see if she can do it. She did it last week, so she should be able to do the same thing this time." Trey kept taunting her, even though Jones had told him to shut up.

"I'm warning you, Trey. Knock it off. Danny, you have problem number three. Trey, you have problem number four. I'll look at the overall site. Like I said, if you need help, find it, but get this project finished now."

As they all filed out of the room, Trey was behind Everly and he whispered, "You think you're such a hotshot, but you're nothing here. Look around you, little girl. Men run the show around here, and we know how to get things done. Not you."

Everly couldn't believe the words that she had just heard. Just because she was a girl, she wasn't good enough to do this job? She had been coding and working on websites since she was fourteen years old, and no man was about to tell her that she wasn't good enough. She would solve these problems and they would get finished before the time she predicted. She would prove to them that she could do it and nobody was going to take that away from her.

Everly went to her desk and immediately started to work. She pulled up the website and started searching for ways to fix the issues. After a few hours, she found what she was looking for. She found the key that would completely fix the website, and not only the problems that she had promised to solve, but for the entire website. She didn't know whether to tell Jones or to let each person work on what they had been assigned. If she fixed it all, it would look like she was showing off, but at the same time, her anger had gotten the best of her after Trey's remarks.

So, she set off to work. She ate lunch at her desk, with both screens on her desk lit up like Christmas trees, checking each line one by one to make sure that her hunches were correct. By the end of the day, she had fixed problem number one. Tomorrow, she would be able to resolve problem number two.

"So, how are you coming?" Trey's voice was now like fingernails on a chalkboard. Everly looked at him, ignoring his question and began walking out of the office. Was he trying to be nice to her, or was he going to say something hateful again?

"I'm doing fine. How are you coming with yours?" Everly asked as she walked toward the elevator doors.

"I guess you'll find out in a few days, huh?" Trey said as they both entered the elevator, along with most of their coworkers. There was silence in the elevator, as everyone only stared straight ahead at the closed doors.

As Everly stood there amongst the crowd in the elevator, she looked around and suddenly felt like she didn't belong. These people were not a part of the world she wanted to belong to. This wasn't what she signed up for when she came to New York. When she dreamed of moving here, the picture she had held for so long wasn't what she was experiencing now. Had she put New York up on a pedestal, thinking that it was going to be the best and only thing for her? Everly truly felt that she would love New York as much as she loved the Florida Keys, but things in her life were suddenly so rocky.

Right now, she could feel the Keys pulling her home. And she didn't want to go. She didn't want to be a failure. Plus, she wanted to prove that she could make it on her own. But, as she walked down the street and towards the subway to go to her apartment, she felt defeated. For the first time in her life, she felt like someone that didn't belong.

33

Once Everly was back in her apartment, she quickly put up her things and changed into something more comfortable. She was going to have dinner at Drew's house tonight, and she was really looking forward to it. She was glad that it was only her, Drew, and Donald that would be sharing the homemade pot pie Drew was cooking. He was celebrating, not only that he had finished a huge article that he had been working on for a while, but the fact that he was getting ready to propose to his love.

She was happy for her friend, but she secretly wished it was her that he wanted to propose to. It was only after what happened to her Saturday night that she realized that she was in love with Drew. Blake had been a distraction. She now knew that she had forced herself to believe there was more between them than there was. He was nice and he was helpful, but he was not Drew.

As soon as she was ready, Everly walked upstairs. When she was at the door, she hesitated. She knew that when she entered the room, it would remind her of Blake, and that reminded her of the weekend. But since he was gone, she felt better about the dinner tonight. Seeing Blake was the last thing she needed after what happened and her stressful day at work.

She knocked on the door, with no response. Once more, she knocked, and no one seemed to be home. Drew had told her about the secret place where they left a key, and that she could come in at any time when they were gone. So, she found a little box that was tucked away in a chip in the planter in the hallway.

She opened the door and let herself in, but saw no one. Just as she was about to take her phone out of her pocket to give Drew a call, she heard movement in the other room. Then, before she could do anything, Blake walked out of his room, naked and laughing, with a girl behind him.

"Blake?" Everly said, shock in her voice.

"What the hell are you doing here?" Blake asked.

"I'm supposed to be having dinner with Drew and Donald. But the better question is, what are *you* doing here? You told me you were going out of town. And who is she?" Everly was now mad for the third time that day. But before anything could be said, Drew entered the apartment, carrying a box. He looked from Everly to Blake, noticing the nakedness of both his roommate and the girl.

"What's going on?" Drew asked cautiously.

"Cassie, go back to the bedroom. I'll be there in a minute," Blake said softly, not taking his eyes off Drew and Everly. The girl backed up quickly, trying to cover herself the best she could, and suddenly disappeared in the bedroom.

"Listen, Everly, I can explain."

"Explain? Sleeping with a woman when you told me that you were going to be going out of town for a few days? Telling me the other night how wonderful things were? Is this all just a joke to you? Are you just using women? Does that girl even know what kind of person you are?" Everly's breathing was heavy and her heart was pounding. She felt Drew's hand on her arm and she jerked it away.

"I'm through. Sorry about dinner, Drew. Tell Donald I said 'hi.'" Everly turned away then quickly walked out the door and down the steps, not waiting for the elevator.

"What the hell happened, Blake? It better not be what I think it is," Drew countered, walking toward him. He watched as Blake tried to find something to cover himself but was having no luck.

"Nothing. I just had Cassie over and things got, well, interesting."

Drew couldn't help what came next. Before he knew it, he punched Blake across the cheek, so hard he hit the floor. "I can't believe I didn't see this coming. I honestly thought that maybe, just maybe, you had changed. That Everly would be that girl that would make you see that life isn't so horrible. Yes, you might have had a shitty childhood. All of us did in some way or another, but using one girl after the next isn't the solution to your problem. You need real help."

"Wow, a lecture coming from a guy that can't get his shit together. Ever thought about how you use Peyton? How you claim to love her, and all that bull? Or is it just the idea that her father has given you a job, something you would have never gotten on your own? You think I don't see the way you look at Everly? Talk about using people. Maybe, we should let Peyton in on your little secret. Whatcha say, pal?"

Drew stood there watching as Blake stood up, wiping the blood from his mouth. He wanted so badly to hit Blake again, but he was right. Drew didn't love Peyton. He liked her. She was fun. But she was also manipulative, controlling, and not the type of woman he was looking for. And he didn't know what he wanted 'til he met Everly in the Keys. Ever since that day, at Abbey's wedding, when they first danced, he knew she was special. That she was the woman he had been looking for all this time.

"You're an asshole," Drew spat at Blake, then turned around and rushed out the door.

■ ■ ■

Everly hung up the phone and it was done. She heard the knocking on the door, but refused to answer it. She was glad that Shari wasn't home, or she would have answered it, letting Drew in. She could hear him saying they needed to talk, but Everly refused to open the door.

She pulled out the suitcases that she had stashed in the closet. Everly took her time and quietly folded her clothes, packing the cases as tight as they were when she arrived here. Within a few hours, everything that she had brought with her was packed, except for what she needed in the morning. Drew had stopped knocking long ago, and she was glad. She didn't want to talk to him, Blake, or anyone. New York was a beautiful city, but it wasn't her. She knew with all her heart that Key West was calling her back home.

■ ■ ■

It was seven o'clock in the morning, but Drew didn't care. He had to talk to Everly, to get this mess straightened out. To let her know how he felt. He knocked several times before he heard someone coming to the door.

"Shari, where's Everly? I need to talk to her. Tell her it'll only take a minute, because I know she must be getting ready for work," Drew said in a rush.

"She's already gone," Shari said with a yawn.

"To work, this early?"

"To the airport."

"What?" Drew asked incredulously.

"We talked when I got home last night. She said she was going back home. Lost her deposit and everything, but said she didn't care."

Drew was trying to think. "Did she say what time her flight was leaving?"

"No, but the taxi picked her up about an hour ago. She must have wanted to get out of here fast. Getting a plane ticket that fast cost a pretty penny."

Drew was just standing there, trying to figure out what to do next, but there was nothing he could do. She was gone. Back to the Keys.

34

Everly looked out the window at the beautiful turquoise water below. It hadn't been too long ago that she had seen that same sight, and she remembered how excited she was that day. Now, she was coming home, feeling so differently. She hadn't even made it one month. The only person who knew she was heading home was Abbey, and she was sure that Zach knew by now, too. But Abbey had promised not to tell anyone. Everly needed some time to come to grips with everything that had happened in such a short amount of time.

Leaving like she did had felt like the right thing to do, but also irresponsible. After what Everly had been through, she knew the only place for her now was the Keys. And as she looked at the scene below, she knew she had made the right decision.

She had emailed Eric last night, telling him of her sudden departure. She was sure this wouldn't garner her a good recommendation, but she did leave on one good note. She fixed all four problems for the web site and emailed the information to Jones. And she was rid of one headache: Trey.

There was nothing left to say to Blake, but she did email him. Whether he would read it, she wasn't sure. He had been exactly what Drew had warned her about. And Abbey thought her brother had relationship issues. They were nothing like Blake's. Maybe, his treatment of women had something to do with his past, and she hoped that he would find a way to become a better man. Between Blake's actions and Trey's demeaning remarks, Everly felt no hope of ever finding someone who wouldn't stomp on her heart or her feelings.

Blake had taken away something very precious to her, but she was at fault, too. That was something she would have to come to grips with. As for Trey, she didn't know if he would ever overcome his complex about women, but she hoped he learned that just because she had a vagina instead of a penis, she could do the job just as well.

Everly felt the plane circling to land and continued to watch out the window, seeing her beloved city. It felt like medicine to her soul. This was where she belonged, not New York City. One day, she would visit again because she had barely scratched the surface of everything she wanted to do, but it wasn't worth it to stay any longer.

She didn't want to face Blake anymore. Drew was getting ready to marry Peyton, who despised her. And at work, the men there thought she was a second-class citizen. Everly knew in her heart that she could have stayed and fought her way through the pain, the heartache, and the work problems, but she had to admit that other things didn't feel right, either. If she was completely honest with herself, New York was exciting, but nothing like she had pictured in her mind. As she looked once again at the stunning water and green islands below, this was where her heart was.

Abbey had told her that she could come straight to their house, leaving a key outside under the flowerpot. She had already fixed up the extra room for Everly, and she could stay as long as she liked. Everly knew that she had to put a new plan for her life in place, but she didn't want to go home to do it. She would use the money she had saved for New York to find herself a place here, in the islands. Maybe not even in Key West, but one of the other Keys she loved. She had friends in Marathon, and Everly could see herself there, too.

But finding work would be a big factor. Everly still had her online side business, but it did not bring in nearly enough money to help her. And going back to Lance didn't feel right. She knew that once he found out that she had left, he would be disappointed. He had done so much for her to get a job in the city, and now she had acted impulsively and just left. At least, she had finished an important job before she took off in such a hurry.

As the plane touched down on the runway, Everly felt tears sting the corners of her eyes. This was not the way she wanted to come back home. She knew that once her parents found out she was here, they would be upset. But she needed time alone. She gathered her stuff, exited the plane, and began the walk to baggage claim. Everly already had money in her hand for a taxi, and was oblivious to everyone around her. She just wanted to get her two suitcases and go to Abbey's. Then, maybe, head to the beach for a while.

The thought of walking in the Atlantic waters was like a dose of healing medicine. The only problem was she had only a few outfits that would work in the warm weather, because she had left all her other clothes behind at her parent's house. She had hoped that they would ship them once springtime was blossoming in New York, but now, she didn't have to worry about that.

"Hello, there."

Everly recognized the voice and looked over to see a very familiar face. The tears came without warning. She dropped her carry-on and put her arms around Abbey. Everly couldn't stop the flow of water coming from her eyes, but felt comforted to be with someone she trusted completely.

"What are you doing here? I thought I was just going to take a taxi to your house. Does anyone know you're here?" Everly sniffled, wiping the tears off her cheeks.

"I told Zach to tell them I wasn't feeling good, which isn't a lie. Just seeing you right now and how upset you are has made me feel bad. I couldn't let you just come to the house with no one there. Not the way you left so fast. I think you need someone to talk to. If you want. I'm not trying to pressure you."

"I know that. I'm so glad that you're here. You're the first person I've seen in a month that I honestly feel safe with."

"Goodness, Everly, was it that bad?" Abbey asked, alarmed.

"Abbey, there is so much to tell. But I just need today to breathe. To think about what happened. Maybe, we can talk tomorrow?"

"Whenever you're ready."

"I'm sorry you took a day off from work."

"I promise, it's no problem. I just had to make sure you were okay, or at least, as okay as you can be."

"I just need some time."

They gathered Everly's luggage and put them in the trunk. Soon, she was settled in Abbey and Zach's spare room. She opened the luggage and dug out her t-shirt, shorts, and flip-flops. She had brought them to New York to remind her of her home, and now, she was glad she had them. Maybe, she'd take a trip to the store tomorrow to pick up a few extra shirts and shorts, 'til she decided to make an appearance at her parent's house. But not till she knew what she was going to do.

35

She slipped into the familiar clothes and felt a sense of peace surround her. This was Everly. She loved the feel of the clothes against her skin. As soon as she gathered some money and a note pad, putting them into her back pack, she borrowed Abbey's bike and headed to Simonton Street Beach. She loved all the areas where she could get as close to the beach as possible, but this was where Louie usually was.

Louie was an older man that had retired to Key West. It was just him and his dog, and Everly always teased him about finding him a lady friend. They would usually run into each other about once a week and had great conversations. Louie was originally from Washington, D.C., but also knew a lot about New York. So, when Everly had told him her plan to move, he was excited for her, but also cautioned her, too. She hoped he was here because she wanted to talk to him.

Everly parked and locked the bike at a vacant post on the beach. She looked both ways but didn't see the man. So, she took off her flip-flops and walked in the small sandy area.

It felt good to have sand between her toes again. And as she looked down, she had to laugh. Her feet felt warm, too, something she hadn't felt in New York unless she had worn three pairs of socks. But this was what she was used to. And this was where she belonged.

"Haven't seen you here for a few weeks. I thought you had already gone." Before she turned around, she knew it was Louie. He looked the same, except his limp was getting more pronounced and he now had a cane.

"I did, but I'm back. Came in just a little while ago," Everly said softly.

"I thought you were moving there, right?" Louie asked, taking his time to sit in the sand under one of the few palm trees. Everly moved slowly over to him and sat down beside him.

"I did. For only almost a month. Pretty pathetic, huh?" Everly said in a downcast voice.

"Nah," he said, taking a water bottle from the little bag he carried with him. "I've seen plenty of people move and come back when they find out what things are really like. So, I take it you didn't like New York?"

"Let's just say, New York didn't like me." Everly sat beside her friend, slowly drawing in the sand.

"That doesn't sound like you. You have a personality that everyone can't get enough of, I'm sure. I know I can't," Louie said with a smile, causing her to grin for the first time in the last few days.

"It just didn't work out. It was nothing like I thought. I mean, the city was beautiful. The buildings, the lights at night.

I got to go ice skating, see snow for the first time in my life, and more," Everly said, recalling some happy memories to relay to Louie.

"Then, why in the hell are you back here?" he asked.

"Too much to tell, Louie. Let's just say that I'm a Key West girl. Born and raised. I didn't realize that I'm not a big city girl 'til I left."

"What is that saying? 'Everyone thinks the grass is greener on the other side of the fence,' or something like that. Well, sweetheart, maybe things didn't work out like you thought, but at least you tried. You know how many people out there have dreams and they never take a chance? You did, and you should be damn proud you tried. I don't know all the details and I don't need to know. But you are one special young lady, and even though you don't feel like it right now, you will make a way. You will find what you are supposed to do, and when it hits you, it will feel like you have been released from a trap."

"Thanks, Louie. To tell you the truth, I was hoping to see you here today. That's the reason I came here." The older man got up slowly, Everly giving him a hand. Then, he reached to give her a hug. "Whatever you do, I hope we can continue these little meetings. I missed them while you were gone."

"So did I." Everly watched as Louie started walking back slowly down the street. She sat back down in the sand and rested her back against the palm tree. Even though she had just gotten back to the island, she felt like she needed to hurry and figure out her next step. But as she sat and looked out at the ocean in front of her, Everly couldn't do it. She needed some time to breathe. So, she put her notebook away and took out her phone to play some soft tropical music.

But one look at her phone let her know that she had twenty-one missed calls from Drew, and just as many texts. She had neglected her phone the entire trip home, not wanting to see anything that might come from anyone in New York. She had said her piece, emailed everyone that she needed to, and headed home, where she belonged.

As Everly looked at the missed calls, she wondered what he would say. But then, she knew she could look at the texts to find that out. Did she want to open them right now, while she felt so raw and bruised inside? No. She would save them for another time.

The bike ride back to Abbey and Zach's house was relaxing. She'd hoped she didn't see anyone she knew, at least, not yet. She put the bike around the side of the house and found that Abbey was still home.

"So, how was the beach?" Abbey asked. She was making some conch chowder for dinner. Just the smell made Everly's mouth water.

"It was nice. I talked to Louie for a bit."

"He is such a sweet old man. I noticed, though, that he's walking with a cane now."

"I saw that, too, but didn't ask." Everly sat at the kitchen, watching as Abbey finished the recipe.

"Everly, what happened? Drew has been calling me all afternoon. I finally answered his call and he sounded so frantic. He wanted to make sure you were okay. And he really wants to talk to you."

"Please, Abbey, let's talk tomorrow, okay? It's just too much right now. I mean, this morning I was in New York, and now I'm sitting in my friend's house in Key West. Everything I had planned and wished for these last few years has suddenly gone completely wrong, and some things happened that I regret more than I can say."

Abbey didn't say anything but continued to look at her friend. Everly was hurting badly, but she knew Drew was, too. When Abbey had pumped him for details, he didn't give her much, but she could tell that he, too, was hurt by what was going on. And for Abbey, who wanted to make sure everyone was happy and okay, this was making her uncomfortable.

"Can you promise me tomorrow night?"

"I promise," Everly said. "By the way, does Drew know that I'm here?"

"I had to tell him or risk him calling your parents. I didn't think you wanted that to happen."

"Thanks." Everly hadn't even thought that Drew or anyone would try to call her parents after her hasty departure from the city. She was glad that Abbey had thought ahead for her.

The door opened and Zach walked through. Everly's eyes filled with another round of tears as she hugged the man who was like a big brother to her. He had known her since she was seventeen and had been the one to both encourage and warn her of her big plans to move away. But he had also been her role model. He had moved out after college, away from everyone he knew, when he came from Galveston to Key West. He had encouraged her, but also let her know that the road could be bumpy. And now, she would tell him the bumps had been more like huge mountains for her.

"Happy to see you," Zach said as he wrapped his arms around Everly. "But I have some news for you. Your boss, Eric, in New York, called Lance today to tell him you quit. But he was impressed that you completed a job that no one else had been able to finish. Eric wants you to call him as soon as possible. It seems that someone likes your work. So, needless to say, it was a bit hard not telling Lance that you were at my house."

"Thanks," Everly responded, giving Zach another hug. "Those guys up there had no clue what they were doing. Well, I should say, one guy named Trey. Talk about an asshole," Everly said. "Sorry, but he was just a real jerk. Told me I couldn't fix any problem they had with a project because I was a woman. I was only one of three women in the office, and the other two, I never even got to talk to or figure out what they did because I wasn't there long enough. I feel like such a loser."

"I don't know what happened, but Everly, you know that's not the case. Sometimes, things just don't work out like you planned. Zach and I are a great example of that. And look at Josie and Michael." Everly then recalled Abbey's neighbor, Josie, who had been left at the altar so many years ago and came to Key West to hide from the world. But her runaway fiancé found her after all these years, and they were now married, living in the Keys.

"It was so different than what I planned. The city was beautiful and I got to do a few of the things I had always dreamed of, but-" Everly couldn't finish the sentence.

"But what?" Abbey asked softly as they all sat down on the sofa in the living room.

"I didn't fit in. It was like I was some little girl lost in a place that just wasn't me, even though I was positive that I would love it there. The people were different. Some were nice, but others…." Everly didn't know if she could finish the sentence as Blake came to mind. "Others just used people. I mean, I've seen that before, but…I don't know, this was just different. Now that I'm back here, it feels good, but a part of me feels like I should have stuck it out. I should have fought harder and I gave up too soon. I know that's what everyone is going to say. I don't know how to face anyone."

"How about just telling the truth? That New York just didn't fit you. But you are glad that you visited for a little while. No one needs to know the details unless you want them too."

Everly sat there for a minute. She wanted to tell them the whole story, but felt so embarrassed.

"You're welcome to stay here as long as you like, but you know, you can't hide forever." Zach softly put his arm around her, giving her another hug.

"I know. I just need to find a place to live and another job, though I do have a good savings account to live on for a while."

"What about your parents?"

"After New York, I now know that I want my own place. You should have seen the closet I was living in. And for nine hundred dollars a month!" Everly exclaimed, feeling frustrated. "And because I just up and left today, I've lost my deposits. Now, I feel like I made the wrong decision."

"Oh, wow!" Abbey said.

"You can second-guess yourself all you want, but you're here, now," Zach said. "So, make your decisions based on living here again. Unless you want to turn around and go back."

Everly hung her head, then put her arms around her knees that she had drawn up to her chest. She felt so confused and conflicted, not sure what she had done, what she was going to do, or anything about her life right now. It all felt like such a blur and she had no direction whatsoever.

"I think, right now, we need some dinner. How about some homemade conch chowder?" Abbey said, moving towards the kitchen. Everly slowly got up and went to help her as Abbey dished out three bowls of soup, along with crackers. Everly decided that, instead of focusing on what happened today, she wanted to hear all that had been happening in Key West since she left. It would be good medicine for her soul right now.

36

It had been over a week since Everly had left, and Drew still thought about the small apartment downstairs that once housed his friend. He and Blake weren't talking to each other after what had happened. Every time he came back to the apartment, it felt like an empty shell. He and Peyton were still on the same path, but when Everly left, Drew knew things for him had changed. He felt totally different about so many things now. He knew, without a doubt, that Peyton wasn't the woman he was supposed to spend his life with. But he didn't know how to tell her, or how it would affect his future at the newspaper.

Blake had been right about one thing that day when Drew hit him. Drew was in love with Everly, and he admitted that, now. But he was still hesitant to break up with Peyton. Why? He couldn't understand why he kept going on in a loveless relationship. Was he really that concerned about his job instead? Was Blake right about what he said? Was he using Peyton? Each day since Everly left, his mind had been filled with nothing but questions, which bothered him tremendously.

As he knocked on the door to Peyton's apartment, he knew what he had to do. He couldn't keep up this façade of a relationship. He wasn't sure what Peyton would think or how she would react, but no matter what the consequences, he had to follow his heart. And right now, it was with a beautiful brown-eyed girl in Key West.

"Hey, sweetheart. Come on in." Peyton was putting her necklace on that would compliment the outfit she wore for the evening. They had made plans to go out to dinner, but Drew wanted to talk to her first. He was sure that after she heard what he had to say, he would be finding his own meal.

"Listen, before we go anywhere, I think we need to talk," Drew said quietly.

"What's wrong, Drew?" Peyton asked, her eyes suddenly looking very icy.

Drew took a deep breath and began. "Peyton, I just don't think that we are meant to be together." Drew came straight to the point. He had rehearsed this conversation in his mind all the way to her place, and it certainly didn't start out with that line. But he just blurted out how he honestly felt.

"Excuse me?" Peyton asked. "Are you saying you don't want to be with me?"

"Peyton, I like you and I think you're a great girl. You're going to make someone so happy one day, but we just have different ideas about our future. We have different plans."

"So, how long have you been feeling this way? Does this have anything to do with Everly leaving New York?"

"This has nothing to do with Everly, and everything to do with you and me," he said hastily. He knew that his words sounded harsher than he wanted them to, but he didn't like her talking about Everly, or even saying her name.

"I'm right. As soon as I mentioned her name, I could hear the tone of your voice change. I should've known better. As soon as I saw how you were taking care of her, I knew there was more to your relationship than just being friends. What I don't understand is how you could want someone who has such little backbone," Peyton said.

"What are you talking about?"

"She couldn't even hack being here in New York City. To be honest, I knew that the minute I met her. It takes a certain type of woman to be able to make it here. You have to be tough and you have to know what you want, and apparently, she had neither."

"Peyton, one thing I will tell you is that Everly has more heart and more kindness than you will ever know or have. I thought that I loved you. And I had already bought you a ring to ask you to be my wife. But meeting Everly was one of the best things that could've happened to me. She showed me what a true woman is really like and how a relationship should be—real and soulful."

"You're weak, just like she is. Too bad you won't have a job after this," she said as she walked back towards her kitchen counter and deposited her handbag and coat there. "When my Dad finds out that you're no longer going to be a part of my future, I'm sure your desk will be filled by someone else."

"So, you're saying that the only reason I got that job was because of you?"

"You didn't seriously think that they gave you that position because of your work, did you?" Peyton laughed. "I told Dad that I thought that you would make a great reporter for his staff. He looked at your work and agreed, but also asked where we stood in our relationship. So, I know – no, I'm positive - that once he hears that you've broken his poor little girl's heart, there's no way you'll have a job come tomorrow morning. Are you sure that's what you want, Drew? Wasn't your dream to come to New York to be a journalist? At least, that's what you've always shared with me- or should I say, bored me with."

"Bored you? If you've been so unhappy, then why are you still with me?"

"Because you had potential. And you were nice eye candy on my arm," Peyton said. She now took a seat at the counter and crossed her legs, looking at Drew with a grin.

There was anger rising in Drew and he didn't want to say anything he would regret. But the woman sitting in front of him now was not the woman he had met that day on the modeling shoot. If it was, she had played him good.

"You know, Peyton, if I don't have a job tomorrow, I will survive. I can get another job. But I know that this isn't meant to be. And if you were honest, you would agree that what I'm saying is true. I never meant to hurt you."

"*Hurt me?* Drew, you're not hurting me. You're only hurting yourself. You know what I can do for you in this city, what my family can do for you if you stay with me."

Drew hung his head and shook it slightly, not believing the words that he was hearing coming out of Peyton's mouth. She was selfish to the core and she didn't care if she hurt anyone along the way. He should have seen this in her so long ago, and maybe, he did. Drew had just chosen to overlook it. But now, to hear her say these things, he was shocked. And very sad. He truly believed that Peyton would never find happiness if she kept this up. Drew was also glad that he had enough guts to end this now, and that the diamond ring was still in his pocket.

Drew quietly walked over to Peyton and gave her a kiss on the forehead, then turned around to walk back to the door.

"Are you sure you really want to leave? Once you walk out of that door, things will never be the same for you," Peyton said.

"You know, Peyton, that's what I'm counting on," Drew said. Then, he turned the knob on the door and walked out, closing it softly behind him.

37

Everly looked around at the place and smiled. The familiar apartment looked good, with her own stuff in it, this time. She was amazed when she found out that Abbey's old apartment had not been rented out yet, and she immediately put down a deposit when she found out the news. It had only been a little over a week since she had left New York, but she was starting to feel more like herself every day.

With a little encouragement from Abbey, Everly was finally able to tell her everything that had happened in New York. But she had left out the fact that she had lost a precious gift to Blake. She still couldn't tell anyone that part of the story yet, and she didn't know if she would ever be able to. She still felt ashamed, and wondered if that was truly what life was about. And if it was, she didn't know if she would ever be able to love someone, at least, not like that.

She stayed at Abbey and Zach's for two days before she went home and told her parents that she was back and what happened. They didn't say anything to her or tell her "I told you so." They just held her in their arms and let her talk. She let them know that, even though she was back, she wanted her own place, now. New York had taught her quite a few lessons, and one of them was that she was a capable woman and could make it on her own. But New York just wasn't the place where she wanted to do that. It was here in Key West, the city that she loved. The city that she grew up in. The city where her friends and family were. For right now, she wanted to stay here.

The Florida Keys were where she belonged. It was like salt water flowing through her veins. Even the sand was a part of her being. She would pick up where she left off.

Next, she'd gone to face Lance. She wasn't sure what he would say, but Everly was confident that he wouldn't be harsh. As soon as he saw her, he put his arms around her and held her. She didn't tell him much, except how the work environment in New York was so different from what she was used to here, with him. She told him about how she fixed the website that no one else could and Lance let her know that Eric was beyond impressed. In fact, Eric had left a message for Everly. He wanted her to work for him no matter where she was. She could work with them remotely, because her work was like nothing he had seen before. But Lance told him that he had first option, should Everly come back to Key West. Everly sat there with a smile on her face as she looked at her former boss.

"So, are you saying that I can have my old job back?" Everly asked cautiously.

"I'm surprised that you even have to ask me that question," Lance replied with a smile on his face. "You know, things just haven't been the same around here since you left. I would be honored to have you back on my team. If you wanted to do some work with Eric on the side, I would be fine with that, too. Eric is a good friend, and it looks like you took care of a big problem for him, and I'm not talking about a website."

"Problem?" The way Lance said "problem", Everly wondered what he meant.

"The gentleman who was giving you a hard time? I think his name was Trey, right?" Lance said.

"Yeah, Trey was a bit of an issue, but I hope I didn't get him fired," Everly said, a bit surprised.

"Well, apparently, Trey had been purposefully sabotaging the project in order for Eric to lose the job and the money they had invested. Trey was interested in working with another firm in the city, and that was going to be his website once he started working with them. He was trying to take business from Eric," Lance said.

Everly couldn't believe the words she was hearing. Why would someone do that, just to get a job? Even though she wasn't in New York anymore, she was still learning so many lessons about life and people.

As Lance and Everly exited his office, they turned to see Abbey, Zach, and Roger all waiting with hopeful smiles on their faces.

"So, are you coming back?" asked Roger. "I sure hope so, because I need you. You don't know how many times I've looked at your desk and wanted to roll over there to get your help."

Everly smiled and nodded. She was finally feeling a little happiness and positivity about her future. She still couldn't erase some of the painful memories that had occurred in New York. But now that she was back home where she belonged, what had happened in the city was going to stay there.

■ ■ ■

"Knock, knock." Everly heard the voice and knew it was Abbey. Everly was sure she wanted to see what her old apartment looked like, now that Everly had put her own special touch in the place.

"Come on in, Abbey," Everly said. "I hope you like what I've done with your apartment."

Abbey walked in and looked around, smiling. "You mean, *your* apartment. This is definitely you, Everly," she said as both women sat down on the sofa.

"I'm really glad you left all this furniture when you moved out. I still don't understand why, because if it hadn't been me, some stranger would be using it now. But I love the bed. Much more comfortable than the one I left in New York," Everly said with a little laugh.

"It's so good to see you smile again," Abbey said. She looked at her friend, taking her hand and giving it a squeeze. "You know, Drew still keeps calling me and insisting on talking to you. I don't know how much more I'll be able to take his constant calls. He also sounds different. I asked him if he was okay, and he said everything was fine, but he just sounds, I don't know, a little bit *off*. I mean, he really, *really* wants to talk to you."

"I'm just not ready yet. And I know why," Everly said quietly.

"You know you can talk to me about anything, right? Don't you want to tell me the whole story about New York? I know there's more than you're sharing with everyone. I can tell when you talk about it."

Everly sat silently for a few minutes, looking at her hands and wondering if she should tell Abbey the little bit of information that she had left out.

"Abbey, I have to tell you. I'm in love with your brother. I knew that from the moment I saw him at your wedding. I knew he was special, and that week when you were on your honeymoon, we had so much fun. But then, I found out about Peyton and I was determined that, since he was out of reach, Drew was only going to be like a big brother to me. Like a best friend." Everly looked around the room and paused, not sure she wanted to go on. But maybe, if she told someone, it would help her put it behind her.

"When I got to New York, Drew was wonderful. He showed me around and helped me try to adjust to the life in the city," Everly said gently. "He was just perfect. But it was clear that he was with Peyton, spending a lot of time with her, which was normal. Then, one day, he came to me wanting to talk about their relationship. He said he wanted to ask Peyton to marry him, and he just didn't know how or when to propose. He asked me for my advice because he basically kept stalling about taking that step with her. And here I was, wanting him to be with me, not her. I felt so confused. And then, there was Drew's roommate, Blake."

"What about Blake?" Abbey asked.

"Blake was nice, at first. He spent time with me, took me places, showed me around New York. One morning, we even cooked homemade biscuits in his kitchen and had a good time. I thought that we were friends and, at one point, I thought that I could see a relationship with him. He made me feel good and took my mind off Drew. Blake was moving a bit too fast, so I told him I was a bit old-fashioned and wanted to take things slow." The memories that were coming back to Everly now were so painful that tears started forming in her eyes.

Abbey could see that Everly was clearly upset and she wanted to help her so badly, but the only way she could was to let Everly tell her story. She saw a small tear slide down Everly's cheek and reached over, gently wiping it away.

"The last weekend I was there, Blake and I had our first official date. He took me by taxi to this beautiful Italian restaurant, right on the edge of Central Park. I hadn't even seen the park yet, and even though it was covered with snow, it was beautiful. I took some blankets with us, because after dinner, we took a carriage ride. It was magical. It was such a romantic date, and when we got back to my apartment, things kind of spiraled out of control."

"Did he hurt you, Everly? Because if he did, you need to let someone know."

"No, Abbey, he didn't hurt me in the way that you're thinking. But we did have sex, and it was my first time. I had always dreamed that making love would be so special. It would be with someone I was truly in love with. Not someone I had barely just met. I don't know why I let things get so out of control. I should've told him 'no,' and I didn't. It wasn't his fault – it was mine." Everly couldn't help it now. The tears were falling faster. The feelings she had bottled up and hidden away were now exposed, and she was relieved to be able to talk to someone.

"Oh, Everly, I am so sorry," Abbey said softly, moving closer to her and wrapping her arms around Everly's shoulders. "It wasn't your fault. It's just something that happened, and though you wanted it to be different, you can't beat yourself up. You need to let it go and count it as a mistake. It happened and it's done. You did use protection, I hope?"

"Yes, thank goodness. But I just feel, I don't know – bad. I feel dirty. It just wasn't what I imagined it would be. I wanted it to be so special, and it certainly wasn't. I wanted to be with someone I loved, and not just somebody. That's not the kind of person I am. It's not the kind of girl I want to be, and I don't want anybody else to think badly of me."

"Why would they think that? Who's going to know unless you choose to tell them? I'm not going to say anything – this stays between you and me. It's up to you, if you ever want to talk about it." Abbey continued to sit by her, trying to comfort her in the only way she knew how.

"Everly, does Drew have any idea that's how you feel?"

"No, I never said anything because I didn't really let myself admit it 'til recently. Plus, Drew is marrying Peyton. He came to me for advice, remember?" she said, laughing through the wet drops that were still falling down her face. "He said he couldn't make sense of why he kept procrastinating on asking Peyton to marry him. Not that I'm blaming Drew, but I think that's why that night with Blake happened. I was just trying to make sense of my feelings for two men, something I had never experienced."

"Well, he sure is checking on you a lot, right now. He sounded a bit perturbed that I won't convince you to talk to him."

"Thanks, Abbey, for watching out for me. I'm sorry that you're in the middle of this. I just can't talk to him. It still hurts too badly and reminds me of everything that happened in New York."

Abbey hugged her friend once more. "I just have to share something with you. I once found myself in your shoes, except I was a senior in high school. I was out on a date with a guy who everyone thought was the best-looking guy in school, and things just happened. Afterwards, he never called, and I felt like I had made a big mistake. But life went on, and I promised myself that I wouldn't let things go that far again. That I was a strong woman and I had the right to say no. But I also knew that I had to have the willpower to do that. Sometimes, it's hard when you get caught up in the moment, so please, don't beat yourself up. Things just happen. It's the lessons you learn that are important. I promise, one day, that certain man is going to come into your life and sweep you off your feet. And it will be almost unbearable not to be with him." Abbey smiled as Everly laid her head on Abbey's shoulder. "That's how it was for me once I let go and gave myself permission to experience the feelings I had for Zach. Now, I can't imagine my life without him. Your man is out there. Just wait and see."

"Thank you for listening and not telling anyone. It feels good to be able to let this out. I felt like I've been carrying around this boulder, and it was wearing me out. But now, I think I can move on. I have my own place and my old job, along with a new one, too," Everly said, finally smiling.

"Just don't take on too much work. You need a personal life, also. But I'm glad that you can show those boys in New York that a girl from the Keys can put them to shame."

"So am I!"

38

It had been two weeks now since Everly had settled back into life in Key West. The wounds from her time in the big city were slowly starting to heal, and she was making a place of her own in her hometown, now. It felt good, and she was beginning to feel happy again.

She grabbed her backpack and opened the front door, ready for a quick bike ride to her parent's house to use their car. Everly was going to Marathon to spend the day boating with her friends. It was the first outing she had been on since coming back to town. She was looking forward to some time in the sun, and maybe, a dip in the crystal-clear waters, if it wasn't too chilly. Most of all, she wanted to be near the ocean water that was so healing for her.

As Everly began to descend the stairs, she stopped quickly, unable to comprehend the sight before her.

"Hi, Everly."

It was Drew. He was standing at the foot of her staircase, looking so good that it took her breath away. That blonde hair with those blue eyes, and the dimples in his cheeks that she could never get enough of.

"What are you doing here?" she asked, feeling as though a shockwave had hit her.

"You wouldn't answer my calls or texts, and my sister was too stubborn to convince you to talk to me. So, I packed my suitcases and came to you, instead. Can we talk?"

Everly didn't know what to think. She was feeling anger, excitement, hurt, love, and anxiety, all wrapped up in one package. Just as she felt she was starting to make some headway in this new independent life in the Keys, the man she needed to forget was standing in front of her.

"I can't right now. I'm on my way to spend the day out on the boat with some friends."

"Then, I'll be at Abbey and Zach's. Maybe, tomorrow? Can we meet for lunch and just talk?" Drew asked calmly.

She descended the steps, her heart pounding harder the closer she came to him. This was the man who had stolen her heart, but she was scared to hear what he had to say.

"I'll call you in the morning." She brushed past him and got on her bike.

"Everly, just so you know, I'm not leaving Key West 'til we talk."

Everly didn't turn around to acknowledge him, but started pedaling her bike down the street. She wanted to turn around and find out what he wanted to say, but a small part of her, which seemed to have the most control, had her running away from him.

Wait. He said "suitcases." When he came for Zach and Abbey's wedding, all he had was a single piece of luggage. Why would he have multiple suitcases?

Everly couldn't stand it. She turned the bike around and headed back to her apartment. Drew was about to get in the car when he saw her.

"Let me put my bike up, and then, we can go to a little place I know to talk. That's your car?" she asked, pointing to the little white Honda Civic.

"A rental, for now."

"I'll be right back." She put the bike in the storage area, then took a deep breath before heading back out towards Drew.

He opened the passenger side door for her and she got in cautiously. *Am I doing the right thing?* Everly thought to herself as she watched him walk around the front of the car. Was she ready to talk to the man whom she was just starting to let go of?

"Where to?" Drew glanced over to her as he started the car engine.

"We're going to go to a little beach I know."

Everly gave him directions to Simonton Street Beach, where she had come almost every other day since arriving back in Key West. Drew parked the car along the side street, and they walked to the little beach, with its couple of Palm trees. Everly sat in the sand, planting her tote on the side where Drew would sit so it would act as a barrier between them. Soon, Drew was there sitting in the sand by her.

"This is a nice little beach. When I was here last time, you didn't show me this place."

"I took you to all the major spots for your stories. This little place is just where I can dip my toes in the sand or the water for a bit. A little spot to just relax. At least, most of the time."

An uncomfortable silence fell between them. Everly wasn't sure what to say, but finally broke the ice. "Drew, why are you here?"

"I'm here for a few reasons, but the most important one is *you*."

"Why me? I left our friendship behind in New York. And aren't you engaged by now?"

"Nope."

"Why not?"

"Because I finally came to the realization that I don't love Peyton."

Everly didn't know what to say. She had seen the relationship- and the friction- firsthand in New York. She had wanted to scream that Peyton wasn't right for him, but she didn't dare say anything.

"So, how did you come to that conclusion?" Everly asked softly.

"It happened the day that I went to your apartment early in the morning and Shari told me that you had left for the airport. I'm sure you saw how many phone calls I left. And text messages, for that matter."

"You did leave a few," Everly said. "But your text messages didn't really say anything other than that we needed to talk. There was nothing to say. I couldn't make it in New York. The guy that I thought really liked me used me." *And the one I wanted had someone else,* Everly thought to herself. "Then, my workplace was chaotic, with some guy who thought that I was just some stupid girl. Then, when I fixed a problem, all hell broke loose. I'm just not that city girl I thought I wanted to be. Or should I say, I'm a city girl, but just not a New York City girl. But how could my leaving affect you?"

"Because, Everly, I love you."

Everly was stunned as she slowly turned to look Drew straight in his eyes. She felt as though she was frozen in place though it was warm on the tiny beach. There were little leaps of joy in the pit of her stomach but she was scared too. Could this really be happening?

"You do?"

"Yes, I do, more than you can imagine," Drew said softly, looking into her eyes.

"What about Peyton?"

"It's a long story, but when I told her that I didn't think she and I were really a good fit together, she said I would regret it. That I would lose everything I worked for. I didn't believe her, but she was right. I walked into work the next day and my boss told me that they were downsizing due to sales lagging, which I know wasn't true. Peyton has a control over her father like I have never seen before.

"The weird thing was that I thought I was in love with her. That we would make a good team. But then, I came to my sister's wedding in the Keys. And I met this beautiful, brown-haired girl that was full of life and love, like no other woman I had ever met before. I remember I told myself that you and I would only be friends, but there was always this magnetic pull toward you that I couldn't make sense of.

"After I went back to New York, I thought I was able to put it behind me, but it came rushing back the day I picked you up at the airport. You were so excited and I couldn't help but want to be around you. But I was torn, because I felt my loyalty to Peyton. It got complicated and I didn't know what to do. Then, I went and asked you for marriage and engagement advice," Drew said, laughing. "I'm really sorry about that."

Everly now had a smile on her face remembering that day. "Sorry I couldn't help you, but I'm not sorry that you and Peyton split up. I knew from the moment I met her that she wasn't for you, but it wasn't my place to say anything." Everly sat there quietly, wanting to say the words and so scared at the same time. It was now or never. "Drew, I love you, too."

Drew smiled and slowly removed the tote that was separating them, moving closer to her. When his thigh touched hers, Everly took a swift intake of breath. It was as though electricity had passed from him to her.

"You don't know how hard it was to be around you in New York. It helped that I thought Blake liked me. I thought he was interested in a real relationship, but I found out the hard way that he wasn't. He only wanted one thing." Everly hung her head, then looked out over the ocean.

"Did he hurt you?" Drew asked delicately.

"I don't want to talk about that right now, maybe later. But he certainly made me question relationships. To find him that morning with that other girl. All the lies." The memories came flooding back, but Everly held her tears in check.

"Well, if it makes you feel any better, I gave him a nice black eye and a bruise on his cheek." Drew dared to put his arm around her shoulders. As soon as he did, just the touch of her soft skin confirmed everything he had been feeling for this wonderful woman.

"You hit him?" Everly said, startled, but didn't move an inch as she settled into Drew's embrace.

"He was another reason I was able to face my true feelings. I guess, he could tell that I was in love with you, and not Peyton. He called me out on it after you left that night. Things got a little heated."

"Maybe, I should have stayed," Everly said with a smirk.

"No, I'm glad you left. I've known Blake a long time, and I should have told you more about his ways long before you even got to New York. I'm so sorry you even got mixed up with him."

Once again, there was a silence between them. They watched a few children with their parents, playing and splashing water along the small shoreline.

"So, what do we do now?" Everly asked. "I don't want to go back to New York, but I do know that I want to be with you. I've wanted to tell you those words for so long, probably since Abbey and Zach's wedding. You're so different from other men I've met. And I do love you."

"I'm not sure what to do now, except this." Drew reached over with his hand and softly caressed her cheek. Then, his lips met hers so tenderly that Everly felt a flush of love sweep through her entire body. She moved closer to him and one kiss was followed by another. It was as though, suddenly, they couldn't get enough of each other.

"Now, that's what I call a public display of affection." Everly and Drew pulled apart and Everly smiled. It was Louie. She jumped up to hug the older man.

"I was hoping to see you here today. Louie, I would like you to meet Drew, my friend from New York."

"Friend? If that's how friends say 'hello,' I'm doing things wrong." Louie laughed. "Nice to meet you, Drew." They shook hands.

"Same to you. So, you and Everly are friends?"

"Yep. It's been several years now, right, sweetheart?"

"That's right. Louie and I met here one day, just talking. Now, we usually see each other every week, even have a sandwich together whenever we can. But I didn't bring anything today," Everly said, looking at the sweet man.

"Yes, you did." Louie took his cane and pointed it at Drew. "And it looks like you were having more fun with him that you ever had with me."

"And you, sir, are one big flirt," Everly laughed as she blushed at his remark.

"I do my best. Well, I'm going for a short walk, then back home. You two behave yourself. Drew, will we be seeing more of you around here?"

"I hope so. It's up to Everly," Drew answered, looking over at her.

Without taking her eyes off him, she answered the man. "Louie, I'll let you know. We're still working out the details."

"Good luck, young man. Just remember – that's one special girl. Not everyone will go out of their way to bring dinner to an old man like me. Be good to her if she lets you stay."

"I promise," Drew said.

They both watched as Louie walked down to the water's edge, now talking to the little children playing in the water.

"So, what do you think about me staying here?" Drew asked. He gently wrapped his arms around Everly as they stood under the Palm tree.

"I thought your life was in New York?"

"Now, I know that I belong wherever you are."

"But what about your work and your apartment?"

"I can get someone to rent my room 'til the lease is up. And the job, you already know about that. Once I decided to come be with you, I didn't look for any work in New York. But I did go online to look for jobs here. I want to live here, where I have family and someone that I love."

Everly could feel the tenderness coming from him. She didn't know how it felt for him, but to her, it was like she was being pulled toward him by invisible bonds that would not be broken. And she wouldn't fight the feeling anymore.

"I would love for you to live here. To be a part of my life. To introduce you to my parents, if you're ready for something like that. And I just happen to know an apartment that's available," Everly said, and kissed him once more to seal the deal.

39

"Are you sure this looks okay?" Drew asked, as he looked in the mirror one more time. He had on a royal blue polo shirt, khaki pants, and loafers. He was so used to button down shirts, dress pants, and heavy coats this time of year that he wasn't sure that the clothing he had on was appropriate for a job interview.

"Take it from a Conch girl, you look just fine," Everly said sweetly, and gave him a soft kiss on the cheek.

"A Conch girl?"

"Key West is the Conch Republic, so we call ourselves Conches. Well, those who've lived here all their lives. Maybe, after a few years, you might earn the title. We'll have to wait and see," she laughed.

"If I can just get this job with the newspaper, it would be great. Though, I think I will be traveling up and down the Keys."

"Is that such a bad thing?"

"Not down here." Drew turned to take Everly into his arms. "Each day I'm here, I see why Abbey moved here so quickly after just one visit. I especially love my next-door neighbor. She is exceptional in every way, and she's one hot babe."

"I sure hope you're talking about me, and not Ella, downstairs." Everly giggled.

"Ella, who?" Drew said, before backing her gently against the wall and kissing her 'til she could barely breathe.

"I like living next door to you. At least, for now," Everly said. She could have had Drew move in with her, but after what had happened in New York, she still needed space. And she wanted some independence. But having her boyfriend next door was a special treat. She was just grateful that the place became available right before Drew showed up on her doorstep that day.

"Okay, mister, you have to stop." Drew nibbled on her earlobe and, in truth, Everly didn't want the sensation to end. "I have a job to get to, and you have an interview. If we keep this up, we might not be going anywhere."

"That sounds good to me, right now," Drew said with a sexy grin on his face.

Everly couldn't get enough of this man. Drew was everything she ever wanted, and she was so glad that he had followed her back to the Keys.

ACKNOWLEDGEMENTS

For me, this is always such a tough part to write. The main reason is because so many people have helped me along the way as I make my journey as an author that I'm afraid I'll forget to thank someone. If I do, please forgive me in advance.

First and foremost, I wouldn't be able to do any of this without the loving support of my wonderful husband, Jeff. As I have said before, he truly is my rock and does so much for me to be able to achieve my dreams. He will be the first to cook, clean, get groceries and more so I may sit at my computer and bring my characters to life on paper. I love you my dear husband.

My mother, Irene Slusser, is the best mom ever! I know everyone says that about their mothers but she has helped me so much on this journey. From letting me bounce story ideas off of her to reading and editing my books – she is such a giving person with a beautiful soul. Love you and I'm so proud to call you my mom!

My father, Sonny Slusser, is also the best dad ever! Can you tell I have great parents? He helps so much with guidance for the business aspect of being an author and also helps me with marketing. His ideas are amazing and I'm one lucky girl to have such an incredible father. I love you Dad!

And what more can I say about my wonderful best friend Donna Gauntlett? She has been an incredible accountability partner, helping me to stay on track with all my projects. Even telling me when I need to take a break since I have a tendency to just keep going when its time to slow down. She has been there through the cheers and the tears. Thanks for being such an incredible friend and the sister I never had. Love you girl!

Thank you Sheri Leonardo for your wonderful information about New York City. All the little tidbits of information you shared helped me formulate Everly's world once she reached the big city.

To all my fans and readers – a huge thank you for continuing to support my writing endeavors. It means more to me than I can put into words.

Finally, as silly as this may sound, I'm grateful for the wonderful place called the Florida Keys. After my first visit there, I fell in love with the area. I was already a beach girl at heart so I felt like this was the place I truly fit in. To all the people that live on these little islands – thank you for welcoming us tourists that love your little corner of the world.

Love to all,

Miki

PS – To learn more about the Florida Keys, please visit www.mikibennett.com.

Other Books by Miki Bennett:

The "Florida Keys Novels" series:

The Keys to Love
Forever in the Keys
Run Away to the Keys
A Wedding in the Keys

The "Camping in High Heels" series

Camping in High Heels
Camping in High Heels: Las Vegas
Camping in High Heels: California

ABOUT THE AUTHOR

A number one best-selling author, Miki Bennett is the winner of the Authors Talk About It Romance Novel Contest. She is the author of two well-received series: *The Florida Keys Novels* and *Camping in High Heels.*

An artist and tech geek who loves the beach, Miki lives in Charleston, South Carolina, with her husband, Jeff and little dog, Emma.